Shemar's fingertips glided from Marita's hair to her neck, which he began to massage. "Do you like that?" He leaned down over her.

"You're an expert." She felt her limbs loosen as his hands caressed down to her shoulders. Her pelvic muscles tensed from the rush she felt there. "Umm."

"Yes, I am an expert. In more ways than you know." He moved his massaging toward her back. "But I'm obliged to help you discover. Lay on your stomach." His voice was a whisper.

Aroused to an aching point, Marita did as he asked. Feeling his hands moving around the back of her dress to the straps, she invited softly, "You can pull it down."

From behind, Shemar did as she wanted, hardly able to sit for the firmness he felt amid his thighs. He looked down at her bare back for a moment. Overheated from the sumptuous sight, he swiftly took off his shirt. What would he do if she turned around? Could he resist tasting her sweet mounds? He'd always imagined how they would look and taste.

Shemar couldn't resist gently brushing the sides of them as he continued to massage her back. "How's that?" He needed to unzip his pants to relieve the pressure. The softness and roundness were killing him to feel more. He needed something. He needed to be inside her. He could hardly breathe, he wanted it so bad. And it turned him on even more that she wanted the same.

Marita heard his breathing, matching her own. She felt the heat from his body bearing down on her sultry back. She was on fire, feeling the pleasurable aching ocean of desire that he stirred, teasing her, making her squirm so she had to have him.

"Shemar," she whimpered.

"Yes, Marita. I'm here." He lay down in back of her.

Marita felt his muscular chest against her naked back. She felt him pushing her dress down lower toward her hips.

"Oh . . . Shemar."

BOOK YOUR PLACE ON OUR WEBSITE AND MAKE THE ARABESQUE ROMANCE CONNECTION!

We've created a customized website just for our very special Arabesque readers, where you can get the inside scoop on everything that's going on with Arabesque romance novels.

When you come online, you'll have the exciting opportunity to:

- View covers of upcoming books

- Learn about our future publishing schedule (listed by publication month and author)

- Find out when your favorite authors will be visiting a city near you

- Search for and order backlist books

- Check out author bios and background information

- Send e-mail to your favorite authors

- Join us in weekly chats with authors, readers and other guests

- Get writing guidelines

- AND MUCH MORE!

Visit our website at
http://www.arabesquebooks.com

DANGEROUS PASSIONS

Louré Bussey

ARABESQUE
BET BOOKS

BET Publications, LLC
www.bet.com
www.arabesquebooks.com

ARABESQUE BOOKS are published by

BET Publications, LLC
c/o BET BOOKS
One BET Plaza
1900 W Place NE
Washington, D.C. 20018-1211

All Kensington Titles, Imprints, and Distributed Lines are available at special quantity discounts for bulk purchases for sales promotions, premiums, fund-raising, and educational or institutional use. Special book excerpts or customized printings can also be created to fit specific needs. For details, write or phone the office of the Kensington special sales manager: Kensington Publishing Corp., 850 Third Avenue, New York, NY 10022, attn: Special Sales Department, Phone: 1-800-221-2647.

First Printing: April 2001
10 9 8 7 6 5 4 3 2 1

Printed in the United States of America

Prologue

From the moment Marita saw that fine creature, there was something about him that exuded danger and irresistible excitement. It was Friday afternoon. She had come straight from campus to Roberta's Unisex Hair Salon to get her hair styled for all the events taking place during the weekend. One of Roberta's assistants was just putting the last touch on her upswept hairstyle when she spotted him through the window. Slightly bopping, he was coming from across the street toward the shop. Seeing him from a distance, about six feet, broad-chested with melon-stacked muscles bursting from underneath his white T-shirt, Marita couldn't help staring harder. Lord, he was handsome. With that golden-brown skin complementing sultry, hypnotic eyes, and the fullest lips, he was the kind of handsome a woman never forgets and can never ignore.

"How you doing?" he said to Roberta as he swung in her shop, bringing a woodsy scent with him. His rich, masculine voice matched his sexy looks. "Can you hook me up?" Gently, he pinched one of Roberta's plump arms. "I have a big night tomorrow. I want to look good."

"You look good enough, baby," one of Roberta's

bold patrons injected loudly, making him and everyone else in the salon chuckle.

He peered over at the petite, freckled girl. She was sitting near Marita. From his embarrassed but amused expression, everyone could tell that he was about to make a flirty repartee. Except when Marita saw him noticing her for the first time, and their gazes locked, his comment never left his lips. He stared, appearing as momentarily speechless as she was. If eyes could talk, she knew his were telling her something she'd never heard, something so arousing it caused her heart to race and face to warm like it never had before. Realizing how foolish she must look, Marita forced herself to look away, and instead nodded at her finished hairdo in the mirror.

As she paid for her services, all the ladies in the shop admired the glistening locks piled atop her head with a few long tendrils spiraling along her neck, shoulders, and back. Tons of praise circulated around the salon for the hairdresser's special touch. Above all, though, no compliment meant more than the one Marita heard before exiting the shop. It came from him when he opened the door for her. As he did, his woodsy cologne and seductive voice seemingly stroked over her. "You look so beautiful. I hope your man appreciates you. I hope he knows what he has."

"Thank you." Marita flashed her biggest smile, while making sure she took a last look into those eyes, along with the incredible rest of him, too. She even swished a little as she left the shop. It tickled her to entertain the piercing eyes she felt on her back.

Now why couldn't she have a man like that? Marita

pondered that question as she sauntered down the avenue, proceeding to DC's tourist district to get those outfits she had wanted for so long. That was a man who could really turn her on. The heat that still inflamed her cheeks proved that. His effect on Marita felt like something she'd read about in one of the romance novels she loved to read so much. Just as sweet, it was unmistakable that she affected him, too. Would she ever get those eyes out of her head—not only the eyes, but also the way they stared at her? Marita had to. She had to be grateful for who she did have in her life. That someone was Harry. Old dud-head Harry, she thought to herself with a smile.

He'd never made her feel like the sexy guy did. Even when she was in his arms, not a ripple of desire shot through her, particularly not when he often butted foreheads with her in his anxiousness to kiss her. Sensuality eluded her, too, during other moments with him. When they were at elegant restaurants, they shared a dinner because he was too cheap to buy two. The passion was missing again in their secluded times together, when Harry would chatter about his beloved biology course, all the while throwing in jokes that Marita never realized were jokes until he told her so.

That being as it may, Harry's kindness toward her redeemed him. He was also one of the smartest guys at Howard University, the university they both attended. What's more, just like Marita knew she was going to be a lawyer and studied hard to earn excellent grades, Harry knew he would be a doctor and did the same.

After arriving at the boutique, Marita eyed all the outfits she'd been drooling over for months but couldn't afford. With much of her salary from her part-time job going toward university expenses, little was left over for clothes. Fortunately, she'd learned through her upbringing how to scrimp and save.

After stepping out of the boutique with a stuffed shopping bag, Marita window-shopped at other more expensive stores. It was one of her favorite things to do. She liked to imagine the comforts she would one day be able to give her mother and herself once she became one of the fiercest lawyers to ever grace a courtroom. Enjoying this simple pleasure, she only became distracted when she noticed that someone was behind her, practically on her back, trailing her every movement. Guilefully maneuvering around to see who was behind her, her heartbeat surpassed the pace it had escalated to in the salon.

"You following me?" the handsome guy from Roberta's teased with a grin.

Marita couldn't believe it was him again, and with his hair now freshly cut, he was more gorgeous. "No, I think you're following me." She laughed to disguise the nervousness besieging her.

A twinkle shimmered in his warmth-inducing eyes. His mischievous grin spreading, his long fingers rubbed his chin, and he stared at Marita, seemingly contemplating what to say next. With his attractiveness stealing her breath away, she was defenseless against staring back. At the same moment, a white Mercedes-Benz pulled up near them. An older, light-skinned fellow was beaming from the rolled-down window. He called, "Yo Remmy. Have to talk. Pronto."

So his name was Remmy, probably short for Remington, Marita thought. It suited him.

Marita watched Mr. Fine stride toward the Mercedes, but she was distracted by the driver's fishlike eyes lingering on her. The gawking was making her uncomfortable, so she pretended to see a fascinating item in the store window. Glancing back in their direction, Remmy was in heavy discussion with the guy. She looked away once again, then couldn't help finding her way back to Remmy. He granted her one last look and smile before getting into the car; then it took off.

Deeply regretting that their encounter hadn't lasted longer, or led to exchanging phone numbers, Marita strolled on her way. Although it didn't feel like it at that instant, she guessed it was for the best. She had Harry. They'd been dating for nine months. She had to forget this stranger. So what if she was madly attracted to him? She didn't know him. There probably wasn't anything of substance beneath that beautiful exterior of his. At least that's what she tried to convince herself.

On Saturday night, Marita wasn't her normal jeans-wearing self as she sashayed into the much-hyped spring break party, featuring the band, Cool Breeze. She was a slinky-dress-wearing enchantress, and Harry's bright eyes couldn't stop looking at her.

The band was as sensational as the promoters claimed it would be, playing R&B and jazz tunes. Marita was having a decent enough time with Harry. They were dancing. He was even surprising her with some moves that weren't as bungling as his usual ones. However, when it came to just being alone with him, like when they went outside for air, Marita noticed that they were all talked out of their usual subjects. A strained quiet hung in the air. Desperately, she tried to think of something to say—something fun, like any woman would at a party where she was having a wonderful time with her date. She could see Harry's desperation in trying to do the same. Since the words wouldn't come, Marita presumed it was best if they rejoin the festivities. She grasped Harry's hand, attempting to guide him back inside. In turn, Harry grabbed her, all of her, accompanied by sloppy, slobbering kisses, then brazen sexual advances.

"Stop," she urged, her head forced back by his mouth kneading lower and lower on her neck. She couldn't stand it. "Stop it! Please, just stop!"

As if her brusque tone pushed the Off button on him, Harry did as she demanded. Only his eyes moved then, shifting across at her with a mixture of anger and sorrow. "You don't feel for me like I do for you, Marita, do you?"

"Harry, don't get all serious on me."

"You don't. I can tell. I can't ignore it anymore."

"What's wrong with taking things nice and easy, like always? Why do you have to get so mad because I'm not ready for sex with you?"

He started shaking his head. "It's not the sex, Marita. It's that you don't care about me like I care about you. I won't wait for you to feel something for me that just isn't there. You're just not into me like I'm into you, and no matter what I do or how I treat you, it never seems to change. The feeling just isn't there on your part. And I'm tired of how much it hurts. So that's why I'm mov-

ing on. It's over, Marita. Over and done with tonight! I hope you brought cab fare."

Just like that, he went back inside to the dance
floor. More nervy of him, he pulled another
woman on the dance floor and laughed with her
as if nothing eventful happened during the night.
For a moment, Marita observed him prancing with
the woman like a donkey hopping over hot coals,
all the while reeling in the shock of being
dumped. Even if she wasn't passionately in love
with Harry, did she deserve to be treated so
coldly? She was standing there, staring at Harry
and wondering if she ever really knew him, when
suddenly she felt a presence behind her, a presence that was oh so familiar as he neared her and
she inhaled the woodsy cologne.

Marita turned around, and the room came alive
when she saw Remmy standing there in a dark
blue suit. Several other guys who had been standing with him dispersed throughout the room as
he gave Marita his full attention.

"Not you again?" His sweltering gaze slipped
over her approvingly. "I can't believe I'm seeing
you again. These must be my lucky days."

Marita hid the hammering in her heart that the
nearness of him created. "Yes, it's me. Maybe it's
my lucky day, too."

"You look real good. Want to dance?"

"Sure, I'd love to dance."

A ballad was the prelude for sweet perfection.
As her body came close to his, and her arms
folded around his massive shoulders, she instantly
felt a madness in her flesh that she'd never experienced before. There was breathless rapture entering her being when she touched this man, and

extreme excitement when his hands came around
her tiny waist, and he asked her name. As easily
as anything, they engaged in a conversation above
the resonant music. Whispering in each other's
ears, they became introduced into each other's
lives. From what they shared, they had so much
in common, from the love of soulful music like
what they were dancing to, to having tiny imme-
diate families but lots of crazy cousins, on to a
love for movies, particularly ones reflecting con-
temporary black life. Smoldering around their dialogue was the fevered mist of so much sensuality.

After the record was over, Marita could tell that
Remmy's insides were filled with as much desire
as hers were. When he escorted her outside, she
found herself in the parking lot near a black, shiny
Jaguar. He moved in front of her, while his eyes
filled with something that she knew hers held, too.

"Did you feel it, too?" he asked. His voice was
laden with sensual tension.

Marita stared at his handsome face, knowing exactly what he meant. "Yes, I did." She couldn't
get over how their racing heartbeats swayed against
each other as they danced. She couldn't get over
how she felt like she'd known him longer than she
did. Somehow she knew what types of things he
liked, just like he knew what she liked. Even when
he laughed spontaneously, she knew what he was
thinking, and vice versa. What was happening with
this near stranger was beyond anything she'd ever
experienced before.

Suddenly Remmy's arms came around her. He
pressed Marita against him so tightly she felt his
arousal wedging into her. A breath later, his mouth
covered hers hungrily. The firm sweetness of his

lips writhing across her own and then his tongue
sexily ravaging hers sent her into a delirium. As
his kiss explored and tasted deeper, her body became drenched in divine ecstasy. When eventually
Marita needed air, he reared back, staring at her,
before he asked, "Can I take you home?"

"Home?" She hadn't even considered taking
Harry back to her dorm room, let alone a near
stranger, even if he didn't feel like one.

"To my home," he clarified.

While they danced he'd told her he owned a
condo. It was a gift to himself for working so diligently in his father's real estate business. Marita
was impressed that he'd accomplished so much at
the age of nineteen—the same age she was. Still,
dazzled or not, that didn't mean she was ready for
a personal tour. Alone with him in his home after
they'd just become acquainted didn't seem right.
"I don't know, Remmy. I . . ."

His plump lips suddenly caressed hers, raking up
untamed longing, solving her indecision. Before
Marita knew it, she was sliding onto the leather
seats of the Jaguar. Moments later, she was wandering around the tremendous living room of
Remmy's luxurious condominium. Remmy smiled,
observing her, as he prepared drinks at the bar.

After he finished, his bottom sank next to
Marita's on the thick white sofa cushions. As she
took a sip of the grape cider, she marveled at all
that he had achieved at such a young age.
Remmy's success made her feel like anything was
possible. If she worked as diligently as he did, one
day she could reside in such luxury, too. Greater
than that, she could lavish her mother with such
a lifestyle. She was determined to get her mother

out of the decaying section of town where Marita had grown up.

"I like a man who works hard to achieve his dreams," she said, clutching her glass.

Ignoring the wine he was holding, his eyes drifted over to her. "Oh, you do?"

"I sure do. I'm like that, too. And it's such a . . ." She didn't want to say something that would make him think she was ready for something that she wasn't.

"A turn-on." Remmy finished her sentence and eased closer to her. His lips brushed her silky neck. "I'm so lucky that we keep bumping into each other."

His lips . . . How did they do what they did to her? Heaven help her, Marita was feeling so lustfully taut in her lower body. She raised her glass to her mouth to resist the seductive haze. After several swallows of the sweet frosty drink, she set the cider on a coaster on the table.

Remmy grasped her hand when she let go of the drink. He began kissing her knuckles. "I like that you know what you want." He spoke between tender, moist pecks. "One day you're going to be the smartest and sexiest lawyer there ever was. I hope I'm around to see that happen."

Marita was excited that he was even entertaining the idea of being part of her future, and that he was so encouraging, just as she was excited by the heated finger she felt coasting too near to her cleavage line. Why did it feel so good? Like she wanted to let him delve further and touch everything on her that way. "Thank you. A lot of guys don't understand my ambition or my dream to be wealthy one day. But it's not a selfish hope. I want to enjoy the good things in life, and I also want to help people. It's nice to know that you can be so supportive of someone."

"Of only you." He was inching closer to her breasts. "I feel like I know you, Marita, and I want to know you better."

"Oh," she heard herself purring. She was light-headed from the assault of his seduction. "But . . ."

Lips crushing into hers forced her backward on the couch and hushed her. Feeling his broad back and arms, while being lavished with his luscious kiss, Marita hardly had strength to utter anything except a moan. Yet when she felt his hands reaching underneath her dress, tugging at the elastic of her panties, her panic button went off.

"I can't!" she informed him, trying to catch her breath. She moved back. "And I didn't mean to lead you on. It was just that . . ." He was looking at her, clearly disappointed. She just knew he was going to get incensed, like some guys usually did when they were worked up and not getting any loving.

Marita was stunned when Remmy came closer toward her, cupped her face in his hands, and sounded as gentle as the softness emanating from his eyes. "Baby, we can take our time if you want. Of course, I want you so bad right now, I would think I had died and gone to heaven if you gave me your beautiful body. But it's all right. I don't want to do anything that you're not ready for. I want this to be our beginning, and I want it to start off perfect, with you trusting me and knowing me as deeply as you want. Do you want this to be our beginning, too?"

Marita was stunned at how understanding he

was. "Yes, I want this to be our beginning. And I don't want to move too fast." She lowered her head. "I'm a . . ."

"Virgin?" he guessed. He lifted the soft slope of her chin with his fingertips.

She was touched by that gentleness in his eyes again. "Yes. I'm probably the only one on the earth."

"So what?" He chuckled. "It doesn't matter. When you're ready, then I'm ready. In the meantime, can I have some more of your sweet kisses?"

Marita didn't answer verbally. She simply kissed him for hours and talked him to death for the other hours. The time flew and before she realized it, she had dozed off in Remmy's arms. She'd felt so safe and somehow loved there. And when she woke up well after midnight, she thought she was dreaming when she looked over at his sleep-drugged eyes.

"I think I've fallen in love with you tonight, Marita."

Remmy finally tore himself away from another kissing session to get ready to take her home. He had just swung open the door to leave when company turned up. Marita recalled the visitor instantly. It was that older guy with the Mercedes-Benz. The one with the strange eyes like a fish. There seemed to be so much black in his eyes and not enough white. Or was it her imagination because he looked at her a little too long?

"Yo, Valerian," Remmy said, greeting him with a handshake as the guy stepped inside the condo.

"Who is your guest?" Valerian asked, flaunting a gap-toothed smile.

"This is my lady," Remmy said proudly.

Hearing that, Marita was ecstatic. Along with it,

she wanted to be nice to all of Remmy's friends. Perhaps this guy stared at everyone that way. "My name is Marita." She extended her hand. "Nice to meet you, sir."

"Call me Valerian." His pinkish lips planted a smooch on her hand instead of shaking it.

Remmy grinned as he watched the exchange. "Marita, Valerian works with me in my father's business. We keep these odd hours because we deal with different time zones in the U.S. and overseas markets."

"That's nice," Marita remarked, looping a tendril of hair behind her ear. "There's nothing wrong with working hard if you want to get somewhere."

Valerian winked. "Beauty and brains. I like that. Really like that."

Remmy stared at her. "She is a smart one. She's going to be a lawyer one day."

"Is that right?" Valerian raised a brow.

Marita's berry-glossed mouth spread into a smile. "Yes, one of these days."

"Anyway," Remmy said, changing the subject, "I'm taking her home. Then I'll come back and we can take care of business. So sit around and make yourself comfortable."

He nodded. "I'll do that. And I hope to see you again, Marita."

"I hope to see you, too, Valerian."

On the ride home, Remmy explained that Valerian worked closely with him in the U.S. while his father worked on the overseas deals.

Remmy, Remmy, Remmy; he was her world after that night. Nearly every day he wined and dined her. As he did, she came to know him better, and what she came to know, made her fall maddeningly in love. Remmy was down to earth, sweet, funny, attentive, patient, sensitive, understanding, and generous. He also showed her a side of life that she'd only dreamed about—a life of luxury.

Every type of entertainment imaginable, he treated Marita to it. Showing more generosity, he treated her to a shopping spree every Saturday. He also paid for some of her university expenses. All this he did, and they hadn't been intimate. Heavy kissing and petting yes, but her losing her virginity had never happened. As much as she had fallen in love with him, she held close to an inmost desire—she wanted to only make love to the man she married. So it was her great hope that when she did do it, she would be someone's wife—Remmy's wife, she prayed as every day passed. Each day she felt more and more like he was her soul mate.

Her mother always seemed suspicious about Remmy's generosity. What's more, she always behaved guarded toward him when Marita brought him over to visit her. She was curious about how he accumulated so much money, despite Remmy telling her about his success with real estate. She cautioned Marita that he might be involved in something illegal. Marita resented her wariness. On the other hand, she understood where it came from. Carol Sommers was obsessed with keeping her daughter clear of any man that she sensed was on the fast track to destruction.

She wasn't having for Marita what she'd settled for, herself—a man who got her pregnant at eighteen, worked three months as a gardener to take care of her and their daughter, then decided that

his low wages weren't getting him where he
wanted to go fast enough. After he abandoned his
family, he seemed to vanish from the earth. Struggle was their life ever since.

Remmy wasn't her father. Marita knew that from
the depths of her heart. He possessed integrity.
The sole problem they had was her growing frustration with Valerian. He always popped up at
Remmy's condominium smack in the midst of
their good times. Worse, he continued staring at
her in a way that didn't feel right. But was it her
imagination?

One unforgettable occasion, Marita made a surprise midnight visit to Remmy's place, hoping for
a romantic rendezvous. Expecting her beloved to
open the door, she was surprised when it was Valerian who welcomed her inside the condo. After
calling out to Remmy and learning he wasn't
there, she was filled with uneasiness, but refused
to show it. "Where's Remmy?"

"The kid's handling a business matter," he answered, sitting on the couch, smiling up at her.
"But I can take care of whatever you need." The
smile cut off and his eyes burned into hers. "Have
you ever been with a man, Marita? I mean a *real*
man? One who can show you what it feels like to
be a woman. I am that man. I can show you now."

Valerian stood and started approaching her, forcing her to back away, trembling. Her eyes were
darting between him and the door she planned to
escape through when the doorknob twisted and
Remmy entered the room. She knew she should
have instantly told Remmy what had happened,
but there was something so terrifying to her about
Valerian, she was incapable of doing it. It was

more than the notion that it would destroy his
business relationship with Valerian or rip their
friendship apart. It was an unholy energy surrounding Valerian.

She had tried to convince herself that it wasn't
there, since first meeting him. Every time she was
around him she felt it. Now the evil vibrations she
felt from him warned her that if she told Remmy
what had happened something awful might happen. Her beloved Aunt Dollie had always told her
to never ignore her natural instincts about someone or something. More often than not, they were
right.

Therefore, after hearing Remmy gush about how
glad he was that she'd surprised him, she simply
went inside his bedroom, sprawled across the covers, and listened to Valerian and him laughing and
talking. Lingering with her was the eeriest feeling.

In the days to come, Marita prayed that something would occur to make Remmy sever his ties
with Valerian. Hopefully, it would be a business
matter and he would be out of their lives. After
all, her Aunt Dollie had also said that if someone
was doing wrong in one place they were doing it
in a whole lot of others. Unfortunately, though,
Valerian never messed up with work. So Marita
tried to control her contact with him. She made
sure they were never alone.

On the evening of Marita's twentieth birthday,
she was beyond happy. She met Remmy for dinner.
It was at the most luxurious restaurant she had
ever seen. Chandeliers, candles, a piano, harps,
roses, scenery paintings, and a view of the shimmering Yakima River made her feel like she was
in paradise. The lobster entrees, champagne, red

wine, and sorbet desserts made the evening even more fanciful. Nothing, however, was as sweet as Remmy's words. "I love you, Marita Sommers." He gazed in her eyes intensely, then reached across the table to clutch her hand. "I love you so much I'd do anything for you."

"I love you, too, Remmy," she confessed. "I've never been so happy in all my life." And she hadn't been. It was a down-to-the-bone happiness.

"Well, I want to make you happier." That's when Remmy pulled a ring out of his pocket. Not just a ring, but the biggest, prettiest diamond she'd ever seen. "I want to be your man, forever, Marita. Will you marry me?"

Marita's hand was shaking as he placed it on her finger. Tears welled in her eyes. "Oh, Remmy, you give me so much." She gazed at the sparkling diamond. "You give me everything and I never have anything to give you. And I doubt I can help you pay rent and other expenses that wives usually do. Do you really want to marry me?"

Remmy looked at her with water glazing over his own eyes. Seeing that, Marita knew whose name he was going to mention. He only looked like that when he spoke of his deceased mother. The love for her reflecting from him always touched her.

"Marita, baby, my mom used to tell me something that I will never forget. And I want you to never forget it, either. She said that if a person really loves you, they just want to *give you*. Give you and ask for nothing in return. But if a person lusts after you, they just want to *take from you*. Baby, you do give me. You give me so much love I can't live without it."

Against her mother's wishes, Remmy and Marita

became engaged. They were even planning a trip to Caracas, Venezuela to celebrate their engagement. There Marita planned to finally give Remmy what he'd been so hot for. Admittedly, she'd been hot for him, too. A week before the trip, a Sunday evening at his place, they were packing for the trip when, unexpectedly, Valerian came by. Marita could hardly look him in the eyes since that night. So after saying hello, she returned to the bedroom to pack. She noticed he had two other men with him, big mean-looking guys. The three of them made her feel strange. She shook it off and went about what she'd been doing.

One pair of Remmy's pants was wrinkled and needed ironing before placing in the suitcase. She didn't see the iron lying around anywhere and recalled once seeing him remove it from the closet. Spotting it high on a shelf, she tiptoed and reached, only to clumsily knock down a big black briefcase. It hit the floor hard, popping open. Marita's eyes stretched at what she saw. Sheets of money. Uncut money. Counterfeit money. She kneeled, getting a better look at it.

The sudden sound of punches and groans of pain made her forget the money and dash into the living room. Valerian was striking Remmy, and she was dying from being unable to help him. One of those men grabbed both her arms.

"Where is my money?" Valerian raged. "Where is it?"

Gaping at Marita, his fish eyes snaked down to her hand that wore the diamond. "You brought her a ring with it, didn't you? Didn't you?"

"Yes." Remmy groaned.

Marita started screaming and pleading. "Please

don't hurt him! You can have it!" She reached to
take it off, but the goon holding her wouldn't free
her arms enough to do so.

"Let her go!" Remmy urged.

The man ignored him, only listening when Va-
lerian nodded toward her. Finally he released her.
She ran into Remmy's arms. "Remmy, are you
OK?" She glimpsed a bruise by his mouth.

"I'm fine, baby. I just want you to get out of
here." He eyed Valerian.

"She isn't going anywhere until we get this
straight."

Disgusted, Marita removed the ring and handed
it to Valerian.

"Thank you, sweetness." He accepted it from
her hand, holding it as he did the stare in her
eyes.

Marita switched her concern back to Remmy.
"Baby, I know what you been doing. Why? You
lied to me about the business with your father,
didn't you?"

Valerian laughed. "What father? He doesn't even
have a father. Never even knew the man."

Remmy rolled his eyes at him, then softened
them on Marita. "I did have a wonderful mother.
But she died and I was on my own. I was just
trying to survive. I didn't want to go this way, but
it was hard."

"And so is your punishment going to be," Valerian added. "You fucked with my money, so I'm
going to fuck with something of yours."

"You have the ring," Remmy stressed.

"But I don't have her."

Marita cringed as Valerian's eyes fell on her.

"Leave her out of it. I'm the one who screwed

you. I'll sell the ring. I'll do whatever I have to, to pay you back."

Valerian grinned. "You thought I was a fool, huh? But you're the fool. Your woman wants me."

Marita was astonished. Not even at what he said, but that he looked like he truly meant it. "I do not!" she heard herself cry out before she realized it. "You disgust me!"

The mood in the room changed with the wounded expression on Valerian's face. All it took for him to look like an attacked little boy was rejection. Marita thought it so strange, but her boldness waned seeing the gun he pulled out.

"You can't get away with making a fool out of me. You cheated me out of so much. Nobody does that to me and gets away with it. I'm going to kill you, dump you in the river, then give your woman what she wants, because she's just saying that. She wants me!"

Valerian cocked the trigger. Just as he did, a bunch of gunslingers, men in blue uniforms charged through the door, scattering about the room. "FBI!" she heard one of them yell. "We've had our eye on you for some time, Mr. Valerian Tate. Now put down the weapon."

Valerian continued aiming the gun at Remmy. Even as an agent charged at him, he refused to surrender. Instead, he grabbed Remmy, locking his arm underneath his neck, the gun pointed to his head. Tears as easy as the line of sweat that slid from Remmy's temple rolled down Marita's cheeks. Her man was not going to get shot. God wouldn't let that happen. God wouldn't give her such a beautiful gift and take it away.

"Put it down!" echoed all around them.

Backing up, Valerian dug the barrel deeper in Remmy's head. Remmy looked over at Marita, his eyes seemingly unblinking until a glaze of water covered them. He closed them tight, then opened them again. The water he tried to fight away was so strong it reached Marita. It strangled her voice as she dropped to her knees, pleading, "Please, don't kill him. I'll do anything."

But she couldn't even hear herself over the shouts and orders of the officers. "Put it down! Put it down! Put it down!" All she cared to listen to is the I'll-always-love-you message Remmy sent to her as he stared at her—staring until that explosion closed his eyes.

One

Eighteen years later

Marita tried to put on an excited face for Aunt Dollie as she packed for Bermuda. And she should have been happy for the gift that allowed her to leave DC for the lush island getaway after such a difficult year. Surely, she was grateful to her great-aunt for letting her stay at her town house for the entire summer. Still, Marita could only smile with her lips. Beyond them, within her, she didn't know how to stop the emptiness, the aloneness, the frustration and pain that was overpowering her as of late. The events of the last months had whipped her into a deep black hole. When would she crawl out? If the idea of vacationing in a paradise like Bermuda couldn't lift her spirits, what else could?

Dollie believed she knew, as she thought of her little secret. Her cheekbones became prominent as she smiled. "Shemar might spend a little time at the town house this summer. Might drop by when you're there. For a few days or so."

Shemar's name stirred good feelings in Marita, bringing them to her heart-shaped face. The grandson of Aunt Dollie's best friend, Nell, she hadn't seen him since they were young teenagers. He was a nice boy as she remembered, just so quiet and shy. She guessed that was because he was often teased about those long bony arms and braces. They'd played some sports, went to movies, and did other fun things together. In recent years, his grandmother Nell had purchased the town house with Aunt Dollie.

Occasionally, Dollie had mentioned what Shemar was doing in his adulthood. He was a near genius, and it was no surprise to Marita that he'd become a psychologist. However, her auntie had mentioned that in the last years he'd left his practice and Dollie was forever annoyed that Nell wouldn't tell what he was now doing. She also heard that Shemar was divorced. Nell was hush-mouthed about the reasons for the breakup, too.

"It would be nice if I saw Shemar," Marita said, finally zipping her suitcase. "Maybe we could have a little fun." She stood the heavy luggage on the floor, then caught the sly grin on Dollie's round face. "Auntie, what are you looking like that for?"

"Nothing." Aunt Dollie's cinnamon complexion had flushed.

"It is something." Finding her aunt's expression humorous, Marita folded her arms. She knew what her aunt was thinking. Ms. Nell and she had been thinking it ever since Shemar and Marita were kids. Dollie had only stopped during Shemar's brief marriage. "You're trying to matchmake Shemar and me again?" Marita had to laugh at the idea.

"You won't think that's so funny one of these days."

"Auntie, I'll always think that's funny. Me and Shemar?" Shaking her head at how ridiculous that notion was, Marita bent to zip a portion of the suitcase that wasn't shut. "Shemar and I were young teenagers who liked to hang out together. I never had those kind of feelings for him—not even the kiddy kind. And he didn't have any little crush on me, either. We were kids, just having fun with each other."

"Feelings can change."

Marita shuffled her suitcase out of the way into a corner. "Mine won't for Shemar. Some guys you just don't feel that way about. They're like a brother or a cousin. That's the way I'll always feel about Shemar." She couldn't imagine anything else. She had never seen him in any other type of light than friendship. He had never stirred any type of romantic feeling within her.

Tired of sitting on the bed, Aunt Dollie made it squeak as she stood. "We'll see." She straightened and rubbed her fleshy lower back. "The future is full of surprises. Get as old as I am and you'll see them turn up over and over."

Later, at the crowded airport, Marita gave her aunt a giant hug. Even amid all of the people rushing about, all the talking, it felt as if only the two of them were there.

"Girl, you're about to squeeze me to death."

"I can't help it." Marita couldn't let go even as they made the call for the passengers to board. With her head nestled against Dollie's neck and shoulder, inhaling the violet water she always rubbed there, she felt so emotional. "You've been so good to me. I'm so thankful you're in my life. Again, I'm so appreciative for this trip and you letting me stay at the town house."

Aunt Dollie reared back so that she could grasp

Marita's face in her palms. Simply staring at her for a moment, she never ceased being amazed at what a beautiful woman flowed from her bloodline. "And I'm just as grateful that you're in my life. You and your mama are the children my womb wouldn't bare. And you may not have come from me, but my blood runs in you. You're strong, Marita. You come from strong women. Know that. Your strength, if you just hold on to it, will lead you out of this despair and to some real happiness. You'll see. Bliss is coming to you, baby. I can feel it. God knows that you have so much love in you to give and He's going to send you someone to give it to. And that someone is going to love you just as much."

Shemar Dalton's large fingers grasped the huge bowl of buttered popcorn that moments earlier he'd taken out of the oven. Carrying it toward the living room sofa, his bare feet making faint thumping sounds, sinking into the thick, beige carpeting, he couldn't help but smile when he saw Pamela Wingate's raisin-tiny dimples greeting him.

"You're ready?" His rich, virile voice stroked through the low, torrid music that was playing, like he was about to croon with the passionate female vocalist. He was glad Pam had brought over the Angie Stone CD that everyone was raving about. With each cut he heard, he was becoming her number-one fan. "This looks cool, but it may be real hot inside."

"Sounds like me," Pam joked, as he made himself comfortable beside her. She stared over at his luminous bronzed skin lighting up the candlelit hues of the room. "There's no one to give all my hot love to anymore."

"It can't be that bad," Shemar remarked, resting the bowl on the table. "What's up with you and Joesive?"

"Nothing anymore." She propped a pillow against her back. "I was so into him and I thought he was into me. Then just like that, he says that I'm smothering him and he needs his space. And the thing is, he told me a few weeks ago that he loved me. Said we were going to be together forever. That liar."

"Some guys can't handle commitment." Sighing, Shemar leaned back, pondering his cousin's dilemma. Despite him being a psychologist, he was the last person who should be sharing relationship advice, since his marriage had ended so bitterly two years ago. Yet ever since Pamela had become part of his family as a young girl, she automatically came to him with her problems. Even when they were living states apart, she would call or visit whenever a disconcerting matter erupted.

Shemar never minded. There was no one else for her to turn to. After his Aunt Grace, his mother's sister married Pam's father, a wealthy auto dealer, she should have had a stepmother, stepsister and a father there for her. Nevertheless, no one wanted to deal with her spirited nature. Her stepsister, Naomi, Shemar's blood cousin actually told him that he shouldn't be bothered with Pam. She claimed that Pam was trouble and they weren't actual blood relations. Therefore, he wasn't obligated to deal with her issues. But Shemar cared less about them sharing biological kinship. Pam was family. Family bonded together in good and bad times.

"You just have to get back out there," he advised. "Just like I am."

Pam's red glossed lips puffed open in surprise. "You're back out there? You're dating?"

"Y-yes," he answered. "Well, kind of. I mean, I'm open to dating if I meet the right person." But hadn't he been saying that ever since the divorce from Leslie? In his heart, he knew all women weren't as wretched as she was. He also knew he was giving her power over his happiness by not giving another woman a chance. What's more, he missed the closeness of a romantic relationship. Along with it, he missed sex, too. Indeed, he missed it all. Even so, something within him prevented him from letting anyone near.

Fortunately, since coming to the island three months ago to immerse himself in his passion after giving up his psychology practice, he'd been able to be around the unconditional love of his family. Having recently opened a new health spa, Pam was residing in Bermuda for the summer, too. She was great company for him. He enjoyed being there for her as well.

Pam shook her head as she bent forward, reaching for a kernel of popcorn. "Maybe something is wrong with me." She popped the buttery-salty treat in her mouth, nibbling as she talked. "I just don't understand how he could say that he loves me and just suddenly do a turnaround. Just slap me in the face, dogging me out."

"Because he's a fool," Shemar swore, swiping up some popcorn. "It's him! It's not you." He began chewing. "You're a beautiful, successful, intelligent, good woman, and you deserve to be treated like the queen you are." He dipped his fingers back in the bowl.

Pam glowed from his compliments. "You always know what to say to me, Shemar." Her fingers ran back through her honeyed locks. "Always. Always have."

"I'm not just saying it to make you feel good. It's true."

Her lips curled up gently, her eyes scattering softly over his face. They only ceased by his mouth, where full, moist lips were beset by a neat circle of dark hair. "I believe I'm everything beautiful when you say it."

Shemar and Pam continued conversing about her most recent relationship while enjoying the popcorn. He tried to uplift her with all the tools he possessed as a psychologist as well as what he felt as a man. Through it all, he couldn't help wishing that Joesive was right there. He ached to tell him off. How could he throw her away?

Shemar longed for what so many men threw away—a woman who just desired to love him for himself, a woman to whom he would return just as much love. He would make love to her in every way, and he would do it so well, so passionately from his heart that she would never want for another.

Savoring her favorite snack, Pam watched Shemar walk back to the kitchen. With a stride that was cool and at the same time majestic, his muscular build was talking to her tonight in those jeans and tight black T-shirt. *Fine, fine, fine. Lord knows he's fine*, she thought. More than that, though, Shemar was as much a part of her as her

own breath. She'd felt that way since first laying
eyes on him. That was when she was nine.

He wasn't as incredibly gorgeous then as he was
now. It didn't matter. He was kinder to her than
anyone she'd ever encountered. He took time with
her when everyone else was impatient. He nursed
her wounds, wiped her tears, and held her if she
starved for a hug. When she was flunking out of
college and at every profession she attempted to
do, Shemar assured her that everyone had a gift
to offer the world. He challenged her to do something she loved. Hence, she opened a chain of
health spas, which were a phenomenal success.

Sure, a woman had stolen him from her for a
while. A little while. They were no more. Now, Nell
had provided this lovely place for them to reunite.
Life had come full circle. Her true love was almost
hers in every way. She just had to expose her feelings—expose them when she felt he was ready to
receive them. She couldn't bear turning him off.
Instead, she would do her part and wait for the
signs telling her to go forward.

"Let's go upstairs to Ms. Nell's room," Pam
yelled into the kitchen.

Shemar swung through its doors, carrying two
glasses of grape juice. He handed one to Pam.
"And what's so interesting up there, young lady?"

"Cable," she said, gazing up into his eyes. "You
know the cable reception is better up there. There's
this movie I want to see. I hear it's hot."

Soaring among the sunny skies, letting her mind
drift with the mellowness of the clouds, Marita
pondered Aunt Dollie's parting words. How could

she not listen to a woman who'd accomplished so much with her life? Coming from an impoverished upbringing, she had educated herself, becoming so proficient in her profession that she was the head nurse of ICU in Washington Memorial Hospital.

So how could she not be strong? She had to deal with it. She had to look each pain square in the face and know that it had not killed her. First, her boyfriend of three years, Richard, had announced that he was tired of having a relationship with a workaholic attorney. Then he confessed that he was involved with a clerk who assisted him in his architectural firm. It turned out that when Marita was putting in those long hours at one of Washington, DC's top law firms, he was putting in long hours too—in a bedroom.

But more misery was to come from another source—her job. Her firm was granted the unfortunate opportunity to defend an affluent rape suspect. He plowed more than an abundance of money into the firm, making them overlook everything, especially the evidence that he was guilty. Worse, they wanted Marita to handle the case against a victim who was around Marita's age. Knowing what she did about him, she was vehement about not representing him. Outrage hardly described the partners' reactions. Marita was fired.

The third blow came with her mother, Carol, who was in a near-fatal car accident immediately after Marita was fired. Narrowly escaping death, she then had to battle paralysis. With Marita constantly at her side and paying for the best care she could afford, Carol beat that, too. Even so, her mother needed intensive therapy. The doctor suggested that the best facility was a resort-type resi-

dence in South Carolina. What else could she give
her mother but the best? Wasn't that why she had
become a lawyer? Some lawyer she was now, she
thought, peering out of the window. She had come
from so far, but inside she wasn't any happier than
she was so many years ago. Only once had she
been truly happy. That was the summer of her life
with Remmy.

A taut sensation knitted behind her eyes every
time she thought of him. Always, he lay delicately
in the back of her mind. What's more, there
hadn't been any lover she didn't compare to
Remmy. The magic she felt with him persisted in
stirring up powerful emotions within her.

"Oh, Remmy," she whispered, pressing her face
against the glass. How could someone with such a
good heart do such a bad thing? What kind of person
was she to fall for someone like him? Lord knew she
fought off any attraction to anyone who could have
been another Remmy. The straight-arrows were the
sole men she allowed in her life.

If only she were satisfied with them. Why did none
of them ever give her the feelings Remmy did? Would
there ever come a day that she didn't think of him?
Ache for him? Would she ever feel like she had with
him with another man? If only . . . If only she could
have kissed his lips one more time. Unfortunately,
that was an impossibility. Sometimes Marita even
thought of the one who had made it that way. Did
he curse her for what she did to him? Did he feel
any remorse for what he'd done?

Valerian Tate walked out of the River's Edge State
Prison and glanced back over his shoulder to see the

guards closing the towering iron gates behind him. His stiff, thin mouth curled with his spiteful amusement. They'd treated him like dirt during the eighteen years he was incarcerated. Fortunately, though, he was smart enough to pretend it never bothered him. Good behavior, he knew, would get him an early release. Today that was a reality.

Stepping off of the manicured prison greenery, the summer rays felt good against his pale skin. Clutching the tiny suitcase, which contained everything he now owned, Valerian waved the other hand out along the roadside. A lanky truck driver stopped. With Valerian unresponsive to his endless questions, the driver was glad to let him out at his desired destination—the bus depot in town.

Waiting there, Valerian gazed in wonder at the new-model cars rolling by, the futuristic architecture of some of the buildings, and the short dresses the women wore. He'd missed so much. It all stirred up obscenities that spewed out of him before he realized it. Hearing his offensive outbursts, an elderly lady standing beside him shot him a mean look. With it, she moved away.

Who the hell cares what you think, anyway? he thought, and restrained himself from going after her. Instead, he continued scouring his surroundings. Happy, that's what he was supposed to be. And he had been in the days before his release. Yet in this outside world, with so many changes, so much progress, so much of everything, he felt overwhelmed and somewhat lost. It all summoned up his rage at being cheated. His precious years were gone. His lady friend had stopped writing to him after his third year in prison. Most of his adopted Holy Roller family swore he'd disgraced

them and wanted no part of him. What else did
he have out here? At least his brother. That's
whose home he was headed to. And there was
someone else.

Marita, oh, Marita. Suddenly the smile returned to
his face. Every day he'd embraced the image of
Remmy's stunning girlfriend. And when Valerian's
mind wasn't good enough, he sketched pictures of
her. He could have been a great artist, the other in-
mates complimented him. They had him draw portraits of their families and lovers, and plastered them
around their cells. He'd done the same with the thou-
sands of portraits he'd done of Marita.

She was unforgettable to him long before she
buried him alive at the trial. As soon as he laid
eyes on her, he felt connected to her. She looked
at him like he was the world. He believed she
wanted him. He swore he saw that in her eyes.
Yet, when she sealed such an inclement fate for
him, he knew otherwise.

It was Marita's testimony above all the others
that had sent him to a life imprisonment. Yes,
there were the federal agents who'd been tracking
his counterfeiting efforts, who'd also witnessed
Remmy's murder, along with his cohorts. But it
was Marita's gripping, tearful testimony about her
fiancé being shot to death before her eyes that
riled the jury into giving him a life sentence.

Valerian was given life and then some. Each day
he never missed thinking of the one who had
made it all possible, as he pictured her at this moment. "Marita, oh, Marita," he whispered. "You
have no idea what I have in store for you."

Two

It was another world, and the more Marita drove her little red rental through the enchanting mélange of mostly island lushness with touches of cosmopolitanism, she was swept into the wonderment of it all. Awestruck by every expanse flying by her, relying on her mapped directions to the town house, everything not only looked and smelled centuries removed from Washington, but she felt different.

The tolerable heat was coating her skin like her mother's arms wrapping around her. Blade-leafed palm trees, hills, coves, footpaths, tobacco fields, corn patches, along with a rainbow potpourri of flowers, awakened her with such a belonging to nature. The way islanders smiled at her, bidding her good day, filled her with warmth like she was around family and at home. Marita was lost in this paradise but hadn't even panicked. Lost or not, when she beheld the red-orange-yellow twilight first shading the turquoise waters, she had to stop the car. She had to get near it.

Soon Marita stood by the shoreline oblivious to the beach's legions of inhabitants who delighted in the early evening. Her sandals in hand, her toes embedded in the dusk-brushed grains of pink

sand, she stared out to sea. Silken lengths of the
deepening blue stretched out to what seemed like
the borders of the entire earth. Swishing whispers
played into the air softly. It all soothed her. She
was in another world. One that made everything
that had happened not seem so unconquerable.
Perhaps . . . Perhaps she could be happy again.
Really, *really* happy. That kind of happy that felt
so good all the way to her bones.

"I like to look out at the water, too."

Marita glanced back over her shoulder toward
the sound of the masculine voice. A tall man with
a paper-white smile was approaching her with a
leisurely stride. Wearing a pale blue shirt and
slacks, his face looked sculpted and as if dark
chocolate were painted over him. He was so regally
beautiful beneath the dusk's exotic light he almost
didn't look real.

Unlike when she was in the city, Marita didn't
feel suspicious of the motives of the stranger coming near her. Already the people on this island
had impressed her as being friendly, mellow, with
their guards down and open for whatever enjoyment the day offered, whether it was merely a joke
with a neighbor or the shimmer of sunshine over
the Atlantic.

"I come here and sit for hours sometimes," he
divulged, finally standing next to her.

Marita looked at his chiseled features. "It was
like I was seeing a postcard. So I just had to stop
my car and get a longer look."

"I'm Dr. Clifton Harrison. You can call me
Cliff." He extended his hand.

Marita shook it. "Marita Sommers."

"Marita is a pretty name." He gazed in her eyes,

then sneakily traveled down the length of her body. "A pretty name for a *very* pretty woman."

"Thank you." Marita couldn't miss being checked out.

"Vacationing? I know you're not from around here."

"I'm staying for the summer at a relative's place."

"Great!" he exclaimed. "I hope I see lots of you."

Not yet in the mood for men, Marita took that as a sign to make a gracious exit. "Well, nice meeting you, Clifton. I better head out." She made a step toward the roadside where the car was parked.

He tapped her arm, halting her. "I didn't mean to scare you off."

"You didn't. I'm just in a hurry to get to where I'm going. In fact, I'm sort of lost, too. The rental car agency gave me a map, and I'm not really good with maps. Could you give me some directions?"

"I have my car. I'll show you the way."

"No, thanks. If you could just tell me how to get there, I would appreciate it so much."

After receiving directions from her new acquaintance, Marita watched him lean into the car window as she buckled her seat belt.

"Thank you," she said, attempting to avoid his deep eyes boring hard into hers. "You've been very helpful."

"I can be more helpful and show you around my beautiful homeland."

Smelling his breath mints blowing over at her, she tucked a long dark hair behind her ear. "I'm flattered. And I appreciate your kindness, but I can't just go out with a stranger."

Nodding his head, Cliff started fumbling in his pants pocket. "I understand." Then he stood upright, searching his shirt pocket, eventually locating a card. He handed it to Marita. "This has my home and office number on it. Call me. Then after we talk and get to know each other we won't be strangers."

Marita still had no intention of phoning him. Out of politeness, she accepted the card and placed it in her purse. "Have a good evening and enjoy the ocean." She started up the engine.

He backed up, providing the vehicle ample room to maneuver. "When should I expect your call? I'm single, you know. No kids, either. No ex-wives with hatchets."

Marita's berry-glossed lips curled, feeding off his playful expression. "I'm sorry. I just don't go out with men I don't know."

She drove off, and once she was a good distance away observed him in the rearview mirror. Watching her drive off for several moments, he eventually headed back toward the seaside. Not a bad body, Marita thought. Hell, the man was superfine, she admitted. Of note, too, he made sure she knew he had eminence, announcing that he was a doctor. Even so, she just wasn't in the mood for male companionship right now. Besides that, he was a stranger. Yes, the folks she'd encountered during her first day in Bermuda were cordial. Nevertheless, she couldn't be ridiculous and take chances. She didn't know a thing about this Clifton Harrison. For all she knew he could be a nutcase.

Biting into a sweet cherry she'd plucked from a tree earlier, Marita was glad that her beach pal had claimed she was minutes away from the town house. After all, she was tired. A hot bath with her favorite cherry-scented bubble bath was going to do wonders for her.

Wind chimes clattering against sunset's sultry breeze indicated to Marita that the house she pulled up in front of was Aunt Dollie's and Ms. Nell's. Her aunt had told her that among the neat row of white stone town houses, hers was the sole one that had such an ornament decorating the porch. Marita thought they sounded mystical.

The fading sunset didn't grant her enough light to take in the outside of the lovely home, its garden, and the scenery around it when Marita reached the porch, though she could appreciate the ocean in the distance. It sparkled like finely cut diamonds were poured over it. Every other sight would have to wait until the morning.

Anxious to get inside, Marita opened the screen door and wedged herself between it and the front one. Fumbling down in her pocketbook for the key, she inhaled the salty air exuding from the sea. However, oddly enough, there was another interesting scent coming from beyond the door. The fragrance was of some tartlike incense. Strange, she thought, attempting to contain a wave of worry.

Entering the house, an explosion of the burning scent became more pronounced. Where was it coming from? Was Shemar here? Did he drop by already? After a quick sweep of the soft pastel comfort of the furnishings, she was relieved that nothing seemed in disarray. Still, her concern dared

her farther into the house. That's when she heard
the subtle sounds of music playing. Her kind of
music. A low R&B jam that she remembered from
back in those old days. She recognized the singer
as Jeffrey Osborne and the tune might have been
called "Love Ballad" or something like that.

Marita followed the soulful crooner all the way
to the upper floor, emotionally professing about
never knowing love as deep as he was experiencing. There were several rooms lining the hall. She
spotted a light coming from one of them, the
same room the song flowed from. Curiosity prod-
ded Marita carefully toward that direction. But she
was startled still at the doorway.

A man and a woman were sitting on the bed
laughing and talking. All he was wearing was a pair
of unzipped jeans. She was completely dressed, but
her hair and clothes were disheveled.

The guy was the first to rise when spotting
Marita, his mouth as agape as hers was. His large,
glistening, rippling, bronzed chest stuck to her
eyes even as she spoke. "I'm sorry. I wasn't expecting anyone to be here. You must be one of
Shemar's friends." There had to be a sensible explanation to who these people were, so cozy in
Aunt Dollie's and Ms. Nell's home. There had to
be. "Is he letting you stay here? Did he go out
for a while?"

Staring in speechlessness, the man tugged his
jeans up higher.

Marita noticed how flat his stomach was as he
did it. "You see my aunt told me I could stay here
this summer," she went on. "It's her place, along
with Shemar's grandmother's. I didn't mean to
barge in on you two like this."

Pam Wingate looked from Shemar's handsome face to the much-too-beautiful one that captivated Shemar.

Marita didn't notice. She had moved from that muscled stomach and enormous chest up to his mouth. The goatee surrounding it only made it more obvious. It was almost as if his lips spoke without moving. It was as if they spoke without words coming out of them. Maddening seduction was what they boasted of.

Shemar couldn't react in any other way except to look at Marita standing there. It was actually *her*. Not one of the mirages his mind had created over time. It was the Marita Sommers he'd spent some of his young teenage years with, and from thereafter had never been the same.

The most exquisite creature he'd ever seen, she had continued to bewitch him in so many ways the more time they spent together. She was unlike anyone Shemar had ever known. As poor as dirt, she carried herself like royalty, and expected no less from her future than to become royalty. Wealth would help her escape that monster poverty that had crippled both their lives and families. She always talked about how she would grow up one day, evading such an existence, having every material possession she ever dreamed of. She would become as rich as the boys who fascinated her. They were the ones who came from the right families, lived in huge homes on the upscale part of town, and were seen riding with their prominent fathers in the most expensive cars ever made.

Shemar had tried to make her see him. They'd spent day after day together, and never could she see him the way he wanted her to. Even though he was as drowned in the dregs of impoverishment as she was, he yearned for her to see him as more than a good friend, or a confidant who she talked to about the boys she had crushes on. Shemar wanted her to see him and how much he felt for her. He longed for her to feel all the emotion for him, too.

She never did. That was clear to him when Marita forgot he existed. His family relocated to Michigan and there was no further contact. There were so many letters he wrote to her. All were unanswered. There were long-distance phone messages he'd left with her mother because Marita seemed to always be out somewhere. With each, he assured that Marita could return the call collect. He would pay for it by working extra hours at his McDonald's job. Again, there was no response. There was even a train ticket he sent her. It was a surprise, inviting her to his high school graduation. Once more, he wasn't acknowledged.

Over the years his grandmother had kept him informed about Marita's life. There was a counterfeiting fiancé who gave her everything in the world, who'd been murdered. There were a select few other boyfriends. None of the relationships had led to marriage. Sadly, her mother had recently been in a horrible car accident. He felt terrible about that, but was grateful that she was recovering.

Shemar also knew that Marita was a lawyer, earning a fantastic salary. However, she had run into some problems and was fired. Well, he wished her well with that, he thought, still staring at her, wondering how it could be possible that she . . . that she could be even more . . . No, he didn't even want to think it, admit it, say it.

He suspected that Marita was too much like his ex-wife. They were shallow down to the bone. Possibly that's why it seemed like time was suddenly still for Shemar. Of course Marita and he were mature adults now. Nevertheless, if Marita had an ulterior motive for coming here, she had another thing coming. If money was her goal, she might as well have turned back around toward home. His grandmother, who had clearly set this up, had apparently let slip what he was doing with his life, and that's why Marita had made her sudden appearance. She had no income and was searching for a meal ticket. Why else?

"You really don't know who I am, Marita?" Shemar spoke unexpectedly, reaching over to the nightstand. He pulled his T-shirt over his head and down over his chest.

Marita. The way he said her name echoed like she was in a dream. It made her look at his eyes, and behold the familiarity. At the same time, there was also something about them so indescribable, so intense, so sensual, it lured her down to Shemar's lips. They, too, were familiar, but something about them was so inexpressible her breath quickened.

"Shemar?" Marita hadn't meant it to, but his name came out in a whisper.

Pam, running her fingers back over her short tresses, trying to make them neater, didn't know if this woman was an ex. She didn't know what this woman wanted, but she was determined not to behave uncivilly. Surely that would turn Shemar off. "You two must be old friends?"

Neither one seemed to heed her. Pam merely watched as the woman who she hoped was a long-lost blood relative, approached Shemar with her toned arms opened for a hug. In turn, Shemar stepped toward her. Observing the display, Pam did feel relieved about one thing: Shemar didn't seem glad about this reunion. On the other hand, there was something unsettling about all this. Maybe it had to do with how uptight Shemar now seemed. Did they have a thing that he'd never gotten over?

Marita reached her arms around mountains of chest, noticing that Shemar seemed reluctant to return the cordiality. Once he did succumb, she felt his thick arms and rock-hard chest enclosing her. For a moment, she couldn't resist closing her eyes and simply holding on. It didn't even feel like she was hugging her old pal Shemar. Just as she couldn't describe the look in his eyes, she couldn't describe what his embrace felt like. It was a sensation she wouldn't easily forget.

Shemar hadn't wanted to touch her. He had hoped maturity and time would have opened his eyes to seeing the lack of depth within her to the point that she would have no sensual affect on him. To his regret, that part of him remained weakened. So many years had passed and now he stood afraid. Afraid that she would feel the fierce drumming in his chest that reminded him that some fires could never be quenched. If anything, with time they burgeoned beyond control. And knowing he was holding her much too long, Shemar forced himself to release her, deciding to introduce his two guests. "Pam, this is a friend of the family, Marita. Marita, this is my cousin, Pam."

Marita reached for Pam's hand and smiled. "Nice to meet you."

"You, too." Pam's tiny dimples blinked at her. "So you're visiting? Where are you from?" But right after asking the question, she realized she already knew. She remembered Shemar speaking of Marita before.

Noting for the first time that Pam didn't have an accent, Marita was about to answer, but Shemar spoke first. "She has lived in Washington, DC all her life." He still couldn't get over that Marita was actually in front of him.

"So you've been keeping up with me?" Marita joked.

Shemar couldn't find anything funny. Actually, he hadn't made a hint of a smile since Marita entered the room. "My gran tells me things, just like your aunt tells you I'm sure."

Aware more and more of his coolness, Marita wondered what was up with him. She hadn't seen or heard from Shemar in years, and this is how he behaved when they met up again? Could it be that he was annoyed because she had intruded on a moment with his cousin? "Enjoy the rest of your evening. I'm going to hit the sack. And again I'm sorry for interrupting. I'll find Aunt Dollie's bedroom. She told me it was the pink room. Good night."

"Sweet dreams," Pam returned.

Shemar remained quiet, listening prudently to her footsteps on the lush carpeting, then to the door down the hall as it opened and closed. Pam crawled back atop the cottony covers and resumed her position on the bed. Yet it was clear that the romantic atmosphere had been ruined for Shemar.

"Is she more than a family friend?" Pam asked, as Shemar relaxed next to her. "Is she also an ex?"

"No. Marita's a family friend like I said."

Marita definitely figured in Valerian's mind even as he stood ringing the bell at his brother's doorstep. Scanning around the picturesque moderate-sized home setting in the midst of Silver Springs, Maryland, he could see that his younger brother, Kenny, had done well. Before Valerian had gone to prison, Kenny was working by day as a clerical worker while attending night school for teaching. Back then Valerian had patted him on his back for his efforts, outwardly cheering him on. Secretly, he hoped Kenny would get a rude awakening to the world and learn like he did that he was not going to get anywhere on that simple brick road that all law-abiding citizens skipped along. Then he would join his operation. The murder sentence thwarted that.

So, Kenny did get a little further, Valerian thought, looking at the home, and the sensible little car parked neatly in the driveway. His brother had done all right. Not like *he* was planning to do with Marita's help, but Kenny was a far cry from where they'd been. And where they'd been, Valerian would always remember, was hell.

Impoverishment had surrounded them throughout his childhood. Yet what made matters worse were his parents. His father was a womanizer who eventually left the family for another woman, some singer. Valerian remembered they lived not too far from the dilapidated tenement where he'd grown up. Sometimes in playing with Kenny and his other friends, he would even see his father with that woman, and the baby they soon had. His father would kiss all over that little baby, while pretending that he and Kenny didn't exist. He would walk right by them, not even acknowledging them with a hello or a smile, as he might have done walking past a stray dog in the street.

At home with his mother, things weren't any better. She would yell at Kenny and him for just about any reason. Each time, she had to put their father's name in it, stating that they were nothings, like he was. Eventually, she became so sick of the sight of them, she dragged them across town to a sister she hardly had contact with. His Aunt Libby and her family were religious fanatics. according to her mother. Even so, her mother must have thought religious fanatics were good enough to raise her children. Because on that day, she told her sister, "I don't want these children anymore. I can't stand them anymore. I just don't want them. Do you?"

Valerian never forgot those words. They became especially poignant because even though Libby took them in, she seemed to feel the same way his mother did. Yes, they were cared for, went to school, and continuously went to church, but he never felt loved. Their eyes would never light up when he came into a room. Their voices would never soften when they spoke to him. His good grades in school were never acknowledged. Kenny and he were just there.

When Valerian became older he found a way to be wanted. Engaging in various criminal activities and being so proficient that he was never caught, gained him instant respect from those who shunned the ordinary life. Beautiful women, and everyone flocked to him for his genius. He would see that look in their eyes. He was wanted.

Wanted like when he opened the door, and Kenny's eyes lit up. They hugged, and as Valerian caught sight of something exquisite his eyes lit up, too. There was that look in the woman's eyes who stood behind them—a look that told him he was wanted.

"And is this your wife?" Valerian asked, letting go of his brother, stepping toward the hazel-eyed beauty who seemed fascinated with him.

Tearfully happy and revealing the same gap-toothed smile that Valerian had, Kenny turned toward Jatique. "Jatique, this is my brother I was telling you about. Valerian, this is my lovely bride. Can you believe I've been married three years?"

"That's something," Valerian said, smiling at his sister-in-law. He kissed her hand. "Thank you for taking such good care of my brother."

She half smiled as she gazed at him playfully. "I'm going to take care of you, too, while you're here."

Valerian walked inside the house. Checking out the modest furnishings, he was really starting to feel like he was out of prison now. He was going to have a life again. He'd stay with Kenny for a while, make his contacts so he could get things in order for his plans for Marita; then he would flee the country and live like a king. Yet as he turned toward his brother's wife, and saw that certain something in her eyes as she stared at him, he knew he was going to feel like a king before he left. He hoped Kenny's bed had good springs. It had been a long time since he'd been with a woman.

Three

As tired as Marita was, it was hard for her to get to sleep during the night. It was Shemar's aloofness that kept her awake. Why had he been cold toward her? Was it really the intrusion? Had he hoped to have the house the entire summer for him and his cousin? Wondering and wondering, she eventually drifted off to sleep.

The next day when she woke, she hoped he would soften toward her. His cousin Pam wasn't around. Maybe they could get a chance to catch up on each other's lives. How wrong she was. Not only was Shemar aloof that day, but the entire week. They were like passing ships in the house. She'd initiate some type of conversation. Halfheartedly, he would answer. The dialogue wasn't even that demanding of him, either. It was small talk, about the weather, the island, or the sightseeing tours she would go on each day. All in all, it was meaningless chitchat, but something she hoped that would connect them to talking like they used to. She wanted to know about him. She wanted to do more than just look at him. And that she couldn't help. Shemar had surely changed. And from the looks she kept getting from him, she didn't look the same to him, either. There was that something in his eyes that she'd seen in the room when they saw each other again.

After showering one morning, she started to go downstairs and get some of whatever was smelling so fried and also so sweet, while wearing the big sloppy T-shirt that she'd slept in. Except for some reason she felt like looking together. After pinning her hair up in a bun, dabbing on a little eyeliner and raspberry lipstick, she completed her look for the day with a denim top with matching pants, along with brown midheeled sandals. She heard his cousin as she made her way down the stairs. She'd only seen Pam in passing during the week when she came over and she and Shemar went out. They hadn't really had a chance to talk.

Shemar and Pam were enjoying an assortment of breakfast delicacies that he'd prepared out on the patio, when he was distracted. Marita was coming toward them from in the house. He looked, then was unable to resist looking again as she approached, before making himself concentrate on his food.

Pam hadn't missed the way Shemar's eyes lit up and was anxious to see what was so interesting. When Marita finally emerged into the sunlight on the deck, she soothed herself that Shemar had just been looking at Marita's outfit. The midriff denim top with the matching pants wasn't a bad combination. That's what it was. Just the ensemble.

"Cute outfit," Pam complimented Marita. She wondered how much she worked out a day to have a stomach so flat.

"Thank you. And good morning to you both."

Shemar looked up. "Morning." He sipped some of his fresh-squeezed juice, then set it back down.

"Sit down and have some breakfast." Not the slightest warmth accompanied the invitation.

Making herself comfortable in the straw deck chair, Marita pondered what was holding Shemar back from being pleasant to her. Was he angry with her for some mysterious reason? "It smells delicious."

"It is," Pam declared, forking a small greasy sausage. "I don't eat this bad all the time. Actually, I try to eat like Shemar does, but I slip sometimes. He knew I would want some of this naughty food, so he made it for me. Think he's trying to spoil me." She bumped her elbow against his mischievously.

With a slight smile, he bumped hers back. "I shouldn't have made you that. You should be eating fruits and whole grains for breakfast."

Marita was intrigued. Shemar had a dish of fruit in front of him, along with a grainy cereal in another bowl. "Are you a vegetarian?" She slid her chair slightly, avoiding a streamlet of sun bearing down on her face.

"Not completely," he answered, reaching for the newspaper instead of meeting her gaze. "I do eat baked chicken occasionally."

"He's good, though," Pam gushed. "This man eats so healthy, and cooks such delicious, nutritious foods. Even these pancakes I have here are made with whole wheat."

"Ooh, let me try that." Marita reached for the pancakes. After putting some on her plate, she poured a layer of strawberry syrup over them.

Shemar glimpsed away from his paper for a second to see if she liked it. Her orgasmic smile screeched volumes. The way her lips moved struck

him, too. He glanced at them several times. They
were bigger than he remembered.

"Delicious," Marita uttered, as she tasted it.
"Umm."

"Glad you like it." Avoiding looking at her as
he spoke, he turned a page.

"That's why he looks so good," Pam raved. "If
you eat all healthy food all the time how else can
you look?"

Glancing away from the newspaper, Shemar
blushed. "You trying to embarrass me?"

Marita searched for the truth of Pam's words in
Shemar's face. What she saw compelled her to
stare.

Shemar caught her and found staring irresistible,
too. The sunlight seemed to beautify every sensu-
ous feature of Marita's face, altogether giving her
an angelic glow. It even reminded him of a bizarre
experience he had several weeks ago. Although it
was only when he realized that he couldn't have
Marita thinking he was attracted to her, that he
forced his attention back to the news.

Marita thought the same about Shemar, forcing
her attention to her food. She bit into a juicy ba-
con strip. "I eat well sometimes." Pausing, she
chewed, savoring the salty, thoroughly seasoned
flavor, before swallowing. "I was in such a high-
pressure job and constantly on the go, lots of
times I was just hungry or ate whatever was
there."

Pam looked curious. "What type of work do you
do?"

"I'm a . . . I mean I was an attorney." Frowning
from the sun, she shifted from it again.

Shemar pretended to read another page.

Pam couldn't see her as a lawyer. Ms. Sex Kitten, sitting there in her belly blouse and hip hugging jeans didn't look that bright. Then again Marita said she *was* one. "You're not practicing law anymore?"

Suddenly Marita picked at her food because she had to figure out how to respond. She didn't want the baggage of lying just to save face. Neither did she want to get into the ugly details of what had occurred with her last case. "Well, I'm contemplating a career change. I'm going to do that while I'm here this summer."

Liar, Shemar thought, and was drawn to the place again where that lie came from—those lips.

"That's interesting." Pam sipped some orange juice, then set the glass back down on the table. "Real interesting." She wasn't referring to the career or the possibility of changing it. It was the length of time Marita was staying around that lingered in her consciousness. The night when she arrived Marita had mentioned it. Today, it was just settling in for Pam. Marita was going to spend an entire summer in the house with Shemar.

Marita dug her fork into another chunk of pancake. "And what do you do, Pam?" Chewing gently on the strawberry-glazed morsel, she couldn't help sneaking glances at Shemar. Time had truly blessed him. The sunrays streamed across his bronzed skin, highlighting the mountains and depressions of his extremely developed upper body, all revealed in his black tank top. Equally as accentuated in the vivid light was the chestnut hue of his eyes, his full mouth's moistness, and the blackest, shiniest, neatest hair. *Lord, if you haven't*

blessed him I don't know the meaning of the word.
Blessed. Blessed. Blessed.

"I own four health spas."

"Oh, wow," Marita declared, jarred back to Pam by her enthusiasm. Striving not to look Shemar's way anymore, she was truly impressed with his cousin's achievements. She loved the way sisters were really pursuing their dreams these days. "Where are they?"

Lounging across from Marita, Pam tried to appear humble. True to heart, though, she really wanted to boast that she was rolling in millions to this so-called lawyer. Except she knew how humble Shemar was. The epitome of modesty, he admired it in others. "The largest one is located here on the island. And I have a midsized one in New York, another in DC, and another in Michigan, where I'm originally from."

"That's so wonderful. I have to check it out one day. I work out."

Shemar could see that she most certainly did work out. She had worked out so phenomenally, he wondered if it was actually the increasing heat that was starting to make him sweat.

Dabbing a napkin at the beads of perspiration she saw popping across Shemar's forehead, Pam hated that she had to leave for the spa this morning. She dared not imagine what could happen between Shemar and this woman from the time she left to the time she reunited with them again. It had bothered her all week to leave them alone, but she had meetings that she couldn't cancel. At least today she could cut her day in half since it was the Fourth of July weekend.

"I better get going to the spa," Pam admitted. "Though I'm only working a half day today."

"You are?" Shemar was surprised. Normally, she worked the entire day on Fridays. "Because of the holiday weekend?"

"Yes. And I wanted to go shopping for something hot to wear, because I wanted you to take me dancing tonight."

Marita smiled. It had been such a while since she went dancing. With the problems with her mother, the firm, and Richard, her world had been so woeful she forgot enjoyment like dancing ever existed. Shemar treated Pam well.

Speculating, Shemar rubbed at the hair fringing his chin. Despite the holiday, he had planned to work at his computer tonight. On the other hand, he missed simply hanging out to have a good time. "Yes dancing should be fun."

"You used to love to dance," Marita thought aloud.

Shemar couldn't help the hint of a smile that slipped out of him. "I still do."

"You were good, too. Just not as good as me. You know how I used to throw it."

Did he know! That perfectly round booty of hers was all over the place, and his eyes followed it everywhere it went. Thinking about it, an exhilarating rush filled him.

Then Marita finally saw it. That broad, sensual smile that lit up his incredibly handsome face. Though no sooner than it appeared, it disappeared. Replacing it with a stern countenance, he asked, "Would you like to come with us?"

Pam wanted to kick something. Going dancing was supposed to be her time alone with Shemar, for afterward, she was planning to try to seduce him with her luscious dessert. *Be cool,* she chastised herself. *Be cool if you want to win Shemar.* In fact, she could use this to her advantage. If Marita accompanied them, she was going to make sure Marita met a guy at the club. She was going to be her best girlfriend and hook her up.

"You know," Pam said, "if you don't have anything to wear, they have some really hot stuff in the shopping district. Maybe you can come shopping with me this afternoon?"

Marita didn't know what to say. On the one hand she did want to shop. Shopping was one of her favorite things to do, especially clothes shopping. It was so fun and relaxing at the same time. What's more, she did feel like dancing, even if not really meeting guys. She just wanted to have some fun. But was Shemar really asking because he wanted her to come? Or was he just being hospitable because it was the right thing to do?

"I better leave you two alone," Marita announced. "It's a family thing."

Shemar shook his head. "Unacceptable. You're coming. When your aunt calls, I don't want you telling her that I went dancing and didn't take you. Now Ms. Dollie knows that if there is some dancing involved you're going to be there. Am I right?"

Marita was tickled. "You're right."

"And I don't want her telling my gran that I'm not treating you right. So you're coming."

Marita leaned back, giving him a *you-have-nerve* expression, while studying him. She could tell he was stifling a grin. Why wouldn't he laugh? Why wouldn't he just be the old Shemar with her?

In the midst of this interchange, Pam felt like screaming. She didn't like what she was seeing. She didn't like what she was hearing. Mostly, she didn't like what she was feeling—like this chick was trying to steal a man from her who wasn't even hers.

Turning to view all the angles of her figure in the boutique's mirror, Pam just knew the red mini that hugged her athletically feminine form was going to make Shemar foam at the mouth. She had to make him see her in another light. She was sure this outfit would make him lose his self-control.

"What do you think of this?"

Pam swiveled toward Marita coming out of the dressing room, and her spirits sank. The royal blue knit number she was wearing looked beyond incredible.

"Your dress looks so beautiful on you," Marita complimented Pam as she walked toward the mirror, soon sharing it with Pam.

Pam persisted in not commenting as Marita viewed the dress from all sides of her doll-perfect figure.

"You look fabulous in that," an elderly Asian patron strolling by threw over Marita's shoulder. "If you got it flaunt it, girlfriend!"

Marita laughed. "I do like it."

"You do?" Pam mashed up her face sourly. "Isn't it too tight around the hips?"

Marita turned backward, looking over her shoulder at herself in the mirror. "No, it's just the way the dress is supposed to look."

"It is," the salesgirl injected. A tall, slender young lady, she was nearby, fixing items on the rack. Pulling away from her responsibilities, she winded through some garments to get nearer to Marita. "That dress looks perfect on you. You don't need a bigger size or anything. It really shows off that shape of yours. Girl, what I'd give for a body like that."

Pam rolled her eyes.

Marita was convinced. "Thanks. I think I will take it."

"You will?" Pam interjected. "It looks tight to me."

"It doesn't to me."

Pam hunched her shoulders. "OK, suit yourself. You're wearing *that* to the club tonight?"

"I certainly am. I think it's me."

As Marita paid for her dress, Pam scrutinized herself in the mirror again. For some reason, her dress didn't look as spectacular as it first did. She knew of another boutique with really head-turning dresses down the street. In there she was sure she'd find one that topped the one that Marita had bought. No way was she going to allow Marita to outdo her tonight. Not when Shemar was at stake. She knew that he already loved her. But she was going to look so beautiful he would love her in a much different way.

Trying to complete the outlines for his work presentations, Shemar was sitting at a table on the porch with his laptop in front of him. He couldn't seem to focus, which was unusual for him. It was bizarre for him because he loved his work so pas-

sionately. When a taxi drove up and the driver
pulled open the back door for Marita to get out,
he was certain his concentration wouldn't improve.
From where he sat, he took a long, lazy look at
her in that belly revealing blouse with snug, matching pants.

Admittedly, Marita was superfine when he knew
her years ago. But now . . . with the way her face
had become so . . . but now with the weight she'd
put on in *those* places. Well, she just made Shemar
think of things. So much so, he was soon swallowing the lump in his throat.

However, what he didn't relish watching was the
interplay between Marita and the driver. Old
enough to be her father in Shemar's opinion, the
cabby was obviously flirting with her as he un-
locked the trunk. Together, among laughter and
chatter, he and Marita unloaded all the packages.
There were so many of them, mostly inscribed with
designer names. For a second his ex-wife crossed
his mind. What a shopping maniac she had been.
Nonetheless, Leslie was instantly forgotten when
Shemar spotted three of his male neighbors approaching Marita and the driver. Wearing their
construction clothes, they were evidently coming
from work.

They were in no hurry to make it to their
homes, either. They also laughed and talked with
Marita while unloading her packages. After all four
men deposited the bags on the porch, and flirted
with Marita some more, they left, headed to their
various destinations. Shemar gave the men the
steady evil eye until they disappeared into their
respective town houses.

Eventually, he granted Marita his undivided attention. "You know, you just can't be friendly to anyone, even here in peaceful-looking Bermuda."

"I know." She was getting a kick out of how he was looking and acting. If she hadn't known better she would think he was jealous. She guessed that protectiveness that he often showed her long ago was still there. Considering how he'd behaved thus far, that made her feel good.

"We were just talking," she said, smiling. "Nice neighbors."

"They're OK. But it's best that you stay away from them."

"And why is that?" She noticed he was barefoot. *Big* bare feet; she knew what that meant.

"All three of those guys are married, for one thing. Just hang around a while and you'll see their wives . . . and kids."

"That's a sufficient reason."

"I'm glad you think so. And why did you come home with that cab driver? Where's Pam? I thought she was taking you and bringing you back."

"She was beeped. An emergency at the spa. She said to tell you she's looking forward to dancing later."

Nodding, he scanned the porch. Packages of every size were everywhere. "I see you bought out the town."

"I hadn't shopped in a while. Thought I'd treat myself."

He nodded again, this time with an introspective expression. "You said you would buy what you wanted when you grew up."

Marita looked touched. "So you remember how

I used to go on?" She leaned back against the
banister.

"Oh, yes, I remember how important money was
to you. Still is, I see." He was noticing all the designer names.

Marita sashayed over to his computer, positioning herself so she could see what he was doing.
"What's this?"

"Work." He closed the top.

It made Marita curious. "What type of secret operation are you doing?"

"You know what I'm doing." He studied her to
see if she really did. He knew Pam wouldn't have
told her, because he always stressed to her about
how private he was about his work. Yet his grandmother's mouth was another story.

Marita looked baffled. "No, I don't. I know you
were a psychologist. But Aunt Dollie said Ms. Nell
won't tell her what you're doing now. And you
know how nosy my aunt is, bless her sweet heart.
So tell me what it is."

With squinted eyes, Shemar continued studying
her. She almost looked like she was telling the
truth. Still, he wasn't sure. He'd even called his
grandmother during the day to find out if she'd
been telling everyone his business. He'd only
made contact with the answering machine. "You
really don't know what I'm doing here in Bermuda?"

"No, I don't. Tell me."

He sat back, looking up at her. "I'll tell you
when I'm ready."

She sighed, not understanding all the secrecy.
"Whatever you say." She began picking up all her
new things when he stood.

"Don't bother with those. I'll take them in."

"That's nice of you."

His eyes clung to her hips swaying as she headed toward the door. "And don't bother with that trouble down there."

She curved around to see him throwing his head toward the neighbors' houses. Marita smiled. "You're mighty worried about what I do."

"I'm not worried." He began picking up the bags. "It's just that I feel responsible. I—"

"Responsible?" She stepped inside the house.

Carrying the bags, he followed. "Yes, while you're here, staying here with me, I am responsible. If anybody touches a hair on your head, Ms. Dollie and Gran are coming after me. So if that means I'm responsible, I am."

"Whatever you say." Amused and warmed by all this, she headed up the stairs. "I'm going to shower and take a nap before we go dancing. You can leave the bags by the bedroom door."

Shemar couldn't hear those parting words because he was too busy listening to the other sounds. They were made as he watched her walk up the stairs. They came from those dungarees. Those back pockets on those dungarees had rhythm. Boy, he was sure entranced by the song they were playing.

Aunt Dollie was playing some stirring tunes of her own shortly after entering her home. It had been a long day at work. Sighing, exhausted as she plopped back in her green-plushed recliner, she hummed with Shirley Ceaser praising the Lord in her fervent, powerful voice. Gospel music always did something magical to her. It always uplifted her. After witnessing all the suffering and demise at the hospital, Dollie was transported to colossal hope with the holy sounds of a spiritual.

In love with nursing the sick as she was, that didn't prevent her from getting depressed from her job at times. There was constant stress, rude doctors, prolonged hours, and patients she wanted to help, but the help they needed was no longer in any man's hands. Sometimes she even debated leaving it all behind and just traveling on those all-expenses-paid trips Nell was always offering. In these last years it seemed like her best friend had hit the lottery the way she had all this excess cash. She even suggested paying for all of the town house in Bermuda. Dollie had too much pride to allow that.

Still, it made her wonder. Where was Nell getting it all from? Her husband had died many years ago with no more than a few thousand in the bank, along with a small insurance policy. So maybe it was her children and grandchildren helping her out, Dollie guessed. They were middle-class professionals, all with cushy salaries. Perhaps they had plenty to spare. In any case, she was sure happy that Nell and her family were so blessed.

The phone suddenly rang, and Dollie was sure it was Nell. There were times Dollie was thinking of Nell and just like magic, she would pick up the phone and her friend's shrill voice would be on the other end. Nell had claimed the same happened with her.

Whenever she couldn't see her, Dollie always looked forward to hearing from her by phone, too. Nell loved to tell Dollie all the happenings at

the senior center she had joined. She had plenty
of gossip to tell. Particularly so since some new
beefcake had entered the scene. Nell swore he was
checking her out. She claimed that he was always
winking at her. Moreover, one of these days she
was going to investigate what that wink was all
about. What Dollie wanted to know was did he
have a partner? She'd thrown her no-good man
out years ago. Now she was ready to do some in-
vestigating, too.

Her chubby hand reached at the receiver from
the diminutive mahogany stand at her side. "Is
that you, foxy mama?"

She heard nothing.

"Hello?"

Nothing still.

"Hello?"

Now there was breathing. Was it one of the elderly patients, who'd become winded in their walk
to the corridor phone? That had happened before.

"Mildred, is that you?"

Click.

"Hell no!" Valerian blasted after slamming down
the phone. "Hell no, it's not no damn Mildred!
It's your next visitor. Just checking on your schedule. Seeing when is the best time to catch you in.
Because, lady, you are going to tell me where that
fine-ass niece of yours is. Yes, you will. You will."

"Who will?"

Valerian turned around and looked from her
feet up. With a tight red jumpsuit splashed over
her big-boned figure, Jatique was smiling.

"Was that your girl you were trying to reach?"

Staring deep in his eyes, she eased down on the sofa. She crossed her legs, looking up at him. "Seems like you've been on the phone a lot trying to reach someone."

Valerian loved the way those hazel eyes were looking at him. It reminded him of how Marita used to look at him. She wanted him. Bad. "No, I'm not trying to reach a girl. Just handling a little business. It's going to be my ticket."

"To where?"

"To the world and everything I want in it."

She patted a spot next to her. "Come sit next to me and tell me what you want. Maybe I can help." Her red lips spread into a cunning smile.

Valerian glimpsed up the stairs. "Where's Kenny?"

"Sleeping. He sleeps a lot."

"All that work teaching will do that to you." He joined her on the sofa. "But what I want to know is, what will *do it* for you?"

Four

As Shemar and Pam waited downstairs for Marita to finish dressing, Pam twirled around repeatedly for Shemar. She was modeling the dress she hoped would raise his temperature to that unbearable level of no return. She was also pondering what a surprise her dress would be to Marita.

Standing by the mantel, sipping from a chalice of sparkling cider his broad smile warmed her as much as his words. "Very nice. Very nice."

A light gray suit molded perfectly over his muscular physique. "Sweetie, you are one hot-looking man tonight. Not that you don't look hot every night." She eased back toward him, gazing up into his eyes. "Maybe I'll get a chance to see how *hot* you are tonight . . ."

"Sorry to keep you guys waiting." Marita was walking down the stairs, but halted midway when she took a look at Pam. Shockingly, they were wearing the same dress. The last thing she wanted was to be a grown woman dressed exactly like another grown woman who wasn't her twin.

Pam's dimples were twinkling. "I liked the dress, too, so I went back and got it." Though when she looked up at Shemar to see what he thought about the two of them wearing the same royal blue mini number, it was as if he didn't even notice the similarity. With his lips parted wordlessly, he was admiring Marita in her dress in a way that he clearly hadn't admired her in hers. It was all in the eyes.

Pam cleared her throat, drawing his gaze to her. "So what do you think?"

"About what?" He set the chalice on the coffee table.

"About Marita and I wearing the same dress?"

Marita feigned a smile rather than asking what she truly wanted to. Why had Pam purchased the same exact dress? At least she could have bought it in another color. But the same dress. She felt silly.

"It's all right," Shemar answered Pam. He noticed Marita's shawl draped on the white couch cushion. "Do you want this around your shoulders?"

"I didn't want to wear anything over my dress," Pam volunteered.

"I do." Marita smiled, wishing that Shemar's sweetness would last. If that was so, she would have believed the look in his eyes really meant something wonderful was happening.

"Here." From behind her, Shemar took his time in gently laying the lacy fabric across her upper back, shoulders, and around to the top of her chest, inhaling something cherry-scented as he did. On her it was so beguiling.

Marita's face flushed as his fingertips gently traipsed across her skin, and a tingle fluttered over her, making her wonder if she was aroused because a man hadn't touched her there in so long, or because this man had touched her. What was happening to her? She couldn't have been attracted to Shemar. "Thank you."

"My pleasure." He was standing behind her, amazed that Marita had turned out to be even more . . . No, he was going to entertain the thought.

Pam was beaming, faking a jubilance and calmness she didn't feel. "Are we ready to party?" She started jiggling her hips, doing a little dance. She couldn't wait to dump Marita off on some character at the club.

"Ready," Marita said, heading out the door first. She had become so warm she needed some air.

Tropical Rhythms, adorned with a gigantic purple blinking neon sign, was a tremendous-sized club, taking up an entire block and ranging up four stories. After Shemar left his Jeep with the valet, he escorted Marita and Pam past the myriad people who were laughing and talking outside the entrance. Upon entering, an amiable sound system was welcome to Marita's ears. She loved partying once in a while, but was sometimes temporarily deafened by the thunderous sound systems some establishments were known for.

"Where do you ladies want to sit?" Shemar asked, ushering them through the packed establishment. "And what do you want to drink?" The place was flooded with people. It seemed he had to utter "excuse me" to make each step.

"I'll have whatever you're having." Pam was shaking her butt, scanning the surroundings, trying to find Marita a man. It wasn't going to be too hard. From her perspective, every male eyeball in there seemed to be looking their way. *Shucks,* she thought. If she wasn't so into Shemar, she would have definitely had some woman leaving with one less man than she'd come in there with.

"And what about you, Marita?" With her back toward him, he watched her bouncing her head to the music and was glad she seemed to like everything thus far.

She spun around to answer him. His eyes fell straight down in hers. "This is a nice place. I'm glad you asked me to come."

"Just want you to have fun."

Pam saw too much lingering of gazes for comfort. A table she spotted was a necessary distraction. "Let's get that one before someone takes it."

Marita and Pam soon became comfortable at a corner table, while Shemar went to the bar. Shemar had mentioned he was getting sparkling cider. Marita wanted the same.

Pam ordered it, but only because Shemar wasn't a big drinker. She could have taken on some real juice on this Fourth of July night. "So you're watching what you drink tonight," she remarked to Marita. "You don't want to get too zooted in case you meet someone and he tries to take things too far."

"Not at all." Marita was slightly bouncing in her seat to the nice but unfamiliar song. "I don't drink. And I'm not looking for anyone, either."

"So you have a man?" Pam hadn't planned to ask. It sprang out of her desperation. Actually, they hadn't even approached the subject of relationships as they shopped during the day.

Marita didn't feel comfortable enough with Pam to spill the intricate details of her love life. So she

was more than ecstatic when one of her favorite
songs came on to rescue her from responding. A
deep one, the story behind it was a man finding
that he was the *other* man in a married woman's
life. The new vocalist Carl Thomas was *sanging* it.

"This is one of my favorite records," Marita
cooed. She was swaying her head from side to side
with the soulful vocalist's emotional delivery.

"Mm-hmm." Pam nodded in agreement. "It's
mine, too."

Enjoying the music, Marita was also scouring the
crowd for Shemar. He seemed to be taking a long
time. As her eyes wandered, a familiar face captured her attention.

Pam saw who she was looking at because he
waved his hand among a bunch of revelers.
"Who's that?" Pam studied the dark, handsome
man approaching. "He is some kind of fine. You
better grab on to him."

Marita wasn't in the mood for him. However, before she could do anything, her acquaintance was
rushing over to the table.

"You didn't call me," Clifton Harrison pointed
out, his smile as bright as the day Marita had seen
it on the beach. "Why not?"

"How are you?" Marita avoided his question.

"Spectacular, now that I've seen your lovely face.
Come dance with me."

"I . . . uh . . ."

"Oh, come on." He reached down at her hand,
pulling her up and onto the dance floor.

When the next song began to play, Marita and
Cliff continued dancing. Pam loved it when Shemar returned to the table and saw the two of
them. They were really hamming it up. They were

laughing, talking, and he was whispering in Marita's ear, too.

Shemar could hardly sit for watching the two of them. "Who's that guy Marita's dancing with?"

"Maybe her next boyfriend," Pam said, clutching the cold glass he'd just set in front of her. "They sure make some pair."

Shemar gazed out at them for a few seconds more, then turned his attention to Pam. "You want to dance?"

"With you? Oh, yes."

Managing to find a vacant space on the crammed dance floor, Shemar flaunted his smoothest moves for Pam. Pam was loving it. Gazing into his eyes, she was strutting her most seductive prancing. That is until she saw his attention wander, accompanied by a sudden scowl. Following his line of vision, she saw what Shemar saw. Marita's dance partner was getting too close and moving his pelvis too close, and too carnally toward her backside. Marita was trying to move away, but the guy kept pulling her back by the waist.

"Excuse me for a second, Pam."

Within a breath Shemar stood beside Clifton. "What are you doing, man?"

Clifton stopped dancing. "Who are you?"

Marita stepped between the two, looking at Shemar. "It's all right. I'll handle my business."

"You weren't handling it. This guy was all over you." He was sneering at Clifton.

Clifton glared back. "I don't know who you are, but you should mind your business. This lovely lady and I were having a good time. She tells me how far to take it, not you."

Raising his hand to emphasize his point, Shemar said, "Look here—"

"No, you look and come with me." Marita grabbed Shemar by the hand, not stopping until they were outside the club and alone near the road.

Marita flung his hand lose. "There was no reason for you to do that! You're taking this responsibility thing a little too seriously."

"And you're letting guys just do what they will with you."

"I am not!"

"You are so. Look at you with the neighbors. Who's next? But that all depends on how much they have to offer, doesn't it?"

That one threw her a step back. "What? What are you talking about?"

"Nothing." Shaking his head, he turned his back to her.

She came around in front of him. "No, there is something. There's been something since I came. You've been giving me this nice-nasty, hot-cold routine. I have no idea what I've done. But I don't like being played with."

"And you were playing with fire in there with that guy. I know you don't know him."

"I know enough to dance with him. I wasn't taking him home. Just dancing. And he's a doctor for heaven's sake."

Shemar grinned. "Oh, that's what it is. Doctor. Doctor equals dollars. You're so much like my ex-wife."

Marita frowned with bafflement. "What are you talking about?"

"You and the Benjamins. I know you were fired from the law firm you worked for."

Marita winced. Why had aunt Dollie told her business? "That's none of your concern."

"So you're thinking the money is going to get low. You need someone to take care of you now."

"I don't need anybody to take care of me." Her head rolled with her conviction.

"Sure you do. So you can keep buying all those designer clothes like you bought today."

"I can buy what I want. I worked for it, so I can spend it."

"And you want to spend some rich sap's, too. It's all about the money with you. You haven't changed, Marita. Always things, things, things. That's what matters to you. You're still the same."

Her mouth opened with astonishment. Marita couldn't figure him out. She couldn't understand where this was coming from. "The same about money. About wanting some? Hell yes, I want money. Try and live without it for a while, and come tell me about how glorious your experience has been."

"Money isn't a bad thing." He stared hard into her sparkling eyes. "It's just that people like you, like my ex, you're greedy and materialistic. That's why you're down here in Bermuda in the first place." He was almost certain his grandmother had told about his fortune. "It's all materialism. All you care about are possessions. You don't care about anything important. You don't care about things that really matter." He thought of how she used to overlook him for those rich guys, of all the letters unanswered, of all the calls. "You don't care about what's inside someone. All the good.

It's all the exterior with you. You're so materialistic."

"Materialistic!" Marita was so fed up with him she felt like her head was popping a vein. "You have the nerve to call me materialistic! Man, do you know I gave up a $270,000-a-year job because of something I believed in? Now that's nowhere near wealthy, but that's a helluva lot for a little black girl from the 'hood. I wasn't doing too bad."

"Granted, you did well."

"Hell, yes, I did more than well. I worked my butt off, and now you have the nerve to tell me that all I care about is money. You have no idea what you're talking about. You have no idea what I been through and where I came from."

"Oh, yes I do. I came from that same place. From dirt poor."

"And you made it out early. You had parents, two parents at that, who were courageous enough to try and move forward. And they did from what I heard. But not me! My mother was a waitress. A damn good one, too, despite her hating her job. She was tired of it. Tired of the long hours and low pay. But unlike your parents, my one parent didn't have courage. She let the world beat her down. And she didn't even know it. Still may not. But I know. She could have applied for school loans and grants and went back to school at night. She could have tried to start a business on the side. She could have done something to improve our situation. But she didn't have courage to move her in that direction. She was deathly afraid.

"The world had the wickedness to tell her that she was a poor black woman and struggle would be her life. And she accepted that. She was scared.

Too scared to try to make a step out. Scared out of her mind that she might fail, that we might wind up homeless or starving. So she settled. Her only hope was for me. That I might do something. That I might even marry someone rich to help us make it out.

"But seed of her womb that I am, I knew better than my mother. I have courage. I wasn't scared. I was poor, but my spirit was rich, and I could see my way out of my circumstances just as clear as I breathed. I wasn't going to be poor and a victim. I was going to be victorious and do my blackness proud. Hard studying, hard working, hard sacrificing, hard believing. I did it!" She beat her chest. "I did it! And not with any man's money! On my own! So don't you dare stand there and belittle me by calling me a gold digger! Don't you dare insult me! You don't know me!"

Before Shemar could stop floating from the waves of her upset, Marita ran off in tears. Shemar went after her, but he wasn't in time. She fled away in a taxi before he reached her.

Shemar rushed toward Pam, looking as if an earthquake had swallowed the world outside.

"What happened? What's wrong?" She touched that big muscle poking out on the arm of his jacket that she'd yearned to touch all night.

"It's Marita." He sighed.

Oh, no. That wench has done something to make him chase after her. "What's wrong with her? I hope she isn't hurt."

"Not physically. Look, do you mind if we leave?

I'll make it up to you, I promise. But I just have to get home to her."

Pam wanted to shake him. Didn't he know the game Marita was playing? "What happened?"

He sighed again. "We had words and argued a little and she left in tears. I just don't feel right about it."

She made him jealous. Dirty trick "Was it about that guy she was dancing with?"

"It was about a lot of things. I have to get back to the house and just check on her. My gran and her aunt wouldn't let me have any peace if I did something to really make Marita miserable. You see, she's been through a lot lately."

Pam put on her most compassionate face, hoping she didn't look as silly as she felt. "It's no problem. I understand. We can leave right now."

Moments later, Pam held back the sailor's curses bursting to be freed from her throat as Shemar drove up in front of her house. In leaving the club, she had no idea he would take her home, then go check on Marita. Pam assumed that she was accompanying him to the town house.

She restrained herself from looking or sounding upset. "Shemar, I thought we would hang at your house tonight. I mean after you smooth things over with Marita."

Shemar didn't want her to think he was deserting her like the rest of the family would usually do. Still it was best she didn't come. "I need to clear things in private with Marita. Please understand."

"What kind of things?" she asked before she realized it. She prayed she didn't sound jealous.

He knew what she was referring to, the relationship thing. "No, we . . . We never had a thing going on, if that's what you're wondering." At least not outside of his wild imagination. "It's just other stuff." Looking off into the darkness outside the front window, he took a deep breath. "There are misunderstandings. Issues. That's what it is."

"All right. No big deal."

After Shemar escorted Pam to her doorstep, she went inside the house. Casually, she dropped her beaded purse on the plush white sofa. Telling herself there was nothing to worry about, she proceeded to her kitchen. Maybe some of her favorite ice cream would further allay her mind. She stopped at the door, kicking the blanched oak hard with her pump sandal. A quarter-sized chip fell to the floor.

"I hate this! I hate it!"

Letting her supple body drop on the sofa, Pam removed each of her sandals. Now a wee more comfortable, she folded her athletic legs across each other like she'd done when she was a girl. That was a memorable time.

Her mother had died from an asthma attack shortly after Pam was born. Her father and her grandmother had raised her in luxury. Never did she want for anything except her father's time. Since he was preoccupied with maintaining the prosperous auto dealership that he owned with his brothers, his mother attempted to give Pam the nurturing she hungered for. The old woman not only overindulged her in affection and her every whim, but every material possession that she desired. Devastated and lonely were understatements of Pam's emotions when her grandmother passed.

Life didn't become easier when her father married a widow, Shemar's Aunt Grace. Pam had instantly disliked her and her daughter, disliked that they were both stealing what little affection her father had to spare. Hence, she'd rebelled, often misbehaving in school and instigating fights and arguments with others. But no matter what she did, Shemar was by her side.

Everyone else tried to be supportive of her, but Pam was a magnet for trouble. Their patience began thinning and completely waned when she slept with her stepsister Naomi's fiancé at sixteen. After Naomi caught them in her bed, all in the family seemed to drift away from her. Everyone except for the one who was always there—Shemar.

And yes, she had let him get away once with his wife, Leslie. Yet, never again would she suffer with the heartbreak of him loving another woman. Now that fate had wound their paths together again, Pam vowed that she would never let him go.

Shemar loved being barefoot, and became so instantly after he entered the house. He was soundless approaching Marita's room. Believing she wouldn't open the door for him if he knocked, he took a chance on opening it. Relieved that she was dressed, he stood still for a moment gazing at her with her back toward him.

The stockings were a perfect color for her sensually proportioned legs. He determined their color was French coffee. Gliding his scrutiny up further, the royal blue dress hit midway the back of her thigh, and moving higher, her buttocks were as round as melons. He began to sweat. Taking out a hanky, dabbing at the droplets of water lining his forehead, his interest climbed further. Long dark hair spilled across her back, the pillow, and the bedspread. It all reminded him of touching her hair when she was younger. She had loved for him to give her a scalp massage and simply play with her hair. She would close her eyes and moan as if in some sexual frenzy. It would make him entertain the ways he could please her further. They would work him into a sweat like the one that he was feeling at this moment. The air conditioner circulating around the house couldn't help him, either.

Marita felt someone sitting on the bed behind her. Before she could turn around to confirm that it was Shemar, a chill quivered over her as hands touched her hair. Curving around, she looked up into Shemar's eyes. They were slowly dragging over her face, making it warm from his expression. It was almost as if he were starving for something he was looking at. Yet Marita knew she had to be wrong there. The way he'd talked to her earlier proved his resentment toward her.

"I didn't hear you come in here." She turned fully around. "What do you want?" She glimpsed the opened front of his shirt. Like his forehead, it was wet and shimmering with perspiration.

"I wanted to apologize." He peered down at her tearstained face and began stroking away the wetness on her cheeks. "I went too far in what I said."

Marita just stared up at him for a moment as he touched her, fighting a desire to close her eyes and beg him to continue touching her face. "Yes, you did go too far."

"I just didn't want you to come here on this island and get in trouble. These guys can be animals around a beau—well, they can get out of control."

She pondered why couldn't he just come out say the word beautiful. Despite that, it delighted her that he viewed her that way. What else did he see? Did he see that she was a woman now, the same way she most certainly saw that he was a man? "Why should I accept your apology?" He stopped wiping her tears, and again, she fought an urge, this time to place his hands right back on her facial skin, and even on her lips. Was she crazy for wanting a man to touch her who'd been so cruel merely moments earlier? "You said some pretty nasty things to me."

"And I was wrong." Looking at her, at how *ripe* she looked lying there beside him, he had to force his hands down. He had to force everything down or he would have to surrender to what he'd been battling so hard since she arrived. "I took some things out on you and it was unfair."

"What kind of things?" She watched his lips trembling as he grappled with what he wanted to say.

"My ex-wife situation. Things were bad. She was wrong and I had no right comparing her to you."

"What did she do to you, Shemar?" She sat up, drawn by the emotion building in his face. This woman had clearly hurt him.

"Let's just say that she loved what I had to offer her more than she did me. And I had no right putting off her negative qualities onto you. I've used all the tools of being a psychologist to help myself, but after two years I'm still a work in progress."

"What happened?"

He looked off, seeing his mind's images. "We married when I had a thriving psychology practice. When I decided to give it up, to pursue something else that was risky, but something I felt a burning passion to do, I told her we would no longer have what we had. We would have savings to live on, but until I excelled at this next venture, we would have to budget our finances. And she wasn't for that." Why had he told her all that?

Curious, she sat up even straighter. "What was this venture?"

"I'll tell you one day."

Marita was amused by his secretiveness. "Are you doing well at it?"

"Very well."

"Good. I really admire when someone has the courage to admit what they're doing is not for them, and pursue something else. Sometimes I wonder if the law is for me."

"You do?"

"Oh, yes. That's one of the reasons I came to the island. To think about what I really want to do. Thinking, along with just having some peace. That's why I came here."

"Really?"

"Yes, really." She was puzzled by the remark. He almost sounded like he didn't believe her. "What other reason could there be?"

He just looked at her for a moment. Was she telling the truth? Or had his grandmother blabbed his business. "Why did you lose your job? You said you gave it up rather than being fired like I heard."

She took a deep breath with her disappointment. "It just got to me. The work, the injustices, everything else with it." She looked off, seeing the day in that courtroom. "My firm was defending a man who was accused of rape, a very rich man. I came upon some evidence that undoubtedly proved that he had raped that woman. A woman of about my age. I brought this evidence to the partners in the firm, and they stated that we had an obligation to our client to prove his innocence. I wanted off. They wanted me on. They threatened me with losing my job. And now I have."

"You stood up for your principles like that?"

"I had to. Every time I saw that woman, that poor woman who this animal had exploited, I was so tired of it. So tired of just working and working for money, and all the injustice."

Shemar was amazed. He leaned back, simply staring at Marita. "That's how you lost your job? That's the *real* story?"

Marita was getting tired of his questioning her answers. "Where is this distrust coming from? Every time I tell you something it's like you don't believe me. I just can't win with you, Shemar. I come here for relaxing, and my aunt even mentioned that you might stop by, and I'm thinking that if he comes by we'll have some fun. And it's been nothing but hell with you."

Frustrated, she turned her back to him. "Leave me alone. I've had enough of this."

Pulling her by the arms, Shemar curved her back around. "I don't mean to offend you, Marita. Please forgive me. I know it's been a long time since we've seen each other, but I still care about you. You have no idea. I care about your well being. I care about what you think and feel. And I care about anyone hurting you, and that includes me. And whenever I do something that offends you, check me. Just because I've been hurt by one woman that doesn't mean I should be on guard with every woman and attribute the negative qualities of my ex onto her. I really care."

She stared up into his eyes. Sincerity glistened from them. "I care about you, too." From the way her heartbeat was increasing with every second, she was caring too much. "I feel bad for you—the way your wife thought. If you love someone, you want them to be happy. And if you were happy doing something, you would do it so well the money would come. She should have stuck by you."

Shemar was touched. It was almost as if she read his soul. Like she'd read one of the pages he'd written. "That's how I felt about it."

"And it wasn't like you were depending on her or leaving the two of you broke."

"No, I wasn't. We had substantial savings. But as I said, we couldn't be extravagant like when I was active in my practice."

"She was foolish. Because you obviously loved her."

"How do you know that?"

"Because I see it in your face. I can hear it in your voice. And besides that, you're still so angry with her, you attribute her qualities to other women, like you did me."

Shemar smiled. "Are you planning to go into psychology?"

She loved his piano-perfect smile. It made her smile, too. "No, not psychology." She sighed. "You know, it's funny. I kind of know what you felt like. Because even before that happened in court, I was so unfulfilled in my work. You see, when I was a kid, it sounded so nice to be a lawyer. I knew they made lots of money, and they had status. But I never really researched what they did to see if I would truly, truly like it."

"Are you saying that you didn't?"

"I tried to like what I was doing. But you shouldn't have to try so hard if something is meant for you, if it's your purpose."

"I agree." *Had* she been reading his work?

"I think when you're meant to do something, it feels so good when you're doing it that you just don't want to stop and the time just flies when you're doing it."

His smile grew. "You are so right, Marita. So right. It's just like when you're with the right person. It feels so right, you don't want to leave them."

His eyes lingered in hers so intensely, Marita felt an inviting pressure in her lower body. She had to remind herself of how cruel he'd been. "I better get some rest. I want to explore this island playground tomorrow." She turned her back, hoping he would get the hint to leave. She could sense that he wanted to do something or say something more, and she knew it had to do with the way he was looking at her, and what she was feeling between them. But maybe . . . Maybe it was all in her mind.

The erotic tension below her navel became more

intense as she felt his fingers comb through her hair again.

"Maybe this will help you fall asleep," he said, feeling his chest rising and falling with his racing breath. "Remember how I used to do this to you?"

Fighting not to recall it, her eyelids surrendered to his touch, and closed. "I remember."

Shemar's fingertips glided from her hair to her neck. He began to massage it. "Do you like it?" He leaned down some.

"You're an expert." Marita felt her limbs loosen as his hands caressed down to her shoulders. Her pelvic muscles tensed from the rush she felt there. "Umm."

"Yes, I am an expert. In more ways than you know." He brought his expertise toward her back. "But I'm obliged to help you discover. Lay on your stomach." His voice was a whisper.

Aroused to an aching point, Marita did as he asked. Feeling his hands moving around the back of her dress to the straps, she invited softly, "You can pull it down."

From behind, Shemar did as she wanted, hardly able to sit still for the firmness he felt amid his thighs. He looked down at her bare back for a moment. Overheated from the sumptuous sight, he swiftly took off his shirt. What would he do if she turned around? Could he resist tasting her sweet mounds? He'd always imagined how they would look and taste.

Shemar couldn't resist gently brushing the sides of them with his fingertips as he continued to massage her back. "How's that?" He needed to unzip his pants to relieve the pressure. The softness and roundness were killing him to feel more.

He needed something. He needed to be inside her. He could hardly breathe, he wanted it so bad. And it turned him on even more that she wanted the same.

Marita heard his breathing, matching her own. She felt the heat from his body bearing down on her sultry back. She was on fire, feeling the pleasurable aching ocean of the desire that he stirred, teasing her, making her squirm so she had to have him.

"Shemar," she whimpered.

"Yes, Marita. I'm here." He lay down behind her.

Marita felt his muscular chest against her naked back. She felt him pushing her dress down lower toward her hips.

"Oh . . . Shemar."

Five

"Yes, I know." He couldn't stand it anymore. He reached one hand beneath her side until he reached the front of her. The other hand dared to venture to that same place.

"Shemar," Marita cried, as he squeezed her nipples between his thumb and middle finger. With the other hand, he stroked her thigh, moving his fingers, nearing her panty line. The overwhelming pressure way down within her couldn't be withstood anymore.

"Marita," she heard his uneven breaths stopping and starting over her ear. He began to turn her around. "I want you so bad I'd kill for it."

Before Marita even turned halfway, the phone rang. Suddenly snapping out of the erotic haze she'd been swept into, she pulled the cover over herself before Shemar saw her breasts. Afterward, she reached for the phone, trying to catch her breath.

"Hel . . . lo."

"Marita?" Aunt Dollie sounded unsure if she'd dialed the right number. "That you, honey?"

"Yes, it's me." She felt Shemar moving around behind her, soon getting up. "Is mama OK? Is something wrong?"

"No, honey. Your mama's fine. I'm just calling to be nosy."

Marita sighed. "Whooh, thank God."

"Honey, what were you doing? You sound funny."

Marita was distracted. Shemar walked toward the door and stared at her before he left. When the door closed behind him, Marita tried to clear the lingering excitement out of her throat. "What did you say, Aunt Dollie?"

"Child, are you all right? Why can't you hear what I'm saying? What's going on there?"

She cleared her throat again. "Nothing."

"You sure?"

"I'm sure. Just . . . just relaxing."

"With Shemar?"

"Huh?" Marita nearly fell off the bed.

"I'm sure you know by now that I tricked you. Nell told me Shemar was staying there for the summer and I thought that would be wonderful if you stayed there with him. Didn't he turn out to be a handsome devil? Hasn't he changed?"

"Yes, he's too much." Marita brought her hand over her throbbing nipple.

"So what's been happening with you two?"

"Nothing." She stared at the rumpled bed. "Just getting to know each other."

Dollie was tickled. "Good. Now aren't you glad you went on this trip? Hasn't he made you feel better?"

"Oh, yes. He's made me feel a whole lot better."

After completing her call with her great-niece, Dollie relaxed across her bed and pulled out her

Bible. Reading it before retiring always made her have pleasant dreams. Then again, she was in a pleasant mood anyway. Marita had her smiling. Something was up with that girl tonight. She wondered if Shemar and Marita had gotten into some of *that* good trouble. Dollie was bittersweet about that. On the one hand, she wanted Marita to "get her groove on," as the young people said. And Shemar was definitely a good man to get it on with. On the other hand, she was wary about things moving too fast. She hoped Carol had taught Marita how to bait a man. There was an art to it. She sure had enjoyed herself, mastering the art when she was younger.

Dollie had never considered herself a great beauty. Her face and body weren't the kind that made her noticeable to the opposite sex. Yet, she had possessed something that once a man got to know her, it was hard for her to get rid of him when she felt they were no longer compatible. She'd made so many mistakes as a younger woman, letting good men go, and keeping bad ones close. It all had been a lesson. When she finally married, she hadn't learned the grand lesson of love yet. She hadn't learned that it was all well and good to feel a passionate attraction for a man, but that there had to be much more to sustain you through the years.

Whenever she was sick, her husband would toss her a bottle of aspirin, instead of holding her in his arms and attending to her comfort. Whenever she needed support because of a stressful job, her husband told her what she was doing was meaningless anyway. While she desired a mate to build dreams with, her husband was throwing away money on parties, cars they couldn't afford, and sadly, she learned, women. The man had no virtue. All they'd ever had together was passion, and with the tortuous weight of his betrayal, Dollie couldn't feel that for him anymore. She ordered him to get out of her house and life, and go on with his other women. He told her there was only one and went to live with her.

He came creeping back months later. He swore to Dollie that he'd made a mistake. He sure had, she assured him. He was never getting back anywhere near her heart again. One time of breaking her heart was the only opportunity anyone would ever get. Throughout the years Dollie kept all men at a distance. Her nursing career and her family became the center of her universe. It was only now that she'd become of the age where she could sit on the porch in a rocking chair, that she desired someone to rock in a chair next to hers. There was no one. She cringed at the thought of her nieces living with that regret. Some women could do fine without a man. They could step, going about their business, and not worry a second about missing one. Much to the contrary, the women in her family weren't like that. Marita wasn't like that.

She wanted a man in her life. She was even willing to settle for that Richard fellow, the one that Dollie knew she didn't love. The clock was ticking. Time was moving, and she'd just wanted to belong to someone. Perhaps if Shemar and Marita would allow themselves to feel something, they could belong to each other with every fiber of their being. She was a good woman. He was a good man.

The next day when Dollie came home from

work, she was still thinking about Marita, wondering what was going on with her and Shemar. Suddenly, though, there was incessant knocking at her front door. Hoping it wasn't one of those pesky salesman or an equally pestering neighbor, Dollie reluctantly made her way to the door.

The man's face in the peephole made a strange feeling come over her. He looked uncomfortably familiar. Those eyes she had seen before. There was too much black in them and not enough white. They were like fish eyes.

"Yes?" she answered, not opening the door. "Can I help you?"

"Yes, you can, ma'am." Valerian hoped she wouldn't recognize him. With all the years in the prison, he'd aged so. The last time she'd seen him was in the courtroom eighteen years ago. He was about forty pounds thinner, had no gray hair, wore no mustache like he did now, and had far less furrows in his brow. "I want to talk to you."

"You're talking."

"Can we talk face-to-face?"

"About what?"

"I'm a friend of your niece."

"I have plenty of nieces. Which one are you talking about?"

"Marita. Marita Sommers."

"What about her?"

"I work with her." Through myriad phone calls, he uncovered that Marita's firm had tossed her out. He'd also learned that no one knew of her whereabouts but this old woman. She was the contact person if the firm or anyone else wanted to reach her. "I would like to get in touch with her. We have to discuss her situation. Her career."

Dollie knew this didn't sound right. "I'm not about to tell anything about my niece to a nut."

"You are the only contact person."

"And you are not from my niece's firm."

She wasn't as stupid as Valerian assumed. "But I am, ma'am. I can show you credentials. I can even give you money." For the latter, he had a checkbook. Rubber, rubber, rubber is what she would see if she cashed one.

"You're a damn liar, and I don't want your money."

"What's wrong, ma'am?"

That's what I'm going to find out, Dollie thought. She headed toward her phone and started dialing the police.

"Ma'am? Ma'am?"

Valerian wanted to kick down the door or even the window. What stopped him were her neighbors. There were too many outside enjoying this late summer afternoon. More importantly, he sensed the hag was up to something. He'd better get going. It was all right, though. He was going to find Marita. In fact, his contacts would help him, especially since Marita would be of special interest to them. He would be seeing her *soon.*

With her eyes shut tight, Marita soaked in a cherry-scented bubble bath. Her mind still clinging to the fever Shemar had incited in her during the night, she wondered how she could make herself stop reliving those sensations. She hoped the date she'd arranged with Cliff that afternoon would cure her of it. Earlier, she had decided to give him a call. Their time on the phone was lengthy, consisting mostly of him talking about himself and his accomplishments. Even so, she found him intriguing, ambitious, and amusing.

It was funny how when she had met him on the beach, she was certain she wasn't in the mood for any involvement with a man. Yet, since she'd been around Shemar that feeling had definitely changed. The situation with Richard didn't even seem as disheartening. For that matter, she'd barely thought of him these last days. What a relief it was not to hear him repeatedly complaining about her not spending enough time with him. She'd never have to hear him accuse her of not loving him. "Maybe you're in love with a ghost," he would tell her. "Because you're certainly not in love with me."

How could he possibly know what was in her heart? Didn't she have to feel something to stay with his stiff and pressed behind for two years? Of course it wasn't like . . . like it was with Remmy. Yet she did love him. Funny though, Aunt Dollie told her it was the "used to somebody kind of love." Just used to him? Was that all it was? Well, what was it the other times? Those occasions in her life when she really cared about a man? Still, as she looked back, none of those relationships ever worked out for one reason or another. Something was always missing. Something she believed she would never feel. Something that touched her so deep inside . . . like last night.

Getting out of the tub, dabbing at water dripping from her body, Marita gazed at herself in the mirror. Surprisingly, she looked different. Now wet and wavy, her hair seemed to shimmer more than other times. Her eyes caught the light in the room so that their cinnamon hue was enhanced. And her skin looked darker, warmer, exotic, and ready for the touch of another's skin smothering it. Altogether, her bare image looked exotic, even beautiful, as Shemar had almost complimented her. Did she look this way because she was so awakened sexually?

Shemar had no idea what he'd done to her. The feelings he stirred up wouldn't go away. Why couldn't she stop thinking about what happened? Why couldn't she stop fantasizing about the luscious scenarios that could have happened? Marita couldn't remember a time when she was so turned on. Not even . . . with Remmy. In some ways, Shemar and he were alike. In the short time she'd been around him, she could see that. Neither was a conventional man. The world was theirs the way they saw it. They lived it the way they wanted to live it. Proof of that was the way Shemar spoke about abandoning his profession for a pursuit more aligned with him. Yes, just like Remmy, there was something exciting and irresistible about Shemar. Somehow there was even a dangerous edge to him, too. Could that have been what had got to her?

God knows that she'd stayed clear of men with any sign of drama around them after Remmy died. So why did she crave the thrill of Shemar? He wouldn't even reveal what he did for a living. Was the mystery about him what turned her on so?

If he could make her feel like that with her clothes mostly on, what would happen with them off? Where did things go from here? And why hadn't she seen Shemar all day? In the morning when she woke, he'd already left the house.

All in all, she had to just get him out of her mind. She could never entertain what he could do to her body. There were tons of reasons why she shouldn't. There were issues with his ex. There were probably even girlfriends, though she hadn't seen any. Additionally, she couldn't take the continual drama of his accusations and apologies. She didn't need it or want it. Neither did she understand this secrecy about what he did for a living. Shemar Dalton was complications. Complications were headaches she didn't need. She sought a peaceful, fun vacation. So from all perspectives, Shemar Dalton had to be a friend, solely a friend.

With his portable computer stretched across his lap, Shemar tried to work by the seaside. He'd come out there early in the morning, not knowing what to say to her and confused about what he felt within himself. Try as he might to write something, he had to continually start over. Images of Marita were driving him crazy. If he wasn't visualizing and his body reliving how excited he was on the bed with her, his mind was going much further than they had yesterday. In his fantasies, they were totally naked, and he was so deep inside her love that he was nearly comatose from the bliss.

"Stop it," he said to himself, looking up just in time to see a giant wave galloping.

But it had been more than their carnal chemistry that obsessed him. He was thinking about things Marita said to him. They sounded so caring, so unselfish, so what he wanted from a woman. The question was, were they truly from her heart. Did she know about his enormous wealth? Was that her real reason for coming to the island? To seduce him and get her greedy hands on some of it?

He'd spoken to his grandmother last night after their encounter. Vehemently, she denied that she'd spilled what he wanted kept so secret. However, she did admit to setting the two of them up for some romance, along with Ms. Dollie. Additionally, she professed that Marita knew nothing about it. She claimed that she was simply on a much-needed vacation.

Shaking his head, Shemar didn't know what to believe, but he did know what he felt. He couldn't remember a time of feeling it so deeply, not ever. He wanted Marita unlike he had ever wanted a woman. He couldn't even remember his wife getting him that aroused. If the phone had not rung, and if she would have wanted some loving, she would have had his—abundantly. For he was still feeling the aftershocks of being so turned on. All he would have to do is just imagine Marita. All he would have to do is recreate the scenario in the bedroom, and he would feel that concrete firmness beneath his shorts. If only he could stop thinking of the ways he could relieve it. He had to think of his work. The lectures were coming up. That's where his concentration had to be.

Pam drove up to the town house, moments after a familiar gentleman had stepped out of a gleaming red Porsche. Parking her black Lexus in the driveway, she hopped out of it, hurrying up to the doorstep where the man stood.

The sight of the handsome face brought a gigantic smile to her own. She glanced down at the bouquet of roses. "I believe I saw you at the club Tropical Rhythms."

"You may have." He rang the bell.

"You danced with my *friend*, Marita."

"Yes, we danced."

"Lovely flowers. I'm sure you're bringing them for her."

"That I am."

"Going on a date?"

"If that's what you want to call it."

"If that's what you want to call *what?*"

Both swiveled around. Shemar was coming up the stairs and he didn't look happy.

Six

"I'm going to show Marita around this ravishing island," Clifton clarified. Beaming, he hoped his cordial demeanor would rectify the unpleasant start they'd gotten off to last night. He'd been embarrassed afterward. Several friends as well as patients who were enjoying the festive atmosphere had witnessed the display. Some razzed him about it. He couldn't have that happen again. A reputation he prided as sterling was at stake.

Easing by Clifton and Pam to unlock the door, Shemar was intent to behave civilly as well. Not only wasn't it his nature to carry on like he had at the club, but since it upset Marita, he wouldn't do it again. He would just let her handle her own business as she stressed. His innate distrust for this character had to be kept to himself—for now at least.

Pam strode in first after Shemar opened the door, helping herself to her preferred spot on the sofa. Clifton swaggered in behind her. With his hands in his pockets, he stood around granting Shemar a silly grin.

Shemar rested his laptop on a nearby table before approaching Cliff with one of his hands extended. "Let's start over. Shemar Dalton."

Clifton met his handshake. "Dr. Clifton Harrison."

Pam curled her lips admirably. "Do you have a specialty?"

"Orthopedics."

"Wonderful."

"And Marita tells me you had a psychology practice," Clifton addressed Shemar. "So what fills your time now?"

"Sit down, man," Shemar avoided answering. "Make yourself comfortable." He walked toward his laptop, arranging it better on the table. "And about last night—that was last night. I'm all right with you. As long as Marita is content, I'm all right. It's just that she's like family, and family is protected."

"Yes, she told me about your families," Clifton responded. "We talked for hours today." He gripped the knee crease in his pants as he settled down near Pam. "And I will be the perfect gentleman. Last night, we were just having fun."

"Fun, huh?" Shemar half smiled to that.

"That's our way on this island."

Pam was studying the awkwardness between the two when she suddenly heard high-heel pumps clacking toward them from the terrace.

Coming into the room, Marita was amazed that Shemar and Clifton hadn't ripped each other to shreds. "I was just soaking up the sunshine, waiting for you," she told Clifton. Warily, she gauged if she'd missed any quarreling.

Clifton's eyes roved over her in a banana-yellow sundress with matching ankle-strap high heels. "You look gorgeous." He stood up.

"Thank you. And hello, Pam."

"How are you doing?" Pam returned, and wondered why Marita had to try to look so seductive
all the time. What was she wearing that for? Suddenly feeling a need to pat her hair, she eyed Shemar for his impressions. His stare told her all she
didn't want to hear.

Edible, Shemar thought, summing up what he beheld. Though careful to hide his attention drifting
over Marita, to him she looked as edible as the
juiciest, most delicious fruit. If he'd tasted what he
hungered for last night he knew he would have
been an altogether different man today. "I, ah . . .
I missed seeing you today, Marita."

Pam threw her eyes heavenward.

"I missed seeing you, too." She couldn't get
over the way the sun had darkened his skin. It
looked glazed with a sheen that reminded her of
his sticky, muscled chest pressed against her back.
"I guess you had things to do."

He scratched at his sideburn. "A few things."

"Thought you might like these." Clifton handed
her the roses.

"Oh, they're so nice." Marita accepted them, immediately inhaling the scent.

Shemar looked away, seating himself at the table
where the computer was.

"Aren't those nice?" Pam remarked to Shemar.

Not looking up toward the flowers to which she
was referring, he began signing on-line. "Very
nice."

Marita glimpsed Shemar. Afterward, she hurried
to find a receptacle for the flowers. Quickly locating a vase in her room, she came back downstairs.
She steadied her gaze on Clifton to avoid Shemar.

For each time she had glanced at him she couldn't help thinking of him in that way. "I'm ready."

"Yes, we better get going." Clifton saluted them. "We're off."

Still not looking at Shemar, Marita shuffled toward the doorway. "See y'all."

The door closing sparked Pam to pull a chair over to the computer table. Sitting in it, scooting her chair close to Shemar, she leaned on his shoulder, examining the screen. "Everything is coming along great from what I can see. This is interesting."

His full lips swerved up contentedly. "I'm glad you approve."

"But I know you're not going to just work all day." Her head curved aside as she looked at his sexy, bronzed face. She was so near that she inhaled his citruslike aftershave. Would he taste like citrus against her lips?

Shemar leaned back in his chair, taking a long deep breath. "Actually, I was planning to work, continuing where I left off earlier. My lecture isn't far away."

"Work on a Saturday? On a Fourth of July weekend?"

It did seem like he was overdoing it. After all, it wasn't like he was hungrily building his dreams anymore. Back in those days, he worked around the clock. Now things were different. He'd been so incredibly blessed he never had to work again if he didn't want to.

In his psychology practice he had enjoyed his profession up to a point. At the same time, there were some issues that had invariably disturbed him. He was totally against some of the tenets set by psychologists in the earlier times. He wasn't a great fan of Freud. Neither was he in agreement with various studies executed to determine intellect. Many were biased and it appalled him that too frequently they were used in evaluating children in respect to what classes they should be placed and what learning disabilities they were affected by. Too many of the young ones were misdiagnosed.

Shemar had been disgusted first in his work in hospital and school settings, where patients were medicated much too often, rather than being guided toward dietary, spiritual, and educational alternatives. That is why his practice had been so successful. He wasn't so fast to suggest that a youngster be put on medication. His advice was love, attention, a nutritious diet, and an education rigidly tailored to the child's individual needs. He wasn't so quick to urge a divorcée who was feeling a little suicidal to take a tranquilizer. Instead of directing her to a pill, Shemar suggested to her to reacquaint herself with God, her soul, and her dreams. Shemar felt in his spirit what he bestowed to them: a natural approach to healing. Now he communicated that on a far deeper level in his work.

Healing the Soul had been his first nonfiction work. Shemar had felt a great desire to express not only all the knowledge, emotion, and learning he'd acquired as a psychologist, but as a man. The book made the bestseller list in one week. Three other bestsellers followed. Shemar had never dreamed that following his bliss would lead to such blessings. His only way to justify it was that if you follow what's in your heart, it would lead you to dreams beyond your imagination. Now all he needed was someone to share his dreams and his heart with.

"What about a compromise for what we'll do today?" he suggested.

"How so?"

"How about you helping me a bit with the lecture, and later we go and do something? Dinner, a movie, or whatever you want."

Whatever she wanted was definitely to be in his arms. "OK," she agreed. "I'll help you with preparing for your lecture. I'll pretend I'm the audience and you just lavish all that brilliance on me. After that I want to go swimming." She'd planned the swimming thing last night. She even wore a sizzling pink bikini beneath her culottes.

Shemar loved swimming. Unfortunately, during his time in Bermuda, he'd been so busy preparing for his lecture and working on a new book, he hadn't had a chance to dip himself in those inviting blue Bermudan waters or even the pool in the backyard. "Sounds good."

"Good." A flirtatious curl formed on Pam's lips. They would swim all right. Once she got Shemar in some water, her bikini would have a pesky problem with falling off. Shemar wouldn't be able to resist her nakedness. Pam smiled and smiled, picturing it all. *Too bad, Marita. After I'm through tonight, he's going to be done. My body is going to work a spell.*

A plethora of kaleidoscopic flowers and fruit-bearing trees lining the roads and hillsides mesmerized Marita. Clifton drove by them leisurely so that she missed nothing from her window view. Flowing by her as soothing as the warm breeze dancing across her face, tangling her hair, were some thin, pointed leaves and other eye-catchers with lengthy protuberant pistils. Arrayed in vivid pink, red, white, peach, and yellow, he called them oleanders and hibiscus.

Other scene-stealers were wildflowers ranging mostly in purple, along with cherry and citrus trees. Orange and yellow pear-shaped fruit dangling from the trees further captured her tourist's watchfulness. Declaring that they were loquat, Clifton ceased driving, picking her a bunch before continuing on their jaunt. Biting into one, Marita found its taste sweet and somewhat pungent. She liked it. In fact, she liked every splendor of this tropical Eden. Peering up into the backdrop of highland hills, against a brilliant, azure sky, it wasn't merely another world. It was paradise.

Later, walking in the direction of the cruise ship that Clifton had planned for them to sail upon, Marita did a back step as they passed a shoe boutique. She'd always had a love affair with pretty shoes. A pair of white sandals in the window that stringed all the way up to the knee had Clifton trailing her into the store. Browsing around inside, she saw other attractive styles for her Aunt Dollie, her mother, and some girl-friends. When she finally made her decisions of which to purchase, the salesgirl carried them to the counter. A hefty sum was rung up. After mentally calculating that the amount was correct, Marita extended the bills to the cashier. Clifton put his Visa card in the woman's hand first.

Marita spun around to where he stood behind

her. "Cliff, I certainly appreciate your generosity, but I'd rather pay myself."

Beaming, Cliff winked at her. Stepping beyond her, he nodded at the cashier. The young girl began the transaction.

"You're already doing enough. I'm sure I will enjoy the boat ride."

"I'm sure you will, too."

"But I'd really rather pay for these items."

He continued to look amused, eventually taking the shopping bags off of the counter. "We'll ask the captain on the ship to put them in a safe place."

Marita didn't feel right about it since she was just getting to know Cliff. Regardless, she didn't make any more fuss as they boarded the ship *Master Blaster.* A tremendous ocean liner with an art deco design, it exhibited a buffet of assorted seafood and a dynamic reggae band. Although it was flooded with people, Cliff and Marita managed to find a secluded spot overlooking the waters. They had danced several times and just wanted to cool off.

"Having a good time?" he asked, leaning over the railings, and looking much too boldly over her body.

"Yes, I am having fun. Thank you, Cliff. This was a good idea." She leaned over and gazed out, also. There were small and large ships floating about on water that looked sometimes turquoise blue and other times more of a green hue.

"You know you are such a gorgeous woman."

Marita smiled as she looked over at him. "Thanks." She started to tell him how handsome he looked also, but with the way he was checking her out, it might have given him the wrong idea.

"I bet it's hard for a man to resist you."

"Men hit on women all the time," she said laughing it off, trying to make light of his comment. It sounded like he was getting at something she didn't want to get to. "That's life among the sexes." She laughed again.

A first for him today, Cliff wasn't amused. "I bet it's hard for *him* to resist you."

"Him who?" But she knew who he was referring to. It was the same *him* who she'd struggled not to think about. Yet even in the midst of the joyous outing, Shemar was lingering in her mind as near as her breath.

"You know who I mean," he went on. "Your *family* friend. I'm a man and I know how men think, and I know how they act, and I know how men look at a woman they want. He doesn't feel like family. He feels like he should be your lover. I saw it in the way he defended you in the club. I especially saw it today in his eyes when he looked at you."

Marita felt uneasy discussing Shemar with Cliff. For one thing, it wasn't right to talk behind his back. For another, she was afraid of what might be revealed if Cliff studied her when she talked about Shemar. He was clearly an observant man.

"Shemar is like family," she declared definitively. "And that's all we are to each other. But about you. You were telling me about yourself in the car."

Clifton brightened at that. She could tell he prided himself on his accomplishments. She thought his success as a doctor was wonderful, too.

His being able to pull himself up from the dregs of poverty as she had done should have been lauded. What she didn't find so appealing was his disinterest in her life. There were no questions about her likes or dislikes, her career, family, or childhood. Cliff talked constantly about his practice, his two homes, his fleet of cars, his wardrobe, his furnishings, his investment portfolio, and his desire to be the richest man in Bermuda.

If that wasn't taking up the conversation, there were the stories about the women who chased after him who weren't good enough for him. There were the offers he'd received to be a kept man by women more affluent than himself. There was reminiscing about the countless times he been approached about becoming a male model or entering body-building contests, which he stated he would have clearly won. There was his hope to marry a beautiful woman who would look the same as when he married her for years to come, because if she ever allowed herself to gain too much weight, he was filing for divorce quicker than one could blink an eye. All Marita could think was heaven help the poor creature, because it sure wasn't going to be her.

His depthless soul aside, Cliff did indulge her in lots of fun. They danced some more. And true to a promise he'd made when they'd talked by phone, he didn't get fresh as he'd done at the club. They also ate ravenously and had many laughs. Marita was grateful to him. For he did make her feel like she was on vacation. However, there was one thing all the merriment couldn't do. Not for one second did the smoldering mist of

Shemar go away. A part of her was always wondering. What was he doing at that moment?

The sun was melting into the orange-yellow cast of dusk. Shemar had just finished rehearsing for his oration and headed upstairs to change into his swimwear. According to Pam, he was ready, practically a master at communicating his momentous messages. He did feel great about his work. If only he'd felt as magnificent in general.

Curiosity about Marita and that guy was agitating him ever since they went out. Shemar hoped she would have better sense than to kiss him. What's more, he couldn't imagine anything more provocative than that. For he'd heard the stories about female tourists coming to the island and just losing every sense of themselves. Would Marita get that crazy? Especially since she'd had a rough time lately. Could she be so vulnerable, hoping to abandon her troubles via a fling? *Stop it, Shemar,* he admonished himself, like he'd done before. *Get her off your mind.* Perhaps the swim would make him stop thinking of her—and them together.

Stepping out onto the warmth of the backyard, Shemar found Pam immersed up to her head in the pool.

From the water, she gazed up at him, loving the way the orange-yellow hue of sunset cascading over his skin made him look like a bronzed warrior. Those tiny black shorts made him all the more irresistible. She couldn't wait to give them a little downward tug.

"Yummy," she remarked and her heart beat fiercely with anticipation. She felt it was time to let him know what she was feeling. Especially with Marita hovering about, she had to make her move.

"Are you saying yummy because you just ate something tasty?" Shemar joked, trying to fight off the weird sensation her compliment had given him. Was it strange for one cousin to say such a thing to another? Or was he just a prude making too much of nothing? Telling himself that of course it was nothing, he relaxed on the side of the pool, his legs sinking into the water.

Light lapping sounds trailed Pam as she made her way over to him. "I'm saying yummy because I want to eat something tasty." Her tongue licked provocatively around her wet lips.

Shemar frowned and gawked at her, this time telling himself that this couldn't be happening. "I'll fix you something to eat if you're hungry."

"No fixing necessary." Pam finally reached him. "My meal is ready." She stared softly in his eyes.

His scowl progressing to an anguished expression, Shemar stared back. Except he was seeing what he'd been too blind to see before. Pam had endured so many letdowns from family and boyfriends he'd become her everything. He was safe for her. She knew he wouldn't hurt her. "Pam, you don't mean what you're saying. You're confused."

"I'm not confused, Shemar. I've never been confused in my feelings about you." Positioning her torso between his legs, she rubbed across his crotch.

Promptly, Shemar gripped her hands and raised them. "Don't do that, Pam."

She stared up into his face. "You love me, Shemar. And I love you."

"Yes, I love you." He nodded his head as he gently released her. "But not in *that way.*"

"We're not really related. You know that. And I've never felt that. I've always been so attracted to you. I've always been in love with you. Deeply. When you were married to Leslie, I was so unhappy, I cried every night. And I prayed that you would see her for the gold digger she was. She didn't deserve you." Staring up at him with pleading eyes, she eased her body nearer to his. "I prayed that you would leave her. And now you have. And now we can be together. It was meant to be. It feels right." She reached up to his chest.

He eased her hand away. "It feels wrong! I don't feel the way you do, Pam. You've always been my cousin, and you'll always be my cousin. Nothing more, nothing less. I can't help what I feel."

Loathing that nothing was going as she hoped, Pam felt anxious, panicky, and desperate. It all made her float away from him. She wanted to grant Shemar ample distance to view what she was about to reveal.

Shemar observed Pam untying the straps behind her neck that held up her bikini top. "No, don't do that, Pam."

"Why?" She was amused by his uptightness. "Scared of being too tempted? You don't want me to stop." She continued.

"No. I mean it. Stop! Keep your clothes on!"

His stern tone felt like he'd smacked her. "Why, because you would rather *Marita* take hers off!"

She swam to the poolside, quickly stepping out onto it. Drying off with a nearby towel, she soon felt Shemar's presence near her. She hated having

an outburst like that. The last thing she wanted
was to sound jealous of Marita.

"Pam, I think you need to spend time with another man. A good man. Then you'll see this attachment you have to me—"

"Attachment?" She was insulted.

"No one has been there for you. So you've at-
tributed your gratefulness and all your other emotions onto me. It may seem like that kind of love,
but I don't believe it is."

"Don't give me a diagnosis, Shemar. I'm not one
of your patients!"

"I'm sorry if it sounds like that."

"Well, it does." Pausing, she fought back her
tears with angry thoughts. "I can't help thinking
that this might have turned out differently if it
wasn't for . . . for your so-called family friend."

"It has nothing to do with, Marita. But I will
admit . . ." He looked off.

"Admit what?" she asked, drawing his gaze back
to her.

Looking down, he took a deep breath before
seeking her eyes. "I, ah . . . I couldn't even admit
this to myself; that's why I couldn't admit it to
you, but a long time ago I was attracted to
Marita . . . and I think it's still there."

Pam began massaging her temples. She didn't
want to hear this. He wasn't telling her something
this horrible. But he was. He was!

"Pam, maybe we need to get a little space from
each other."

So you can be with her every second. "Fine with
me." She rolled her eyes.

"And I don't mean to make you angry, but
maybe we have been spending too much time to-

gether and you've been missing opportunities to be with someone who could have a future with you."

Like he can't even consider a future with me. She couldn't take anymore. Gathering her belongings, she began muttering, "If it's space you want, it's space you get. You're right, I do need to see another man. A real man who can deal with me!"

Shemar didn't argue with her. He simply watched her until she was no longer visible, then gazed up at the enigmatic sky. This would pass. As soon as Pam had some time away from him and met someone, she would realize how crazily she'd behaved tonight. They would laugh about it.

On the other hand, was he partly to blame for Pam's feelings for him? Had he unknowingly led her on? He hoped not. He had adored Pam. He just hadn't known *how* she adored him. It all made him feel off balance. Though, when he really acknowledged how he felt, he was dispirited the entire night. He couldn't stop wondering what Marita was doing.

Was she truly enjoying spending time with that Clifton? Was he getting to know her better than Shemar had? He felt strangely connected to her but there was so much he didn't know. What had her life been like after they lost contact?

Dollie put on her silver rimmed reading glasses. Afterward, she picked up the tattered yellow news clipping she kept in a shoebox on a shelf in the closet. It smelled like the mothballs she often placed in dark, sealed places. She couldn't help but scowl at the brittle paper that detailed all the trouble Marita was in years ago.

There were days that Dollie thought about her young niece's boyfriend who was killed. What would he have been today? A lawyer like Marita, or perchance a state senator? Was his family coping with the heart-wrenching loss any better than she had years ago? Or did the missing of Remmy still ache like it was yesterday? Dollie had to remember to say a prayer for that family tonight. Anytime people just came up in her mind like that she took it as a sign to pray for them.

It was a shame, Dollie thought, overlooking the text of the article to analyze one of the pictures beside it. It was of the man who'd murdered the boy, and as Dollie inspected it, a sickness surged through her stomach. "Jesus." Shave off some years, weight, and that mustache, and it was the man who'd come to her door. That's why she'd took out the clipping. Something told her it was him. She needed to be sure.

The cops had come promptly after her call. But her visitor had vanished, and the officers had given Dollie a look like she'd wasted their time. Well, she was about to waste their time again, she vowed, picking up the telephone and pressing the buttons. The authorities had to be alerted. A murderer was on the loose. The prison couldn't possibly have let such a psychopath out. He'd definitely escaped. Marita . . . Marita was in danger.

Seven

Carrying her purse, shopping bags, and the shoes she'd worn, Marita entered the town house. Tossing her belongings and purchases aside, she immediately plopped down onto the sofa cushion. Her feet were tired. Her neck, back, and butt were tired. Everything on her was tired. Still, she didn't feel like trudging upstairs and succumbing to slumber. She wanted to see Shemar before she went to bed. She didn't want to talk about what had occurred between them. She just wanted to see his beautiful face and be assured that the closeness they'd been approaching the other night hadn't disappeared with day. But as she lay on her side she realized it was unlikely to happen. She could only imagine what he thought of her after she'd gone out with Cliff.

Too comfortable to budge, Marita dozed off. It was a restless nap, and the man soon appearing in her dream had appeared there many times before.

"Remmy," she whispered, reaching out to him in a room that had no ceiling or floor. Were they floating on air? He was so beautiful in that blue robe. His skin was so clean. His smile was so like the angel he looked like. "Remmy, why did you leave me?"

Remmy moved an inch closer. "It was my time, baby."

"I miss you. Sometimes I want to be with you . . . be with you there. *I haven't been as happy since you left me."*

"But you'll be happy again. It's coming. So much joy is coming to you, Marita. Right now you can't see it. But life can change in a second."

"No, my happiness is gone forever. I want to be with you."

"But He's not ready for you. He has so much for you to do."

"You're wrong. There's nothing for me to do. I don't have anything. I'm empty inside. Every day I feel empty. Take me, Remmy. Take me with you." She extended her hand.

He didn't reach back. "Your place is where you are."

"But it's not! Sometimes I feel like crying for nothing because I'm just so unhappy. If I was with you I would laugh every day, every second of every day."

"No, Marita. Be patient. Don't let go of your will to live. Believe in His word and know that He wants you to be joyous. Happiness is coming. But you have to let me go. Let me go and hold on to him. Hold on to him. You're going to need him soon."

Remmy paced back further and further, soon disappearing inside a white fuzz of light. Marita struggled to catch up to him. Except the more she ran, the more it seemed like she remained in one spot. "Remmy, Remmy. Remmy."

She was jerking from side to side when Shemar came toward her. "Marita, wake up. Wake up." Gently, he patted her face. "You're having a bad dream."

Marita felt a tender palm that caused her to shiver. Languidly, her long-lashed lids separated.

She gazed up into Shemar's tense expression. He was sitting next to her. "Shemar, I . . ."

"What?" He longed to protect her from whatever it was. "What can I do?"

"I was having a dream."

"I know." He helped her sit up. "One that really got to you."

Marita wakened more, leaning into the curve of his side. "It was about Remmy." She still felt dazed from it all.

"Who's Remmy?"

"The man I loved. A long, long time ago. He did some bad things and I still can feel love for him. What does that say about me?"

"That you're human. We can love people who aren't upright. Actually, we can't help who we love. We just don't have to be around that person or have them in our lives. We can love from a distance."

"I can't. I can't say to him let's have some dinner and catch up. Can't even call him up to just say hello."

"Why not?"

"Because he's not down here on earth anymore. Can't *ever* say anything again to him down here. Couldn't let him share my happiness when I graduated law school. And when I won a big case, I couldn't feel him patting my back or telling me how how proud of me he was. No, I can't do that."

"Gran told me that you had a fiancé that was murdered. Is that who you're talking about?"

"Yes." She was so disheartened that Remmy actually wasn't with her, she dropped her head on Shemar's shoulder. Dreaming of him always drained her. There had been so many dreams of him. "Sometimes when I dream of Remmy it's so real I can actually feel him, just like his being is right there in front of me. Isn't that strange?"

"Not at all, Marita," he said.

"And I get so emotional in these dreams."

Shemar glanced down sideways at her. "Want to talk about it?"

"It was just him in the dream, telling me things. And I was telling him things."

"What kind of things?"

"For one, he was telling me that I was going to be happy and that I should hold on to someone. He kept saying hold on to *him*." She paused, thinking about that. "And I was telling him how much I missed him and how empty I felt." She tensed at his side.

"Empty?" He slipped his arm around her shoulder to comfort her.

She eased deeper into his side, inhaling citrus. "Yes, empty. I've felt like that for so long." She looked off, seeing flashes of her life. "After he died, I felt like I would never connect with anyone that way again. It was like I would never feel so close to someone, and they feel so close to me. And you know what? I never have. And then there's the law situation. I wanted to be a lawyer because it seemed like a respected, high-paying profession. But soon after I was there, I wasn't happy. I didn't like the justice that I saw. The guilty were practically going free. Black folks were being punished for being black. Women were getting killed by scorned lovers. Children were left parentless and bumped along in foster care, never feeling loved and often being abused. I felt powerless. Utterly powerless. You want to do something, but nothing you do is enough. You want to give, but you don't have anything to give. You want to run, but there is no place to run to. You feel trapped in a little box.

"I hated my work! This wasn't what I was meant to do. I shouldn't have had to dread Sunday nights because I had to go to work on Monday. Every day that I set foot in that place and sat at my desk, I knew it wasn't my soul's calling. Because if it were, I wouldn't hate it."

Shemar was struck by the emotionalism of her profession. "You're right. Your soul's calling would feel wonderful when you're doing it. But there are people trying to do something about injustice." All the children's foundations and other charities he'd donated exorbitant sums of financing to came to mind.

Shemar thanked God every day that he'd been so blessed that he wasn't powerless. His fortune had enabled him to do things to make those little innocents lives better, to make even many adults lives better. Nonetheless, he didn't feel secure enough with Marita to share this all with her. He needed to know more about her. Most of all, he wanted her to feel what he was beginning to feel, and he wanted to make sure his money had nothing to do with it. "You'll find out what you're supposed to be doing one of these days, Marita. And you won't feel empty. You'll even find that person."

"I don't know about that. Sometimes I tell myself it just doesn't matter anymore. Maybe I'm better off by myself."

That tickled him. "You sound like me after my divorce."

"How?"

"I was ready to throw in the towel on women. But then I said no way I'm giving my ex power over me like that. Just because she betrayed what we had, I'm not going to let her stop me from loving any other woman again. No way."

Marita raised her head from the shoulder that felt so wonderful to lay on. Being this close to him made her feel so secure that she said things she hadn't planned to, and now as she stared into his eyes, they filled her with something so warm and so welcome. "What did she do to you, Shemar? What did your wife *really* do?"

Shemar gazed into Marita's eyes, and felt his heart's untamed thumping shaking his entire body. But in opening up, he saw a place that had been too painful to visit with anyone else before. "Leslie and I had met at the hospital where I once worked. She was a receptionist there. Very attractive, but I was even more intrigued by her personality. She had all these dreams and hopes. She was so upbeat about everything, so sure of herself, just like . . ."

"Like who?"

"Like you used to be." His eyes lingered on hers. "I loved that about you, Marita. A person felt good just being around you. I know that I did." He brushed her cheek with his finger.

Marita felt a chill come over her. "So, ah . . . what happened after that?"

"I thought she was the one for me. We married, and I noticed she was a shopaholic and on the materialistic side, but she was my woman, and I was going to give her what she wanted. But then she didn't act like my woman when I wanted to pursue my dream and we had to cut back. With the lowering of our income bracket, there was a lowering of her support and love. Ultimately, she filed for divorce. She only wanted me for my money, Marita. Only money. That was the sole reason. Do you know how that makes a person feel?"

Dreadful, she imagined. "I have some idea." But how could a woman not fall in love with Shemar? Looking at him, it mystified her.

"It's worse than awful. You know why?"

"Why?"

"Because there is nothing—not anything on this earth that is more precious than being loved."

She was touched. "Do you really mean that, Shemar?"

"My heart is beating with all my belief. Feel it." He lifted her hand and placed it against his chest.

A raging drum reverberated beneath her fingers. It unnerved her because she could feel her own beating the same way. She reasoned it to be the emotion this conversation had stirred up. It couldn't have been because of the way he was looking at her. Neither was it the sweltering mist lingering so strongly between them.

"What do you want from a man, Marita? What do you need to take away that emptiness? What is it that those other men didn't give you?"

Marita stared into the intensity of his eyes, and had to look away before losing her thought. "They gave me spurts of happiness. Moments where I'd have fun with them, but it never led to that spiritual bond of knowing that this person was your appointed love for life—your soul mate."

"You never know how near what you need is."
He marveled at her lips trembling as she spoke.
What would they feel like on his, and all over him?

"But that true, *true* happiness was always elusive.
The kind where you can smile and it's not just
with your lips. People can see it in your eyes. You
can feel it all through you, all in your soul, and
again, everyone can see that. You couldn't hide it
if you wanted to. It drapes over you and reeks in
everything you do. You can be with that person in
the heat of passion and it will overtake you. At the
same time, you can just be sitting quietly with
them, and the excruciating joy is still ever so present. You don't even have to say anything. It's just
there, alive as we are . . . alive as . . ." *As I feel
with you right now.*

Shemar knew exactly what she spoke of. He'd
expressed it in his works—that indescribable happiness. Moreover, it was a God-designated connection to a certain being. There was just something
about the person that made their mate aware that
this was the person they were meant to be with.
It was something beyond human comprehension.
It was a phenomenal feeling. It was as indescribable as what made him ease his face toward hers.
Every inch of him cried out for her.

Marita heard the moaning among his uneven
breaths as his lips neared hers. "I need you,
Marita."

She looked at his face up close. He was so incredibly gorgeous, and combined with his plea, she
felt tremors stirring within her innermost places.
"I tried not to think about the other night."

"I tried, too." He pressed his moistened lips
against hers. Lightly, he kissed them. She was

softer than he'd ever dreamed. He was more excited than he was before.

Marita breathed heavily, turned on by the sensual fever engulfing her from his mouth. Craving more, she parted her lips.

Shemar opened them wider with his tongue probing forth. "So good," he groaned, thrusting deeper. She was so sweet, so tasty, he swept his arms around her. He couldn't hold her tight enough. He couldn't feel enough of her.

Marita couldn't, either. Weakening with his every luscious suckle of her tongue, she became moist with piercing desire. Squirming, daring to taste him more and more, she carried her damp fingers across his melon-sized muscles, his broad back, resting them behind his neck.

His head fell to her throat. Feathery kisses rained there, and she could stand no more restraint. She rubbed across his bulging zipper.

"Do you like that?" he groaned, returning to her mouth. Like a blazing spear, his tongue darted in and out of it.

"Oh, yes, Shemar," he heard her whimper.

"Because I'd love to give it to you." His probing mouth softly sucking her bottom lip, his body easing atop hers, he coaxed her back to flatten on the couch.

Marita matched his savoring of her lips, while feeling him moving his pelvis gently and forcefully into her. A fiery iron rod seemed to move against her dress, making ultrasensitive the triangle of hair hidden beneath. She unzipped his pants, feeling the knit fabric covering his steel erection.

"Oh, I could come already," he breathed. "I love you touching me, Marita. I love touching you, too." His excitement making him kiss her harder, he reached down to the bottom of her dress.

Marita soon felt tender fingertips climbing to her throbbing folds. "Shemar, what are you doing to me? You're driving me crazy." Feeling her lips crushed with his heat, she soon felt the shock of his fingertips. Anxiously, they tugged her panties aside, and she felt his fingers titillating her. "Oh, oh, Shemar."

"I'm here, baby, and I'm ready." Rising, staring down into her lust-drugged eyes, Shemar hastily lifted his T-shirt over his head. Staring back up at him, Marita worked at his zipper, while he watched her. He couldn't believe what was about to happen.

The phone's ring startled them.

"I better get that." She tried to move up, but he was reluctant to free her from his arms.

"Please, leave it alone!" Shemar begged.

She eased him back with a light nudge. "But it might be important."

"And it might be nonsense." He was so hot he was about to explode.

"It might be about my mother."

Shemar let her pick it up.

Catching her breath, Marita answered, "Hello?"

"Sounds like you were running," Cliff said. "What were you doing?"

"Uh . . ." Avoiding Shemar's concerned frown, she rolled her fingers through her hair. "Just relaxing."

"You don't sound relaxed. Anyway, I was just laying down in my bed, thinking about you."

"You were?" She maneuvered away from Shemar. He was clearly trying to figure out who she was talking to, likely anxious to know if anything was wrong.

"Yes, I was thinking about you. I had a great time with you, you know."

"I had a good time, too."

Shemar made an *oh, please* face. *So that's who she's talking to.*

"In fact," Cliff went on, "I had such a good time, I want to spend more time with you. Lots of it."

"Lots of it?" Marita hadn't realized she'd been that entertaining.

"I want to see you every day this week after work."

"You do?"

"Oh, yes. We're just going to enjoy the island, and if you'd like, we can visit some others. Have you ever been to Jamaica? Negril, in particular. It's spectacular."

"Jamaica?"

Shemar stretched his eyes. He knew Marita wasn't going on a trip with some guy she just met. It wasn't going to happen. Not if he was alive.

"I don't know about a trip," Marita divulged. She shifted to avoid Shemar scrutinizing her every word and expression. "Maybe we can hang out again . . . sometime."

"Am I moving too fast?"

"No . . . no."

"Good. I'm glad you don't think so. I'm just a man who goes after what he wants. How do the shoes look with your outfits?"

"I haven't tried them on yet. But thank you for them."

Thank him for what, Shemar wondered. Though

he didn't have to wonder too long. The shopping bags were right by the couch. *Don't tell me she let him buy her all that stuff.*

Marita paused, feeling unsure about letting Cliff buy her the items. But she was appreciative. Her savings had dwindled terribly. Before she left, she'd written a hefty check to the residence where her mother was for her continued therapy. "Cliff, I appreciate it. But you really didn't have to do that."

They continued talking for a little while longer. Yet, Marita feigned that she was too tired to continue the conversation. For she knew she'd kept Shemar waiting too long already. Winding up the call, they agreed to get together on Monday evening for more fun in the tropical playground.

Shemar looked angry when she hung up. "I don't believe this."

"What?" The mood in the room had certainly changed.

"You, that's what."

"What about me?"

"You're going to see him again?"

She didn't like this possessive act. Particularly when she didn't really know what was happening with them and where it was going.

"I don't like cave men."

"I'm not a cave man.

"You are when it comes to me."

"Because you bring that out of me. You are so . . ."

"So what?"

"I can't even put it in plain English. But you bring a certain side out of me." Then his eye caught the packages. "And how could you let him buy you things? You don't know the man."

"Now that is none of your business."

"It just verifies what I said."

"And what is that?"

"That you're materialistic."

"I am not!" Marita felt fire breathing from her nostrils. "Don't tell me you're back on that again."

"Then why did you let a stranger spend all that money on you?"

"That's none of your business. In fact, we have no more business together."

She flounced toward the stairs.

Clutching her hand, Shemar coaxed her back around. "Where do you think you're going?"

She jerked his hand off of her. "To bed if you don't mind."

"What about what happened here?"

"What about it?"

"We're just going to walk away and not discuss it like before?"

"There is nothing to discuss. It never happened." She flounced away, heading up the stairs.

Shemar soon heard a door slam.

Eight

The singing of the birds woke Marita up the next morning. They urged her to look from the window toward the back of the house where a forest was. She spotted the melodious creatures resting in the blade-leafed trees. A melange of multicolored flowers and a pond with several ducks further fascinated her. Within moments, she'd left the house and found herself in the midst of the tropical wonderland she had beheld. Reposing on the ground, her back flattened against the trunk of a tree, Marita delighted in all the magnificence. The sun rising seemingly higher with each second made it all the more beautiful.

She needed to think. This was the perfect place. It was soothing and distant from the reason for her contemplation. What had she been thinking last night? She and Shemar were playing with fire. Even if the phone hadn't interrupted them, she knew she couldn't have gone all the way to making love with him. They were just getting acquainted again. Sometimes it didn't feel like it. Sometimes it felt like they were back in time to when they were younger. Then at other times, like when she was so turned on by Shemar like she'd never been for anyone else, he felt like an exciting, mysterious stranger. She'd never given her body to a man she didn't know well and

she wasn't about to start. Then there were other issues with him, which made her put up a stop sign
where he was concerned.

Shemar was still mourning his ex. Shemar believed she valued *things* more than all else. And
with what he said about Cliff buying her things,
now he probably believed she was out to get everything she could from a man. Shemar was too
jealous. And then there was that other thing—she
didn't know what he did for a living.

She'd been there with Remmy. She wasn't going
there again. Although last night he seemed anything but mysterious. She felt so good when they
talked. It felt even more than good. There was a
connection. It was so unlike what she'd felt with
other men in her life. She wanted that soul bond-
ing with someone who was going to be part of her
life. Would she ever find him?

Shemar was already up, lifting weights in his
room when he heard Marita go outside. Before
long, he viewed her from the window. How could
he stop desiring a woman that was driving him
crazy? There was no hope for them. She wasn't
what he needed in his life.

He wanted his dream. Someone who he not only
felt extreme passion with, but a woman who loved
him with every fiber of her heart. She would love
him if he lost everything. She would love him forever unconditionally. Marita wasn't that woman.
Passionate as they did feel together, she could
never be that woman. Where the money was to be
found was where she'd be. Look at how she'd let

a complete stranger lavish her with gifts. She was definitely out for what she could get.

So why did he feel so torn?

Last night they were *there*—together in body, spirit, and mind. If he would have made love to her, Shemar knew it would have been one of the most unforgettable experiences of his life. The things she spoke of touched his core. The emotion emanating from her, he could still feel quivers from it. He had been so turned on that he was certain if she allowed him to be swept into her sweet walls, he would have never wanted to leave. A part of him was screeching to get deeper with her as powerfully as another part was warning him to keep things at bay.

Now he was convinced that she didn't know about his wealth. But Lord knew what would happen if she did. Wouldn't that same little Marita Sommers he once knew, who was obsessed with becoming opulent, follow him anywhere and say anything to fulfill that destiny? For Marita hadn't changed. It was obvious. For that matter, he questioned the validity of the story about how she'd stood up for a rape victim and lost her job because of it. What's more, she'd never even brought up why she hadn't returned his calls, letters, or the train ticket. Didn't he deserve such a courtesy? Weren't things like that important to her?

He deserved better. He wanted more. He needed a woman to love him with her whole heart. A heart that he could feel raging at the height of passion the same way it could rage in the way she treated him when they were together and even apart. They would support each other's dreams and struggles. Without anything, he would still be

her everything. Somewhere out there in the world
he knew that such a woman existed.

Moments later, Shemar startled Marita when he
met up with her in the woods.

"How are you doing today?" he asked.

Looking up at him, Marita heard none of the
hostility from the former night. "I'm OK. And
you?"

There wasn't anger. Still, he detected formality.
"I'm all right. I'd be better if I knew you weren't
angry with me."

A tiny curve cracked through her pressed-
together lips. "I'm not mad. I was just out here
thinking."

"I was in the house thinking." Dabbing at his
sideburn, he shuffled a few steps toward her.

"About what?" She noticed he was barefoot.

His long boats planted themselves next to hers
as he sat by the tree with her. "About how we can
make this sharing of the town house a pleasant
and peaceful experience."

She looked over at him. As serious as he was
gorgeous in the morning light, he gazed out in
the direction of the pond. "I was trying to figure
that out, too."

"I came up with something." He couldn't look
at her. Couldn't. It was hard enough to keep last
night from flashing in his mind every second. He
had been kissed into madness and his lips were
still throbbing from it. "I came up with the perfect
solution."

"Me, too."

Pausing, he announced, "I believe it's best if we
keep things on the friendship level and never *ever*
cross that line."

With different words, Marita had been about to tell him the same thing. So why did it feel so disheartening to hear him saying it? As much as she knew she shouldn't have, she had enjoyed the sexual tension between them. And that kiss . . . God that kiss. "I was just about to say the same thing, Shemar." She set her sight on a squirrel running about, avoiding his eyes. It was better to say this and not look at him. "We can be friends, buddies like we used to. It won't matter to me what you're doing, because my hea—my emotions aren't on the line."

Shemar feigned interest in a duck circling the pond to evade being weakened by looking at her. "You can go out or flirt with whoever you want, or anything you choose and it can't concern me."

"And you can . . . You can have issues about your ex, or be a dating fool, or do God knows what for a living. . . . You can do whatever and it won't concern me, either."

"We'll just be friends like we used to be."

"Without all that unnecessary stuff." She wrapped her hair behind her ear. "Get to know each other, but not like *that*."

"Exactly."

"That will make things so much easier."

"It sure will."

"Good."

"Yes, good. That's settled." He looked over at her. When would he stop seeing her that way?

Marita felt his gaze on her. She turned aside. How could she stop feeling this way when she looked at him? "Want to shake on it . . . friend?"

Shemar looked at her hand, but was overtaken to sweep her into a hug instead. "We're friends

136   *Louré Bussey*

again." He closed his eyes, feeling his untamed heart.

Marita closed her eyes, too, feeling the rhythm in his chest matching her own. *It's going to stop feeling like this,* she consoled herself. *I'm going to get used to him, and it'll just feel like I'm hanging around my old friend Shemar again. Feelings can go away . . . eventually.*

"Oh, I'm feeling you, sweet thing. I'm feeling you."

Valerian stepped back from the mantel in his room to admire the portraits he just placed there, featuring Marita. Hung above them was the 15 X 15 inch painting of her he'd finished that morning. He pondered if her lips were as plump as his brush had depicted them as being. He never forgot those lips. Those eyes however, were what really enraptured him.

They would be seeing each other. If all his plans fell into place it would be a matter of weeks, possibly less. Valerian had made contact with the people who would ensure his future as a wealthy man. After the meeting he would be having with them, things could move a whole lot faster. Money would exchange hands. That would enable him to know Marita's whereabouts soon thereafter. He would hire a private investigator to handle that. He'd heard they could find someone in as little time as hours or as long as several days. "Oh, Marita," he laughed aloud as if someone had told a great joke.

Parole Officer Johnson, making a surprise visit, heard him outside in the hall. "Tate! Tate!" He knocked hard on the door that Tate's sister-in-law had escorted him to. "What's going on in there? Open this door now."

"Damn," Valerian mumbled. He didn't want him to see his artwork. Yet there was no time to take them down. And why was he popping up all of a sudden, anyway?

"Open this door, Tate!"

"Cool down, brother." Grinning, Valerian opened the door to a bald black man with slightly bowed legs.

Scanning the neat surroundings, Johnson preferred to stand. "What have you been up to?"

"Living on the outside. Just a former convict trying to make it out here."

"You didn't show up at the construction site job I arranged for you."

Valerian looked as if something was funny. "That wasn't me. My brother is getting me something."

"You're lying."

"He is. He's arranging for me to work at the school where he teaches."

Wildly, Johnson shook his head. "Lying, lying." Then suddenly his eyes narrowed as he noticed the portrait and sketches dedicated to Marita. "And what the hell kind of sick shit is this?"

"My artwork. She had a nice face and body and I liked putting it on paper and canvas."

Shaking his head at the bizarreness of it, Johnson snapped his head toward Valerian. "What are you up to? What are you really, really up to?"

"Nothing."

"You draw all those pictures of the woman who put you away for eighteen years. And make a painting, too. Something is going down here. What?"

"Just a man adjusting to life on the outside, try-

ing to keep some beauty in it. I'm even going to
show up to that construction site tomorrow and
get to working like regular folks." He reached for
a pack of cigarettes off of a lace-dressed table. He
extended the pack to Johnson. "Have one?"

Johnson's nostrils flared. "Don't give me no
crap, Tate."

"What stick is in your butt, brother?" Valerian
sat and crossed his legs.

"Don't 'brother' me. Real brothers don't harass
old ladies."

So that witch recognized me. "What are you talking
about?"

Johnson wanted to grab him by the throat and
shake the breath out of him. He hated guys like
this. They couldn't do the right thing to save their
mama's life. "You went over to Mrs. Dollie Brunswick's house and asked the whereabouts of her
niece, Marita Sommers, who testified against you
at your trial."

"That's what this Dollie woman said?" Valerian
was lighting a cigarette.

"Don't play games."

He took two puffs. "She must have mistook
someone else for me."

Johnson observed this rat crossing his legs, observed his whole nonchalant attitude. "You piece
of shit!" He grabbed Valerian up by the collar.
"You better not go near either of those women!
You better go to work somewhere and you better
not do anything out of line, because I will have
your ass back in prison so fast, you'll think you
never left. Do I make myself clear?" Releasing
him, he harshly threw Valerian down."

Hitting a chair, Valerian looked up at him, smiling. "Of course, Mr. Johnson. I just want to be a law-abiding citizen. Really I do."

Johnson slammed the door behind him. Watching it for several moments, Valerian's smile transformed into a glower. "It won't be long . . . sweet thing."

Marita had thoroughly enjoyed a nutritious and delicious breakfast that Shemar prepared for her. Mostly she enjoyed the conversation. They had a lot of catching up to do. She was surprised they still loved many of the same things, soulful music, dancing, great movies, and good books. In fact, Marita expressed how she would spend her day reading. She hadn't just spent a leisurely day reading in so long. She had several romance novels to complete.

"So I'll catch up with you later, sir," she said, walking away from the dishwasher. She thought the least she could do was clean up well after he cooked so magnificently. "And thank you for the munchies. They were really good. I'm going up to read my books."

Shemar watched her walk up the stairs. "And I'm going to lock myself in my room and get to work on my computer. I have lots of things to do and no time to waste."

Marita wanted to ask about that. She was getting more curious about what he now did for a living. However, she told herself it didn't concern her. "See you later."

She proceeded up the stairs, down the hall, and somehow in her lazy strides bumped into a half-open box. A book caught her eye. She pulled back the other side. *Getting The Most From Life* by Sherman Dawes was a fabulous book, she'd heard, and a best-seller. She'd also heard about the author. He'd written many other successful nonfiction books. Unfortunately, she'd been so busy at the firm she'd never had a chance to indulge herself in what others obviously found fascinating. She could see that Shemar certainly was fascinated. Because when she glanced back at the box, there were many copies of that same book inside. She guessed that he probably liked it so much he bought copies for his friends. She had done that sometimes.

Down the hall in his room, Shemar seated himself before his computer, but his heart wasn't with his passion today. Not with that one at least. He'd enjoyed talking to Marita at breakfast so much, he wanted to talk some more. He wanted to do something with her. On a friendship basis, of course. And after all, it was Sunday.

He knocked on her door. "Marita?"

"Come in."

She had changed into shorts. Her shimmering bare legs caught the light and his eyes. He raised them to her face. "I have this great movie on video. I saw it before, but maybe you haven't."

"What's it called?"

"The Best Man. It's just awesome. You have to see this."

She lit up. "I saw that. Isn't it good?" She sat up, closing her book. "I would love to see it again."

"Now watch out for that innocent bride," she said moments later as they snuggled next to each

other before the television. "She's not that innocent."

Shemar reached back behind them to dim the
lights. "You're just like you were when we were
younger." His tone was playful.

"What do you mean?" She chuckled, knowing
what he meant.

"You always have to tell what's going to happen
in the movie. Every time we used to watch reruns
of *Lost in Space* and *Creature Feature* you had to tell
what was going to happen. Big mouth." He
pinched her lip.

"Ouch!" she whined, but loved him touching
her like that.

"Better be quiet before I give you something to
really say 'ouch' about."

Marita smiled with him as they concentrated
back on the movie.

"Now you see there," she pointed out some time
later. "Nia and Taye got over that attraction thing
and are going to be friends. It can happen, right?"
But even as she said that, Marita realized how they
were positioned on the couch. She was snuggled
up against Shemar's chest and his arm was around
her. Their legs were entwined and his free hand
was caressing her thigh. He had been caressing it
for the length of the movie and that welcome fullness in her lower body hadn't wanted her to stop
him.

He turned to her as the credits began to roll
for the end of the movie. "I like doing simple
things with you." His voice was a near whisper and
his lips brushed her neck as he talked.

She was intoxicated by the warm wind of his
breath on her. "It's been a nice day." She turned,

and beheld his face so close to hers. "I better go upstairs."

"Not before . . ." He moved his lips up to her cheeks. Delicately, he kissed it, her nose, her forehead, before treating himself to her lips. "One last kiss."

"The last . . . one." She opened her mouth as his tongue slid inside, and parted her legs as his probing fingers massaged in an upward motion on her thigh. Soon reaching her secret place, gliding his fingers over the fabric, he parted her legs just as he widened her mouth with his thrusting tongue.

"Oh, God," Marita whimpered as she felt him slowly rolling her shorts down her thighs and legs. "We said . . . we weren't."

"Just this one time." Tasting her succulent lips, Shemar was aroused to an aching point. He couldn't get her clothes off fast enough. "Just this one time, baby." Kissing her deeper and deeper, he managed to remove the shorts and fling them aside. "Let's get it out of our system."

"No," Marita cried, feeling his lips divide between her neck, cheeks, and lips. "We can't."

"We can't feel this hot." Shemar's tongue pulsated across her lips, soon meeting her tongue back in the warm sweet nectar beyond her mouth. He played with her top until it bundled around her waist. She wore nothing underneath it. He paused from kissing her just to look at her. He had imagined doing this, but he had no idea how he would feel when he beheld her like this.

"Oh," Marita murmured, feeling her hardened bud between his lips.

Squeezing her, kissing her, Shemar pulled the

top over her head, removing it from her completely. His breath quickened seeing that only her panties were left. "I want you so bad, Marita," he breathed, his fingers rolling the silken fabric off of her.

"Take it off, now! I want you too, Shemar. I need you."

"I'm coming, baby." Staring at her finally nude body, his breath sucked away in his throat. Hurriedly, he pulled his shirt over his head and she helped him out of his pants and soon his boxer shorts.

"You're a creature certainly blessed by God," she managed between her deep breaths. Never had she seen a man so fine and that she wanted so badly she could have screamed if she didn't have him.

He left the room and returned quickly with the little red package. Standing above her, watching her as she so lovingly placed the strawberry-scented latex on him, he rubbed his fingers through her hair. Never had he been so turned on. He couldn't wait to be inside her.

Marita watched him staring in her eyes as he came down. Starting with her feet, he massaged them, tenderly kissing each toe. Shivers propelled through her. The saturation in the bottom of her stomach neared the point of bursting from the pleasure. With his unencumbered fingers, Shemar reached her moist legs, caressing them, before climbing toward them with his lips.

The taste of cherry came to mind as he devoured her legs and controlled his burning arousal, reaching her throbbing thighs. Kissing them, rubbing them, he felt her trembling with every bit as much as desire as he was. This perfect moment was the most ecstasy-filled one that he'd experienced since he'd been on the island, since years and years, and he didn't dare imagine it ending. He wanted to prolong it, and he was determined to give Marita an erotic pleasure she wouldn't soon forget.

Marita played with Shemar's hair as he worked his way up to kissing the patch of hair below her stomach and discovering what sent her into a frenzy.

"Oh!" she screamed as he began to thrill her there with this tongue, while his hands squeezed her breasts. She felt him shaking and looking up into her eyes, his feral stare screeching that he turned her on as much as she did him. Marita couldn't imagine feeling bliss beyond what they were feeling.

Though there was more. He brought his hips up toward hers, laid on her, then guided his body into her. Clutching his back, feeling him delving deeper and deeper, Marita suddenly awakened with life unlike any she'd ever known.

Shemar was a master at loving her. The way he looked at her, the way he held her in his arms, the way he kissed her, all the while moving himself with an erotica that made her shudder with orgasmic rapture multiple times. At times it felt so good, she would just hold him in that position, not allowing him to do anything else but continue what he was doing. Oftentimes screaming her throat raw, she couldn't bear for him to stop.

And he couldn't if he wanted to. Her body was made for him. Every stride, every curve, every touch, every softness of her skin, and every luscious kiss filled his erection with indestructible steel. Orgasm after orgasm would come to heighten and steal the moment. Yet wanting Marita's joy to continue forever, he would hold on with every effort for the strain of the bliss not to break. Finally it did, bringing each of them to an experience of delight that made their limbs reach near convulsions before leaving them speechless and breathless in each other's arms.

All afternoon and part of the night they discovered the astonishing capabilities for pleasure of the human body. Even when Pam dropped by, no one answered her knock at the door; they weren't able to stop. She knew Shemar was home. His car was in the driveway. So was Marita's rental. Were they asleep so early in the evening? Curious, she stepped across the porch, peeking in the window that had a full view of the lit living room. "God, please no . . . No!"

Nine

Shemar had been awake long before the dawn started to rise outside the window. He was busy looking at her. Marita, the Marita he'd been so infatuated with as a young teenager, was actually in his arms. Passionately, and feeling so much passion from her, he'd made love to her over and over and over again. It hadn't been a dream. For at this moment, her warm, naked body was splayed wildly across his as she snuggled against his damp chest.

He'd left for only a few moments while she slept to get a blanket to cover them. As he tucked it securely around them, he wondered if he'd made her too heated. Tiny beads of perspiration were clinging to her facial skin. Every so often, he'd blot them off with a kiss. Something had happened between them. It was beyond a strong sexual attraction being satisfied. For him, it was the ultimate soul connection. There was a bond between them that couldn't be denied. It was expressed in their sexual chemistry, in the way they talked to each other, in the way that they looked at each other. Shemar beheld it as she looked up at him at this moment.

"Good morning." Swiveling sideways to better

see him, she smiled. "I don't even know what to call you after last night." She stretched her lower limbs. "You did me in."

Shemar grinned. "And you were one delicious, one-of-a-kind-of-earth *fruit*. And I'm addicted to your sweetness. I want to lose myself in your tasty juice again." Lifting her chin, he pressed his lips against hers. When she turned back to rest her head, he lifted her face again. A deep thrusting of his tongue overloaded her feminine core with desire. He squeezed her nipple beneath the cover.

"You're a fresh thing," she teased, pulling the cover down from her, allowing him more access.

"You're fresher." He guided her available hand toward his erection.

Marita couldn't believe how ready he was again. "My, my. Aren't you *aiming* for fun?"

"Mm-hmm." His head started moving down her chest, kissing her breasts, then moving lower, planting amorous kisses over her stomach.

Gripping the sides of his face, she raised his face to hers. Her expression was as earnest as her tone. "Last night meant so much to me, Shemar. You have no idea how you made me feel. And I'm not just talking about how good you made me feel on a sexual level. You made me feel like . . ."

"Like I loved you . . ."

The way he said it stirred something in her. "Did you feel it, too?"

"I feel it now." He lifted her hand to his chest.

The wild thumping was almost alarming. "Does this really mean you care about me? Last night just wasn't about sex?"

"I've always cared for you, Marita. Always." The back of his hand slid along her cheek.

"I always cared for you, too. Just not like I do now. You were my good friend. And I felt so close to you like a friend."

"For me, it was different. I used to look at you and just want to kiss you and hold you and tell you what I felt for you."

She had no idea he'd harbored those emotions back then. "What did you feel for me?"

"So much. You were everything. So beautiful. So smart. And you carried yourself like a queen. I admired you so much. It made me feel good to be around you. It was inspiring. You saw your way out of no way. You made me focus on the beauty of life rather than the ugly that tried to consume us in that environment. You made me keep my eyes on big dreams, and music, and movies, and anything good and positive. And though you may not know it, you played a major influence in my life. Some of the things I learned from you, I use in my work."

"What is your work?" She fully faced him. Surely, he would tell her after they'd shared so much. "I need some of that positive incentive that I gave you. Maybe I just gave it out and gave it out, leaving none for myself. Maybe that's why my life is in shambles. Though I must admit, last night it did take a turn." She pecked his lips, then pulled away staring up at his handsome face. "So what is it? Tell me all about what you do."

Shemar rose so he could explain it. He was so passionate about what he did. "I—" A knock at the door cut him off. "Who the hell is that?"

"Why now? What time is it anyway to be barging in on a woman when she just got the best loving of her life?" She winked at him.

Shemar patted the side of her hip, before glancing at the wall clock. "It's two-thirty." He was stunned at the time.

So was Marita. "Two-thirty in the afternoon?"

He picked his pants up off the floor. "That's right, baby. We were doing the *do* all night long. Couldn't get up."

She loved the way he called her baby. Not wanting to get up, she merely gathered up some cover over her. "I'm not moving. You're going to have to get rid of them."

"I will." He stepped into one pant leg. "Because I want a replay of last night, right there on that couch."

"You do, huh?"

"Oh, yes." Hurriedly, he was sticking his foot into the other leg. "Then I'm taking you upstairs and I'll take care of you there, too."

"You will, huh?" She was watching him walk to the door. Heaven help the woman who saw him with all that chest exposed.

"You're only going to be good for rest after all that. Nothing but rest. I doubt you'll be able to even move a pinky." He shuffled by the door. "Girl, you were speaking Chinese and all kinds of languages last night because I had you so far gone."

"You liar!" Laughing, she tossed a small pillow at him.

It hit him on the butt, not distracting him from opening the door. "Yes?" A delivery man faced him.

Narrowing her eyes to see the goings-on at the door, Marita wondered what all those packages were about. "Who's that for?"

Shemar was trying to figure that out himself. He signed the receipt and brought in all the boxes addressed to Marita.

With the cover draped around her, she walked over to where Shemar deposited them on the love seat. Both of them scoured the nine packages of various sizes.

Shemar bent down, inspecting one box for its sender's name. He saw nothing. "Ms. Dollie must have sent you something."

"I know. She's the only one who knows I'm here. Her and mama. And I doubt mama's got the strength to be shopping for me." Marita began to unwrap one package. It was the smallest one. The floral silk scarf she removed came from a boutique. Not only was it labeled so, but she remembered going there with Cliff after they left the cruise ship. Saying "Oh, no" in her mind, she continued opening the packages. Gifts varying from electronics to household trinkets filled the boxes. All were clearly expensive.

Shaking her head, looking down at all the items, she looked up to see why Shemar had become mysteriously quiet. His face now blank, he was holding a card in his hand. It had been attached to one of the wrappings she'd tossed aside.

"Looks like Aunt Dollie wasn't the one sending you these."

"Who did?"

Speechlessly, and sort of angry, he looked at her, compelling her to take the card from his hand. She sucked her tooth while reading it. It was all going back. Right back to where it came from— Clifton. She didn't know the man that well. And although she'd admired these particular items as they window-shopped, she hadn't told him to buy her anything. They were definitely going back.

She began gathering up the items and their wrappings. "I have to talk to him. He and I have to get some things straight."

"What kind of things? Like more expensive things next time?"

Marita's frowning face snapped up. "What?"

"You heard me, Marita. What's he have to buy you next—jewelry? A Mercedes-Benz? A trip to Paris? What does it take next to make your eyes light up?"

How could he talk to her this way after what they'd shared so deeply together? "You have the wrong idea about me, Shemar. I did not ask this man to buy me these things."

"I don't see you in a hurry to send them back."

What did he think she was doing right then? She didn't like this side of him. Worse, as she really thought about what he was saying, she didn't like what he was insinuating. "You're back to that materialism thing again, aren't you?"

"Marita, no decent woman lets a man just buy her things like this when she doesn't even know him that well."

Stomping anger filled her; she wished she could take her loving back. This crazy man didn't deserve it! "Don't you dare insult me again!"

"I'm not!" He tossed his hands out. "I'm done with you. I'm absolutely through with all this. It's not going to work!"

"You're doggone right it's not. Because you're not having me again."

"Fine."

"That's right, it's fine. And this all came up because you're probably feeling a little insecure."

"Insecure about what?"

"About Cliff. He's a successful doctor and he can give a woman anything she wants."

"So?"

"So nothing. And you're a I-don't-know-what, and you probably have nothing to offer."

"That's you again, isn't it? It's all about the bank account."

"Think whatever you want of me. I know who I am. And I was starting to think I knew who you were, but I don't. And now I don't care who you are! I must admit it was some damn good sex! But it will be no more." She marched upstairs.

Shemar went out on the porch and swatted at a fly that buzzed by his nose.

Marita paced throughout the empty house, wondering where Shemar had driven off to hours earlier. Mad or not, she thought he would have at least hollered up that he was going out. Every so often she peeked out the window into the dark, hoping he'd drive up despite not knowing what she'd say if he did. Then she would look at the sofa where they had been so intimate. With vivid memory, her hand had even brushed where he held her in his arms.

It had been more than intimacy. It had been more than unbelievably erotic sex. Shemar had touched something within her that had never been touched before. Sex had always been a take-it-or-leave-it matter. All her life she wondered what was the big deal about. Yes, there had been some wonderful moments with Richard. However, in no way did it compare to what she experienced with Shemar.

It was as if he knew her to her soul in that moment, and she knew him. In some way, it seemed like she'd known him even before their younger years together and even after they went their separate ways. Somehow in that impassioned moment, she instinctively felt that he was the embodiment of everything she desired in a man. Her flesh against his flesh, she'd never felt so like a woman. The experience had been almost spiritual. She felt connected to him. It made her feel that he could protect her, understand her, need her, and even love her.

She had loved it so when he looked in her eyes as he loved her. No man had ever done that. Selfishly, they kissed her, they caressed her, they touched her, but no one had spoken to her with their eyes. And if she could have seen what her eyes reflected back, she knew what they would have said: I'm falling in love with you, Shemar Dalton. Madly, wildly in love.

Yet she had been mistaken. She had been robbed by a shyster. The Shemar Dalton who made love to her was not the man who spoke so rudely to her moments later. That tender man would have known she wasn't a gold digger out to grab everything she could from unsuspecting victims. That passionate dreamer would have known that all she'd ever really wanted out of life was what her mother never had: a constant, reliable wellspring of love from a man. Someone who would be there eternally as her fiery lover and equally as her soul's other half. For some hours, she'd been fooled into thinking she'd found that.

Put him out of your mind, girl, she placated herself, as she walked up the stairs. She had to get dressed to meet with Cliff. He'd phoned earlier, wanting to come over and pick her up for another outing. However, in light of what happened between Shemar and her that would have been awkward. Consequently, they planned to meet at a popular sports bar. Glancing at the clock when she reached the bedroom, Marita saw that she had about an hour to get ready.

Opening the closet, pulling out various clothes to see which she should wear, she realized that she didn't look forward to seeing Cliff again. However, she wanted to return those items to him. She was going to return all those shoes, too. Additionally, she wanted to kindly part ways. It was better than to lead him on. Cliff clearly had ideas about their friendship that differed with hers. That became clear with all those things he purchased for her. Before that, she could have even tolerated his irksome traits such as boasting. For he was fun. Nonetheless, bragging like he did about his prosperity, along with her surprise delivery, it was dawning on her what type of man he really was.

He tried to buy women, whether for a relationship or merely for sex. Marita wasn't up for either. All those sneaky glances slithering over her body confirmed too that he had ideas that he surely shouldn't. She shouldn't have ignored them. Luckily, now she knew better.

She was bent over searching through her dresser drawers for the ideal undergarments to wear with a pantsuit when she heard a bump downstairs. It

startled her into straightening her posture. Was
Shemar home? She sidestepped to the window. His
car wasn't in the driveway. Must have come from
next door, she decided, returning to the drawer.
Riffling through it more vigorously, she looked for
panties that wouldn't show the line and a bra with
good support. Finding a yellow lace set, she
headed into the bathroom.

The shower's lukewarm cascade began pouring
over her face, down her shoulders and the length
of her body. It felt great and so relaxing she could
no longer fight what kept crawling to the forefront
of her mind. Everything was ruined with Shemar.
Now even the friendship was gone.

Another bump coming from downstairs interrupted her musings. Marita froze, then carefully
turned the water dials off. Drying off quickly, she
threw on a terry housecoat. A glance out of the
window made her aware that Shemar still hadn't
returned. While her feet plodded carefully down
the hallway carpet, she scrutinized her surroundings. Then from the upstairs banister, she scoured
as much of the downstairs that could be viewed
from that standpoint. It was soundless and motion-
less.

Picking up an umbrella from a silver receptacle
tucked in the corner, Marita held it tightly as she
stepped cautiously down the stairs. When finally
she stood in the midst of the living room, there
was no one in sight. Neither was anything disar-
rayed. Satisfied that it had to have been a sound
coming from the neighbor's joined house, Marita
headed for the stairs. Except a thought crossed her
mind. She curved around. Could it have come
from the porch? Was one of the hanging pots of

flowers bumping something because of the wind? The wind chimes' tinkling was indicating a summer breeze.

Marita's damp feet stepped over the exterior concrete and allowed the flurry of tepid air to play over her skin. Everything except the chimes was quiescent. She saw nothing to stir her heart until there was a human shadow by the side of her eye. Spinning around, the umbrella fell out of her hand. The unexpected presence moved forward in her direction. Gasping, Marita moved back.

Because of Marita, Shemar was detached from the game as he gazed up at one of many giant-sized viewing screens inside the Champions Sports Bar. The woman had been born who could actually distract him from basketball. It was truly a first. In boyhood his father, Evan, had introduced him to various sports. Of the many he dabbled in, it was basketball that stole his heart. Every aspect of the sport fascinated him. Any team he could join and any chance he had to play was always welcome.

Since being in Bermuda, his preparation for the lecture and writing a new book left little time for his indulgence, but he had managed a few good games. The two brothers Trent and Michael, whom he often played with, were now seated beside him at the bar.

When the game was over, they all found a table in the dining area of Champions. No one was hungry. Their favorite team's loss did that to them. Still, they enjoyed a round of drinks.

"I don't even want to talk about it," Trent lamented. "When my team loses that hurts my heart." Tall and as robust as a basketball player himself, Shemar considered Trent more like him of the two. Since he'd become friends with the guys in this very bar, the threesome usually met once or twice a week to play a game or at least to watch one on the high-tech screens like they had just done. Both Trent and Michael had grown up on the island, left for many years for the States for educational purposes, and returned to engage in their respective business enterprises. Their accents were lost in the migration.

Michael, the younger basketball fan, had forgotten his favorite team as soon as an attractive group of young ladies entered the restaurant. Sipping his beer and watching them standing about at the entrance, he debated escorting them to a table instead of the hostess. All were more than welcome to sit right on his lap. "Check out those honeys over there." He nodded his curly head toward the entrance. A hostess was now escorting the thirtysomething, fortysomething women far out of his view.

"They look like nice ladies," Trent commented. Though that's all he would do. He had a woman he was very happy with.

Michael had a wife. He turned toward his drinking companions. "Boy, if I wasn't married I would be on that."

Shemar was as tickled by him as he was annoyed. "But you are married. Man, don't you ever stop?"

"No way." Michael scoured the place for more appealing bodies. "I'll never stop looking at pretty women. Never. When I stop, you'll know I'm dead."

"And you will be if your wife catches your roving eye," Trent jested.

Shemar joined him in a chuckle and a high-five. Michael gaped at the two. "There is nothing wrong with looking. Just looking, that's all."

Trent shook his head again. "I don't believe that. I know you. If you had the chance you would have done certainly more than look."

"No, I wouldn't have. I never cheated."

"In your mind you have," Shemar pointed out. "And how would you feel if your wife did that to you? From what I know of your wife, she's a good woman."

"Damn right she is." Michael nodded his head with conviction.

"So what are you doing this for?" Shemar leaned across the table closer to Michael. "From what I see it's not her. It's you. It's all *within* you. That's where the problem is. No matter what woman you're with, the same behavior is going to be an issue. Because you can't escape *you.*"

Michael waved his hand at Shemar. "You don't know what you're talking about."

"Truth is what I'm talking about. Whatever you feel devoid of is always going to be there until you take action to do something about it. And all this looking at everything in a skirt is not because your wife doesn't make love to you. It's not because she may not look the same as when you married her. It's not because she doesn't give you attention, or whatever reasons some guys come up with. I heard the cheater excuses all the time when I had my practice."

"I'm not a cheater."

"So you say. But what I'm saying is that it's your

feeling of lacking something within that makes you feel a need to be validated outside your marriage. That's what it is. And if you want to lust after other women, and if you're not happy with the relationship you have and feel something is lacking, maybe you should get some help."

"From you, Doctor, an authority on everything?"

"No, it doesn't have to be from me. But some religious counsel might help. There are some great books that might help. There are spiritual healers and even being introspective and asking yourself what you really want might help. Clearly, you're not happy with your marriage."

"I am so."

"I agree with Shemar," Trent added.

"I am happy."

Shemar sighed. "I don't think you are. Because if you were with the woman that you believe God sent to this earth for you, you would cherish her."

"I'm good to my wife."

"You're not being good disrespecting her like this."

Michael's thin lips inched up in a silly grin. "You're one to talk, Shemar. Your marriage didn't work out. How can you tell me about mine?"

"Because I learned from my mistakes, and I make a point to learn from the mistakes of everyone I encounter in my life."

"Don't seem like you're doing too good to me. When was the last time you had some?"

Shemar shook his head. Michael was always interested in his love life. Nevertheless, he never shared the intimate details of being with a woman sexually with any other man. He shared relationship issues, yes. Intimacy, never. As a boy, when his father first

told him about the birds and bees he cautioned Shemar: don't ever let another man know how much
your woman pleases you. Because more often than
not, he's going to try to discover if your ocean is really
that blue. In any case, Michael made assumptions
based on the lack of an explicit report.

A dispirited haze hung over the table. Michael
suddenly felt bad about turning on Shemar. He
was a cool brother and he wanted to stay cool with
him. "I'm sorry, my brother. I didn't mean to
come off at you like that."

Shemar refused to let himself get riled. "No
harm done. I just let you talk."

"And I know I don't do right all the time. But
I'm working on it."

Trent popped a pretzel in his mouth. "Work on
it some more." He chewed that pretzel, then
tossed another in his mouth as his bright eyes
shifted to Shemar. "So what's going on with that
new houseguest you told me about on the phone
the other night?"

Shemar appeared introspective as he recalled his
confrontation with Marita. "It's not going that
good."

Michael was intrigued. "Is this houseguest a
woman or a man?"

"A woman," Shemar answered, with a flash of
them in his mind, of the maddening lovemaking.
He blinked it away when he noticed Michael grinning at him. "What? What's so funny?"

"She's fine as hell, ain't she?"

Shemar was amused despite not wanting to be.
"There you go again."

"You want some, don't you? I can see it on your

An important message from the ARABESQUE Editor

Dear Arabesque Reader,

Because you've chosen to read one of our Arabesque romance novels, we'd like to say "thank you"! And, as a special way to thank you, we've selected four more of the books you love so well to send you for FREE!

Please enjoy them with our compliments, and thank you for continuing to enjoy Arabesque...the soul of romance.

Karen Thomas
Senior Editor,
Arabesque Romance Novels

Check out our website at
www.arabesquebooks.com

SPECIAL OFFER!
4 FREE BOOKS

ARABESQUE ®

A PRODUCT OF

BET BOOKS™

3 QUICK STEPS
TO RECEIVE YOUR "THANK YOU" GIFT
FROM THE EDITOR

Send this card back and you'll receive 4 FREE Arabesque
novels! The introductory shipment of 4 Arabesque novels – a
$23.96 value – is yours absolutely FREE!

There's no catch. You're under no obligation to buy anything.
You'll receive your introductory shipment of 4 Arabesque
novels absolutely FREE (plus $1.50 to offset the costs of
shipping & handling). And you don't have to make any
minimum number of purchases—not even one!

We hope that after receiving your books you'll want to
remain an Arabesque subscriber. But the choice is yours to
continue or cancel, anytime at all! So why not take us up on
our invitation to receive 4 Arabesque Romance Novels, with
no risk of any kind. You'll be glad you did!

Call us
TOLL-FREE
at 1-888-345-BOOK

face." With his interest in this, Michael started shaking his leg. "And she won't give it up."

Trent threw a pretzel at him. "Be quiet."

Michael ducked, but was determined to pull something out of Shemar. "That's why you were half-ass watching the game tonight."

Trent thought that Michael might have had a point. Shemar wasn't really as involved in the game as usual. He turned to Michael. "Why don't you go get some more drinks?" He knew his brother was anxious to check out the ladies in the place, anyway. While he was doing that he could speak to Shemar in private. "We're low."

Michael glanced at the nearly empty glasses. He knew what Trent wanted. He looked at Shemar. "Sparkling cider for you again?"

Shemar nodded. "I guess I'll have a little more."

"Be back." Michael walked off, soon disappearing into an adjoining room where the bar was.

Glad he was gone, Trent leaned toward Shemar. "So what's going on with your lady guest?"

Sighing, Shemar rubbed across his face. Stopping, he looked over at Trent. "I told you how I felt for her when I was a kid." He laughed at that.

"Right." Trent nodded.

"Well, now, in this little span of time something much deeper is happening."

Trent was baffled. "What's so bad about that? You're not in a relationship with any other woman. Maybe it's your time."

"Not with her."

"Why not?"

"She's not right for me. She has a trouble sign on her just as big as my ex-wife."

"And you say something is happening? I don't understand."

"It's like this. I feel her, man. I can't stop. I just feel so much for her. It's all in here." He brought his fist to his chest. "But I can't. She's no good for me."

"What did she do exactly?"

"She's out for all she can get. A real gold digger."

"What has she done to make you think that?"

"A guy who she just went out with bought her all this stuff. Plus, I know how she was before. She hasn't changed."

"Before, she was much younger. Maybe she has changed. But you're too deep into that pain with your ex that you can't give her a chance."

Shemar smiled at him for a moment. Could he have been right? "You sure you didn't study psychology?"

The men chuckled at that, and Shemar steered them off the conversation. He didn't want to talk about Marita anymore tonight. It was actually painful for him. Yet he was reminded of his pain when he saw an unwelcome sight enter the bar.

Cliff saw him, too. Because Trent and Michael had left by then, he helped himself to one of the available seats.

"Hello," Cliff greeted him.

Shemar nodded, while inhaling the excess of cologne he wore. The scent reminded Shemar of bug spray. "How you doing?"

"I'm here to meet Marita."

Shemar's eyes widened. He watched Cliff stretching his neck, turning from side to side scouring the place. "Why didn't you pick her up?"

Smiling, Cliff focused on Shemar. "I wanted to, but she insisted I meet her. So I gave her directions to this place."

Shemar speculated. Marita probably felt it would have been awkward because of what happened between them. He shifted his attention back to Clifton and was tired already of looking at him. "I better get going. You . . . You two have a good night." He eased his chair back, preparing to stand.

"Why haven't you two ever gotten together?"

Shemar remained in the chair, his eyes narrowing on the smirk. "What do you mean by that?"

"I mean that you two are the same age and everything. And now in a house all alone." Certainly he didn't want a scene, but it was so tempting just to play with the loser a little bit. Cliff concluded that Shemar was a washed-up psychologist. Likely kicked out of his profession. No doctor would just give up a great salary to pursue the "bliss" that Marita had claimed this character was chasing. "I guess Marita is into professional men. Power and money turn women on like crazy. Believe me, I know. The amount of women who come on to me is staggering. And I don't get near most of them. I'm real particular. I think Marita is, too. I think you two are too different. With her being a lawyer, and you being a . . . What did you say you do now?"

"I didn't. But I can tell you what I'm doing right now."

"What's that?"

"Spending too much time looking at one great big fat head." Shemar stood.

Ten

Driving home, Shemar didn't want to think about that jerk. Yet, he couldn't help it since he was thinking of Marita. Why was she with someone like that? He was everything Shemar detested: pompous and showy. But he was assured Marita would see it eventually. People like that couldn't hide behind the pretense of decency for long. The real them would come out sooner or later.

Creep that Cliff had been, Shemar was tempted to tell him some things about true success, but he prided himself on never lowering himself to a foe's low level. He didn't want to take that ugliness home with him tonight. He just needed to sleep everything off. Perhaps tomorrow he wouldn't feel like someone dug his insides out. Though he would feel better visiting the Angels of Hope site tomorrow—an organization that he'd been a major philanthropist for. It was his turn to get out in the field and do some work.

It uplifted his spirit so to get involved that way. Helping the needy in areas of housing, food, shelter, money, and all else, Shemar loved the people, the purpose, and everything they'd accomplished. Whenever he came from there, he felt such a high.

* * *

Marita sat across the table from the elderly
woman she'd discovered on her porch some time
earlier. The source of the bumps she'd heard,
Elizabeth, as she introduced herself, had twice
dropped the fruits she'd picked from the tree beside the outside steps. Tumbling from her crowded
basket, they'd hit the concrete right below Marita's
bedroom window.

Gazing at the woman, Marita saw skin that was like
stretched plastic. Her body was frail and her hands
shook. Marita was glad she'd convinced her to come
inside. She'd only been picking fruit for her grandchildren. There was no food in the house and no
money left to purchase any. Aunt Dollie and Ms.
Nell's tree was the closest fruit-bearing one to her
home. She shared that she didn't have a car or money
for transportation. Unburdening herself more, she
had been too weak to walk to pick the fruits farther
into town where they were more freely available. Occasionally biting on the cheesecake that Marita had
sliced for her, she still looked ashamed about stealing.

"I would have never have bothered your tree,
but I was desperate. Like I said, my daughter is
sick in the hospital with complications from diabe-
tes, and I'm the only one who can care for the
kids. Her husband passed after the last child was
born. He was in New York City, working a good
job, and was mugged. They shot him like he was
nothing."

"I'm so sorry for all your hardship. It's going to
get better. You just have to believe that. That's
what I do, and it may not happen instantly, but it

eventually does get better." Marita reached across
the table, patting Elizabeth's veined hand. "And
it's all right, Ms. Elizabeth, about what you picked.
There is plenty of fruit out there in that tree. You
can take as much of it as you like. No one here
is going to miss it."

She smiled, showing yellowish teeth. "Bless you,
child."

"Bless you, too. Now, I want you to call that
number tomorrow."

The woman's gray eyes peered down at the small
paper Marita had placed beside her saucer. "They
can really help me with all the kids?"

"Yes, they can help you with the kids and all else,
housing, financial support, nursing, baby-sitting. Angels of Hope is a wonderful organization." Marita
smiled with pride at the good they'd done with the
money she'd donated over the years. Rich she wasn't.
Though the organization had made great use of what
she could afford. They had actually used her donations to build several homes for low-income families.
Her benefaction had also provided grooming items
for the homeless. Coincidentally, she'd called them
earlier to find out where their organization was located in Bermuda. Now that she had some time, she
could give more than her cash. She was going out to
the field tomorrow to offer some sweat.

Shemar had left his front-door key so he had to
go around and unlock the patio one. He was surprised by the sound of an unfamiliar voice. Standing out of view, he peered into the dining area
where Marita sat with an enfeebled woman, a
stranger from what he could tell from the conversation. According to what he perceived, she had
lots of grandchildren, a sick daughter, health prob-

lems of her own, and financial woes. Then winding up the warm exchange between the two, Marita went upstairs. When she came back down she placed what looked like two bills in the woman's hand.

"You meant to give me all these hundreds?" the lady asked. "This ain't no mistake?"

Shemar leaned closer to hear the conversation better.

"No, it's not a mistake. I hope that gets what you need until the organization comes through. Is that enough for groceries for you and the three children?"

"Yes, dear." The woman's face brightened like the sun had emerged in the room. "Thank you. Thank you so much." She threw her head back, facing the ceiling. "And thank you, Heavenly Father. You are so good. So, so good. You never let me down."

Afterward, Shemar watched as the two prepared to leave.

Marita opened the front door for her guest. "I'm going to escort you home; then I have to meet a friend." She glimpsed at her watch. Cliff had been expecting her forty minutes ago. At least she'd loaded those gifts of his in her car earlier in the day. That would save some time.

"Finally, you're here" Cliff remarked, as Marita seated herself across from him.

"I apologize for my tardiness." She scanned the busy establishment with the technological design and liked it.

"It's no problem."

She was glad he looked and sounded pleasant. "I was just caught up with a new friend."

"A new friend?" He wondered if it was a male friend. "What does the person do for a living?" Did he have more to offer than him?

Marita perceived the last question as so bizarre she ignored it. "This little grandmother just showed up at my door, trying to get some food. My heart crushed, seeing her so pitiful. At the same time, I really enjoyed her company and was glad I met her. You know, she really made me think. We should appreciate everything we have and take nothing for granted." She eyed Cliff for his reaction.

Disinterested and obviously bored by what she said, he picked up a menu. "What are you having?"

Marita was bothered by his indifference even though she shouldn't have been. She knew what mattered to Cliff. Nothing of any real meaningfulness. "Cliff, I won't be having anything."

Curious, he placed his menu aside. "Oh, no? Not hungry? Did you eat with him already?"

Again, she disregarded his ridiculousness. "I met with you because I wanted to get some things straight."

Cliff frowned. "What have I done? I bought you beautiful things. I've been the perfect gentleman."

"The gentleman part I have no problem with. It's the buying of things that bothers me. In fact, I have the shoes and all that other stuff you sent me in the trunk of my rental. When we leave here, I want you to go to the parking lot with me and put it in your trunk."

"What didn't you like?"

"It's not that I disliked anything, Cliff. I barely know you and you're giving me such extravagant things. It makes me uncomfortable."

"OK, I'll take it back." He slipped his hand inside hers, hoping he could remedy things. "I'll do whatever you want."

"Thank you."

He picked up his menu. "Now, what do you want to eat?"

"Nothing."

The menu dropped, sailing to the floor. Cliff didn't stir he was so busy studying Marita. "Why can't you have dinner with me? What changed? You met someone, didn't you? I'll tell you one thing, it's rare that you'll meet a man who has more money than me on this island. Very rare."

"You see!" She lowered her voice after realizing how loud she sounded. "Everything is not about money with me, like it is with you."

"That's not true. You make me sound shallow."

"I think we're different."

He swallowed the frustration-built saliva in his throat. She wasn't getting rid of him that easy. "What can I do to make things better?"

"I don't want you to do anything. You're you, and I'm me. We can still be friends."

Friends meant no sex, no showing her off as his girlfriend to his colleagues and family, no candidacy for being Mrs. Clifton Harrison, and no making that roommate of hers jealous. "We were meant to be more than friends."

"I don't think we're suited for each other."

"Why not? Give it a chance. Let's get to know each other."

"That's what I have been doing. And I just don't think you're right for me."

"But what did I do? What makes you think that all I care about are superficial things?"

Marita didn't have to think back too far. "For one thing, I just told you about my experience with this pitiful woman and you just didn't care."

"I care."

"Only if she were a paying patient."

He chortled. "You're witty."

Marita wasn't amused. "I'm not trying to be. I'm just stating the facts." She slid back her chair, positioning herself to get up. "Now, I have to get up early in the morning."

"Have a hot date?"

"No." She shook her head at him. "I need to get to bed early because I need an early start tomorrow. I'm going to do some fieldwork for the Angels of Hope organization."

"Oh, yes." He'd heard of the organization. "I donate to them all the time," he lied.

Marita looked surprised. "You do?"

"Of course. I know all about their chapters all over the U.S. and Caribbean. One's right here in Hamilton." They always solicited him. All of their literature and donation envelopes went in the garbage.

Marita eyed him suspiciously. Was he saying this to get on her good side? "I don't know why, Cliff but I don't believe you. I just don't see you caring about an organization like that."

"Well, you're wrong."

"I can check to see who donated."

He cleared his throat. "No need to go to all

that trouble. In fact, I'll prove how much I care about this cause."

"How?"

"I'll right you out a check right now to give when you go there tomorrow."

"You don't have to do that."

"But I want to."

"No, you don't."

"I'm not trying to score points. I'm serious." He opened his silk olive jacket and pulled out his checks from the upper inside pocket. He scribbled on one of them, then handed it to Marita.

The sum that he was donating nearly knocked her off the chair. Warily, she looked up at him. "You sure you want to do this?"

"Of course."

"I mean, really?"

"Without a doubt."

She thought for a moment. It wasn't going to her. It was going to people who needed it like that sweet lady she'd met tonight.

"And you know what else?" he added. "I'll try to join you in the field after work tomorrow.

"You don't have to do that."

"But I want to. If my patient roster allows it, I'll be there."

She hoped his patient roster didn't allow it. "Are you *sure* you want to give this money?" She waved the check between her fingers. "Because you shouldn't do this for me. You should do it from your heart. If you're not doing it for that reason, then take it back."

He smiled. "I'm sure. Give it to them. It'll do someone good."

Later in the parking lot, Marita returned the

items he'd bought her. Afterward, she drove off. A swirl of dust followed her car. Cliff watched until she was fully out of his vision range before getting into his car.

For a long while he merely sat there thinking, his teeth ground hard against each other. "You're not getting away that easy."

Eleven

Visions of Shemar making that sweet love he had made to her, along with so many thoughts about them, filled Marita's head as she drove a dark, lonesome road. It was an alternate route she'd discovered, a shortcut to the town house. If Shemar was home, what would he say to her? How would they act with each other? And when would she stop feeling such a fullness inside her for him when he evidently didn't trust her? He thought the worst of her. He thought she was a gold digger.

Waving arms were caught in her headlights' glare, jarring Marita from her musings. It was a hitchhiker. No, it was someone stranded, she determined, because of the cutoff car nearby. Fearful of slowing down for either situation, she was relieved it was a woman. In fact, she knew this woman.

"Pam?" Marita said, stopping her car beside the idle one.

Pam bent down, leaning into the passenger window. "Marita, I'm sure glad to see you. My car just went out on me."

"What's wrong with it?" Marita looked at the car. "Do you need a boost?" As she kept looking

at it, she realized something. She had seen this
car moments earlier when she first got on this particular road. In fact, it was behind her. Unexpectedly though, it swept past her so fast Marita
thought the driver might have been drunk or on
drugs or something. Marita had had to swerve to
avoid getting bumped. "Weren't you in back of me
and you sped around me?"

"If we were on the same road I probably was."
Beaming, Pam looked hard and long into Marita's
eyes.

"So, do you need a boost?" Marita looked away
from Pam, toward her car.

"I don't think so. Maybe it's the transmission or
the water pump or some other problem."

"Because I do know how to give a boost."

"No. I don't need a boost. I would like you to
drive me home." Again, Pam looked hard and
long in Marita's eyes.

Marita felt a shiver. Was it her imagination? Or
was Pam looking at her strangely? *Must be my imagination.* She didn't feel like driving her home. But
how could she deny a woman stranded on a lonely
highway? "Hop in and tell me how I get there."

Following Pam's directions, Marita proceeded to
her home. There weren't many people out driving,
and combined with the peculiar silence in the car,
there was a dim, eerie atmosphere lingering about.

Unexpectedly, Pam looked over at her. "How is
Shemar?"

"Fine." She tried to appear much more comfortable than she was answering the question. "He's
fine."

"We had a little spat. Decided to make some
distance."

Marita didn't want to know anything. "I just mind my own business."

A strained quiet simmered through the air. Marita was looking ahead at the road, but Pam wasn't. Marita felt eyes on her, just watching and watching her. Finally she looked over. Pam was still staring at her, her gaze unmoving, and her eyes taking on a strange glow, almost an inhuman one. Another shiver fell over Marita again.

When they finally arrived at Pam's home, Marita was awestruck by the immense size of the mansion and the land around it. "Your home is huge; I can only imagine how beautiful you have it decorated inside."

Pam leaned in the driver window after stepping out of the vehicle. "It is nice." Again, her eyes anchored on Marita's. "You have to come by and visit sometimes."

"I will." Marita looked up at the house again, envisioning how lush the estate looked in the daylight. When she brought her attention back to Pam, she was still leaning in the car window. Leaning and staring again. "Pam, is something wrong?"

"No," she said, finally moving back from the car. "Nothing is wrong. Not a thing."

Driving away quickly, Marita tried to shake off that weird sensation that Pam had given her. Those eyes. She had looked at her so strangely. Was she jealous that she had to share her cousin's attention—a little too jealous? For sick as it sounded, sometimes Marita got the strangest vibes from Pam. Like when she caught her staring at Shemar. It wasn't a look she'd given any of her cousins, she was sure. But no, she had to be wrong. She was making too much of the feelings she got when Pam was staring at her.

Dollie's parlor room was her favorite place to lounge. Filled with soft, thick pink cushioned chairs, billowing curtains, and mahogany antique tables and lamps, she would sit in her rocker for hours. The only thing that made it more wonderful was when Nell came over for a visit and sat with her. That's what they were doing this morning.

Dollie hadn't felt like going into work today. Yesterday, she had been too distracted, and rather than risk making a mistake with a patient, she preferred staying home. She had to contemplate what she should do. Was Marita in danger? Did she need to be told that that psychopath was out of prison? Tate's parole officer and other authorities had tried to placate her, telling her that Marita had nothing to worry about. But could they guarantee that? Should she have called Marita and told her this awful news? But wouldn't it ruin her vacation? Lord knew she had needed that vacation after all the stress she'd endured.

Relaxing on one of the sofas with a magazine beside her, Nell stopped turning the pages and looked up at Dollie, smiling. "You know what Henry said to me yesterday?"

"Who's Henry?" Dollie's gaze wandered out the window. What was she going to do? Were those people right? That monster wasn't going anywhere near Marita.

Nell mingled her fingers through her shoulder-skimming gray locks. "Henry is that piece of beefcake I've been telling you about."

"Oh."

"Dollie, child, he was looking at me in a way that I just can't describe. I was switching it, too. Knew he was watching me, so I shook it real hard."

"That's nice."

"I mean, he was looking at me like he really, really cares for me."

"That's nice."

"We talked for hours and hours. We have so much in common. For one thing we're both widowers with precious children and grandchildren, all doing so beautifully."

"Uh-huh."

"And he likes so many of the things I like, too, like reading, traveling, and then there's both our love for jazz and gospel music."

"That's . . . that's good."

"And we have so much more in common." She chuckled. "He even likes to gamble like I do. He hit the number for five thousand dollars the other week. That's when he surprised me with those yellow roses and all those rich chocolates."

"Good."

"And Dollie, child . . . Guess what he whispered in my ear yesterday before I left him?"

"What?"

"You wouldn't believe it."

"Uh-huh."

"And I know it was fresh, but at my age I need a little excitement."

"Yeah."

"You wouldn't believe it. You just wouldn't be-

lieve it." Nell's bronzed skin flushed. "He told me
that he don't need no Viagra."

"That's nice."

Sitting up straight on the couch, Nell sucked her
teeth at Dollie. "That's all you can say?"

"What?" Nell's terse tone made Dollie finally pay
her attention.

"I said is that all you can say? I'm telling you
that I'm about to get a little after sixteen years
and all you can say is 'That's nice'?"

"I'm sorry, Nell. I just have a lot on my mind.
Pressing things."

"Like what?" Nell got over to the rocker that
was a twin to the one Dollie sat in. "What is it,
child?"

Dollie hesitated. "Just thinking about things I
have to do at work tomorrow."

It was a lie. As much as she loved Nell, Dollie
knew she was the most worrying woman ever born.
She didn't want her worrying about something
that she couldn't do anything about. Not only
would she worry about Marita, but she would have
been worried about Shemar because they were
sharing the same home. Nell had had a minor
problem with her heart a few years ago. Dollie
didn't want to exacerbate it with stress.

She wanted Nell to luxuriate in this feeling of
romance she was experiencing. It was a long time
coming, and with their advancing years, they
needed to hold on to everything dear and beautiful about life. What could be more splendorous
than falling in love? She didn't want to steal its
magic with all this news about that Valerian Tate.
This she would keep to herself. For Nell's sake,

and Marita's, too. That animal couldn't get to her. He couldn't.

With a silk navy blue suit slung over his shoulder, Valerian walked out of the cleaners. He'd borrowed it from Kenny and planned to wear it for his very important meeting in a few days.

Watching him from the driver's seat of her Camry, Jatique opened the door for him to get in. "I can't wait to see you in that suit."

Laying the suit in the back seat, Valerian agreed, "I can't wait, either." Shifting his husky frame so that he was more comfortable in the seat, he gazed over at his brother's wife. He sure had been having a time with Jatique while Kenny was at work.

"Where to next?" Jatique asked. "Want to go see a movie?"

Valerian grinned. "I want to make a movie." He stuck his tongue out at her and wiggled it.

She cracked up. "I know what that means. I hope the bed's still warm from this morning."

As she drove, Valerian gazed at her, knowing he would miss her. Everything would go as planned at his meeting. Then he would have to leave her behind for another woman—the one who would play a much larger role in his future. She was going to be so sorry for what she did to him.

Merely the frame of the structure the workers circulated about left Marita in awe when she first arrived at the field site. What she was looking at was actually going to be someone's house. Someone who had probably believed they would never be able to have their own home. It filled her with emotion.

The head of the field team assigned Marita to be an assistant to several professional builders. The scorching sun could have made the physical work unbearable. Except that being part of the construction team and seeing the progress was exhilarating. The people she was working with were so nice. There seemed to be a peacefulness and gentleness about everyone there. These were clearly caring people. Marita could feel it. It was obvious in the way they spoke and the consideration they extended her.

The day was all too perfect. She was holding a hammer for one of the builders, listening to his corny jokes, when she saw a shocking sight. Wearing a hard hat and work clothes, he looked as stunned as she did when approaching her.

"What are you doing here?" Shemar asked. With the back of his hand, he wiped the sweat off his forehead. He'd clearly been working at something strenuous.

Marita gripped the hip of her overalls. "I would like to know the same thing about you." He'd been sleeping last night when she arrived home and was gone when she woke.

"I'm working here." He couldn't understand how she could look like that in all this heat, after so much work. He just wanted to take her . . .

Marita was amazed as she was oddly aroused. "So am I." He looked as sweaty as he did when he'd loved her.

"I . . . I belong to this organization."

"So do I."

Both just looked at each other.

Shemar noticed a line of perspiration running downward on her neck. Trying to cool off, Marita unbuttoned a few top buttons of her shirt. The water ran down to the break where her cleavage began. Shemar followed it to as far as he could. "How long have you belonged?"

"A long time. I just used to give money, but since I'm on the island and not tied down to a stressed-out law firm every day, I can do what I want. So I wanted to come here today and pitch in." She searched through the tender expression on his face.

"That's really good of you. I make donations, too, and since I've been in Bermuda I pitch in." He thought of her last night with the woman. "I walked in when you had a guest last night."

"You were there? I didn't see you."

"I had left my front-door key and come through the patio door. I . . . I didn't want to interrupt. I was really impressed about what you did for her."

Marita smiled, thinking of the sweet elderly lady. "The organization is going to help her. But you know about all the red tape. It'll take a little while."

"They've already helped her."

Marita was astonished. "But how? How do you know?"

"I just do." Picking up some shelving around her, he smiled. "I guess we're going to be work partners. They sent me from another site to pitch in. Let's get to work."

Work they did. Not only working, though. They were talking, talking about everything they'd missed in sharing before. Catching up seemed to take them everywhere, and Shemar seemed even more connected to her than when they'd made love. They had so much in common. They had so many similar views on the same things. He even understood her agony over Remmy, and from a psychological standpoint pointed out that her ex was probably right in assessing that she was in love with a ghost.

Marita could already feel Remmy's presence in her core drifting away with Shemar's real live flesh. And she didn't believe she was attracted to Shemar because he exuded danger and mystery like Remmy. Any man who was donating his time and money to an organization like this had to have something inside that was as warm and tender as he made her feel. Smoldering sensuality seemed to surround their every moment.

At lunchtime she couldn't help noticing that some of the workers had their heads buried in a book by Sherman Dawes. It was the one she'd found so many copies of at the town house. As they munched pizza beneath a tree, Marita couldn't help asking, "Why do you have so many copies of that book that everybody is reading?"

"Oh, you've seen my box at the house."

"Yes. Why so many copies of the same book?" She wiped a piece of pizza off his lip.

He wished her finger could have stayed there so he could have suckled it. "Oh, I know the brother. He gave me promotional copies."

"You know Sherman Dawes?"

"Yep." His finger probed at a piece of pizza on her lip, too.

Marita restrained the urge to kiss it. "But . . . But, uh, nobody has seen him. I've heard on this site today that he's giving some lecture."

"Sure is."

"And that everyone will finally see who he is."

"That's right." He pulled some hair back from her eye and couldn't help wishing that he'd tasted her instead of the food.

"So who is he?" Marita loved the way he was looking at her. She squeezed her legs together, fighting the rush she began to feel there. "Tell me who he is."

He pinched her nose instead of kissing it like he wanted to. "Stop being so curious. You'll find out."

"I will?"

"I'm extending to you a personal invitation to come to his first lecture. Free of charge."

"Just let me know when."

Working the rest of the afternoon, Shemar enjoyed the easy mood between Marita and himself. He was beginning to feel that he'd misjudged her. She wasn't just out for herself. Look at how she'd treated that elderly woman. Look at what she was doing now. Look at how they communicated. And she probably *had* given up her cushy job because of a principle.

He was really enjoying talking to her, playing with her, laughing with her, getting to know her again as much as he was just looking at her and remembering all too well the maddening lovemaking they had shared together.

Nearing late afternoon the field team was intent to continue until the light made it impossible to labor any longer. As they worked, Marita and Shemar were so exhilarated by their conversation and interplay they didn't want to ever stop. Gloom only came over their moments when Cliff suddenly appeared.

Wearing a flawlessly creased beige suit, he stood before them looking very out of place. "I told you I would come Marita." He noticed something in the way the two were interacting. It made him plant a kiss on Marita's cheek.

Shemar made an *oh, brother* face.

Marita appeared annoyed. "Cliff, what are you doing here?"

He started taking off his jacket. "I'm here to work. I told you I would come."

"That is not necessary. Your contribution was enough."

Shemar looked at her. "Contribution?"

"Yes, I told Cliff last night about my donations and work with Angels of Hope and he gave me a check." She gaped up at his suddenly blank expression. "It was a check for the organization. I gave it to them. You can verify it."

Softly, he looked at her. "I believe you, Marita. I think I know you, too."

Cliff noticed *it*. Something was different. Different between the two of them. Something was going on with them. His suspicions were confirmed in the duration of time he lent his labor at the site. They were laughing with each other too much about things that didn't even seem funny. They were engrossed in conversations that no one could distract them from, and their voices sounded gentle in speaking to each other. They were also playfully hitting each other a little too often, in the face, on the arms. Yes, something had changed between Marita and the loser.

When the dark made working any longer impractical, everyone started heading home. Shemar was the first to leave in his car, because he told Marita he was stopping at a health-food restaurant and bringing some nutritious and delicious takeout home for them to have for dinner. She was grateful. She was also so excited. Today her relationship with Shemar had made a wonderful turnaround. She looked forward to what was to come.

She looked almost in a trance to Cliff as she watched Shemar driving off. He came up behind her. "How about some real food? At an elegant restaurant? I heard him say he was bringing home some horse grass for dinner or something."

Swerving around, Marita corrected, "Health food. He's bringing home healthy food. Tasty, but good for you. That's what we're having for dinner."

"What about a juicy steak at the most beautiful restaurant that you'd ever imagine? It's overlooking the ocean."

"I want to go home."

"You mean you want to go to *him!*" Cliff was surprised he'd exposed his anger.

Marita was surprised, too. "Cliff, I don't know what's up with you, but you need to relax."

He relaxed his tone and expression with a smile. "I'm sorry, it just seems like you were ignoring me today, and paying all this attention to Shemar. I'm a big baby. And I'm crazy about you."

Marita didn't want to deal with this. She was tired. Hungry, too. She was also anxious to get home and be alone with Shemar. "See you later," she threw over her shoulder as she started walking toward her rental car.

Cliff hurried behind her. "Wait. Wait."

"What is it, Cliff?" Containing her irritation, Marita turned around.

"Can I see you tonight?"

"No. I told you yesterday how I felt. But we can be friends. OK?" She continued on to her car.

Arriving home, Marita kicked off her shoes and sprawled on the couch. Where was Shemar with that meal? The one he was bringing her to eat, and the one she ached to devour—him. A smile curled her lips as she gazed up at the ceiling. The day had been so much fun. Helping build that home had done wonders to lift her spirits. However, it was Shemar who had truly put the magic in the day. She loved the way they interacted. Loved how he looked at her. His touch was gentle and his voice so sensual. She couldn't wait until he came home.

There was a knock.

Thinking Shemar had forgot his front-door key again, Marita rushed to let him in. Swinging the door open, her expression sank. "Cliff?"

He sauntered in uninvited. "I know Shemar isn't here yet. I don't see his car. So I didn't interrupt dinner."

"Cliff, I'm really surprised to see you again. I told you earlier I just wanted to go home."

"I didn't mean to turn you off by snapping like I did. I'm not jealous of Shemar or anything."

"OK, you're not. But I do think you should go." His desperation was making her uneasy.

"Not until we talk."

"I told you what I wanted to in the bar the

other night. Please go." She moved to show him the door.

He clasped her arm. "I don't want to go. I want to spend a little time. Forget that dinner and come out with me."

"I don't want to." She spoke slowly, easing out of his grip. "You're acting really irrationally."

"It's him, isn't it?"

"Him who?" She really didn't like where this was going.

"Shemar. Something is going on with you two."

"If there is, it's none of your business."

"Oh, it is, goddamn it!"

Twelve

"What?" Marita's heart beat in triple time. "Get out of here!"

Not responding, Cliff walked to the door that he'd left open and slammed it shut. Leering over at her, he locked it.

"Don't you lock my door. I want you out!"

Approaching her, he shook his head. "But I want to stay in. I want to go *in*."

She knew he couldn't mean . . . But with his eyes glaring in hers, he began removing his jacket.

Marita watched it drop to the couch. "Just leave now, and there won't be any problems."

"You're right there aren't going to be any problems." He tugged at his tie, while easing toward her.

Marita backed up. "Cliff, please don't get ugly like this."

"The only thing that's ugly is your being with that loser."

"Leave! Shemar is coming in here any second now."

"Shemar won't be coming anywhere anytime soon. That place he went to is so far out, plus, the lines are so long, it'll be hours before he comes back."

"You touch me and he will kick your ass!"

"You've been sleeping with him, haven't you?"

"Get out!" Backing away as he neared her, she pointed toward the door. "Just get out of my life."

"Easy to say now!" he blasted. "After I spent good money on you."

"I gave you back those things."

"What about the donation? Have me write a big fat check, then toss me aside like a rag picker. Hell no! If he can get it for nothing, I'm damn sure going to get something for all I gave."

Marita turned to dash up the stairs. He caught her by the back of the shirt before she made a step. Like flames grinding into her mouth, he crushed his lips into hers, while his fingers wrestled with hers as he tried to rip her blouse.

Having seen that the lines were too long at the Health Nook, Shemar chose a restaurant closer to home. Hearing the screaming, scuffling, and cursing where he stood trying to open the front door, he knew it was the Creator's directing him that he decided to return earlier.

"Get your filthy hands off her!"

Shemar punched and tossed Cliff around the room like a weightless sack. When it was over, Cliff huddled in a corner, his eye swollen from the blows he'd received. A few ornaments were ruined.

"I'll press charges," he declared, peering up from the floor through his one intact eye. He sounded winded. "I'll press charges against you so fast."

Shemar put his arms around Marita. She was still shaking from the assault. Luckily though, Cliff hadn't been able to remove any of her clothing, merely tear them. "She's the one whose going to press charges. You tried to rape her. You animal! You damn animal!" Shemar was so irate his voice rose octaves. "How dare you try to force yourself on any woman! And you call yourself a doctor."

Cliff touched his bruised eye. It had swollen so he couldn't see anything out of it. How was he going to work tomorrow like this? He staggered up to his feet. "No one will believe I tried to rape her. We've been seen together. People think we're dating. She knows she wanted it." He looked at Marita.

She cringed. "I did not!"

"Hell, she invited me here. She knew it would take a long time with you to come back with that horse food." He sniggered.

"I didn't invite you anywhere. You make me sick."

Shemar hurried to the phone. Swiping up the receiver, he announced, "I'm calling the police."

"No!" Marita put her hand over his, placing the phone back in its cradle. "I don't want to go through all that humiliation or the ugliness." This year had been hard enough. She'd lost a job, lost a man, and most painful, almost lost her mother. She didn't have the strength to deal with anything else that was oppressive. A person could take but so much. She just wanted to enjoy a vacation. She glowered at Cliff. "I just want him to stay away from me."

Cliff was more relieved than he showed. The last thing he wanted was to visit the police station. He knew some of the officers. They were patients. He didn't want his reputation sullied. He'd been bluffing about his pressing charges. He had to say something to rub off some of the rage that he was feeling at that moment. He'd felt so used. "I gave her so much."

"And I gave you back those things," Marita shouted.

Shemar was relieved to hear that. "I'm glad you did. You don't need anything from him."

"She owed me, and she was trying to pay me back." Cliff smirked.

Shemar came up close to his face, noting that Cliff retreated some steps. "Don't be afraid. I'm not going to put any more on you."

"I'm not afraid of you." He hid his hand behind his back. It wouldn't stop shaking.

"I just wanted to enlighten you to something."

"What is this? Words from the nobody?"

Shemar shook his head at how lost Cliff was. "You're not supposed to give a gift, expecting something in return. You give a gift from your heart. When you give a woman something, there is no law on earth that states that she is required to pay you back with her body."

"Please! Let me get out of this dump!" Cliff treaded as best as he could to the door, not bothering to close it.

Seconds later, Shemar and Marita were nestled close to each other on the sofa. Slipping his arm around her shoulder, he gazed down at her. "Are you all right?" His fingers grazed her upper arm with gentle caresses.

"I'm fine now." With his warmth enveloping her, how else could she be?

"Because if you're not, I'll do whatever I can to make it better."

Marita looked up into his scintillating brown eyes. "I believe you would, Shemar. I'm so grateful that you came in when you did."

Shemar stared down at her, his eyes dividing between her mouth and lips. He wanted to kiss her. Yet, with the trauma she'd endured, he knew that Marita simply needed his comfort, and not of the kind that his body was screeching for. "Can I just hold you tonight?" He swiveled sideways, laying back on the couch, and guiding her backward so that her back rested against his chest. "Just lay here on me, Marita, and go to sleep." Tenderly, he brought his arms around her, resting them on her stomach. "Don't even talk."

She was so touched by his sensitivity and caring. What's more, she felt so safe and protected, so secure. Mostly, she felt that whatever had thwarted them from becoming as close as they could before couldn't stand in their way now. During the day he'd somehow confirmed what she already sensed about him, and moments ago, he made her feel a security she'd been seeking all her life with a man. As much a woman as she felt she was, there was someone to lean on, even if just a bit. She snuggled her head closer to the corner of his chest. "I'm so relaxed, Shemar. I could sleep like a baby."

"Sleep, then." Unable to resist pecking the top of her head with a kiss, he sounded as relaxed as he felt. "We'll talk tomorrow. We have *so* much to talk about." Closing his eyes, he smiled.

Not many miles away Cliff placed compresses on his eye until it opened. Examining it in his bathroom cabinet mirror, he observed that it wasn't damaged. He thanked God for that. However, he would have a black eye, likely for a week or so. For that he cursed that Shemar to hell. How would he explain it to his patients? His staff? It was too humiliating to say that another man whipped his behind. What about the bumped-into-a-door explanation? Too stupid. Got mugged? Oh, that sounded silly, too. Oh, what the heck, he wouldn't tell them anything. He'd just say it was a long story and leave it at that.

Leaving the bathroom, he headed to his game room. Playing with the dozens of arcade games he owned was always entertaining for him. Play as he did, though, his nerves remained frazzled from what he'd braved. Wandering throughout his house, he found himself on the balcony of his chateau. He could hardly see anything in the dark. Yet he was assured of what was there and it always made him proud. Every square inch exuded the affluence he'd conquered after being chained to poverty as a child.

He'd made his family proud. He'd made his friends proud. He believed they even saw him as a local hero. The scores of women who'd tried to become part of his life validated his colossal worth to him. Only a select few were welcome into his world, though. He was particular. It really didn't matter if they had a fabulous career or not, either. Or much education. Someone too smart might try to become too independent. She might think she was smarter than him, which he could not have.

However, what he did seek was the looks and class. He certainly couldn't escort someone to medical conventions and seminars who spoke like she'd been raised in a sewer. Neither could he be with someone who wasn't as pretty as a beauty queen. In all this, his ideal woman would know her place. It was way behind his. He would always have control.

He could tell that Marita could have been that woman. She didn't talk too much about her law career. Hence, he deduced she wasn't good at it or didn't like it. He knew he could have easily snatched her away from it with the promise of being taken care of for the rest of her life. Shaking his head, all he could think of was what a fool she was. *Fool.*

And the two of them had made one out of him. Ooh, just imagining them engaged in intimate relations sent his blood boiling. And Cliff knew they had done it. Their interaction was a giveaway. And she had the nerve to withhold it from him. What was so special about that Shemar? Was the bulge in his pants a bit bigger?

Cliff felt that he had much more going for him in every way. How dare Marita treat him so shabbily after that fat check he'd written for that charity? Grinding his teeth so hard that he felt himself getting a headache, he came back in his house. Wandering aimlessly, still attempting to assuage himself, he wound up on the edge of his waterbed. Sitting there, one question turned over in his mind. Did Marita need to be taught a lesson?

The next morning Marita woke up, easing out of Shemar's protective hold of her until she stood looking down at him. He was such a beautiful man. From the inside out he was beautiful. She was so glad they were on the right track again.

She so looked forward to this day with him; not even how awful Cliff had been could linger in her mind long and take it away.

His eyes opened slowly and his lips curled up at her. "Are you a temptress in my dream or are you real?"

Marita smiled. "I'm the temptress in your dream."

"Oh, yeah." He reached up toward her thighs. Caressing them nearer and nearer to her femininity, he saw her eyes fluttering closed. "Looks like the temptress is getting tempted."

"You do that to me." Her face was serious as she gazed down at him.

He stopped feeling and pulled her down on him. Face-to-face, he stared into her eyes. "Are we starting all over? Because yesterday I sure felt close to you. I felt like I was knowing you again."

"I felt it, too."

"Let's spend more time together."

"I'd like that." Her finger strode over his bottom lip.

He suckled it in his mouth, all the while looking up at her for her reaction. Feeling her chest heaving, she was getting as excited as he was. "I can do much more."

"I know you can." She felt his heartbeat synchronize with hers, and his erection boring into her clothes, right above her folds. She ached for him to free her of every stitch. However, she remembered what she had to do. "I have to get to the site again today. I told the field captain I could put two days in."

"Oh, baby, can you tell her you'll come tomorrow?"

"I promised."

"Well, I usually do it whenever I can, so I guess I'm going to have to come with you. I have work to do, but I'll put it aside for you."

"Are you going to tell me what that work is now?"

He grinned. "Soon. Very soon."

"So you're keeping me in suspense." She was certain that it wasn't anything shady so she wasn't upset about his secrecy anymore.

"You just come to Sherman Dawes lecture and you'll find out a whole lot."

"What does Sherman Dawes have to do with you?"

"You'll see, nosy." He pecked her nose.

"OK, keep me in suspense. I'm going upstairs to get dressed."

Flirting with each other as they rode in Shemar's car, Marita noticed that they weren't headed to the field site. "Where are you taking me?"

"I'm going to take you to the field. Don't worry. I'm just taking you for a little workout and then a healthy breakfast before we start."

She marveled at the immense health spa they drove up to. After parking the car in the lot, they were walking up to the door when he announced, "This is Pam's place."

"You wanted to stop off to see her?"

"No, she doesn't get in this early." He opened the gold doors, letting her enter the lobby. "I just thought we'd have a little workout, eat a healthy breakfast, then head to the field. You'll enjoy it, baby."

Stepping up to the registration desk together,

Shemar was sure he'd enjoy it, too. Particularly after the peace he and Pam had made. She'd called and apologized, saying he was right about her behavior. She had even started dating.

Shemar felt so bonded with Marita that he'd shared the entire situation with her by the time they were riding the twin stationary bikes.

"I knew it!" Marita exclaimed. She paused from peddling. "I knew she had a thing for you. It was all in the eyes. But at least she isn't your real cousin."

"She's as real as all my other cousins are." He stepped off the bike, reaching for his towel. Lifting it from a linen cart, he blotted his cheeks and forehead. "Besides, everything worked out. We're cool and she's on to someone she can have a real relationship with. I wouldn't even be in her spa telling you this if things weren't cool."

Marita was speculating. Feelings like that didn't die instantly. Besides that, she remembered that look Pam gave her. "I . . . I hope you're right."

After their workout, they showered, then headed to the dining area. After feasting on big bowls of organic fruit salad and milk made with soybeans, Marita's taste buds were lusciously satisfied. She also felt energetic, healthy, and as sexy as any temptress, from the way Shemar was looking at her. That is until Pam entered the spa while they were on their way out.

Thirteen

Shemar pecked Pam on the cheek. "How are you doing?"

Pam beamed. "Great. Fantastic! So you two are leaving the spa?"

"And we really enjoyed it," Marita raved. "You have a lovely spa. And I loved that fruit salad you have in the dining area. All those exotic fruits. It was so tasty."

"I'm glad you enjoyed it." Pam slung her bag higher on her shoulder. "I'm glad you're enjoying everything. You're glowing, Marita. Has Bermuda captivated you that much? Or is it something else that's making you feel so good?"

Shemar saw some discomfort on Marita's face. "She is enjoying her vacation."

Marita wiped at a little sweat droplet at her temple. "Yes, I sure am. The island is so full of everything wonderful."

"Good. Very good." Pam searched Marita's face, stopping at her eyes.

Shemar began shuffling toward the door. "We have to get going."

Marita followed. "Yes. So have a great day."

"You, too."

Shemar held the door for Marita and she walked

past. Still, something was silently beckoning her to turn around. Somehow knowing what she would see, she did.

Pam was watching. More than that, it seemed like she was looking directly in Marita's eyes. She was looking long and hard, like she had the other night. Feeling a shiver, Marita couldn't look anymore. She spun back around.

After a while of cruising on the road, Marita couldn't keep it inside any longer. She looked over at Shemar. "Pam knows about us."

"What do you mean?"

"She knows we've slept together. And she's mad about it. She's so mad it's scary."

Keeping his eyes on the road, he shook his head. "She doesn't know. How could she? We're roommates just hanging out, for all she knows. And even if she did sense something, like I said, we're cool now. It was just a weird moment she had. Don't worry, baby." He lifted her hand and kissed it.

A ripple of warmth went through her. "You're right. I'm just going to enjoy my day with you and not worry about nonsense."

"Good. Just give in to us having a great day together." He paid attention to the road, then to her again. Looking at her, he was so thrilled by what was happening with them, he wished he didn't have to go to the site today. He wished he could have just thrown her in the backseat and made wild love to her until they were out of breath and drained of all the pent-up desire. Returning his attention back to the road, he knew that at least they would be together all day. And the night . . . A grin spread across his face. He had all kinds of ideas about that.

At the field site, Shemar and Marita picked up their building assignments from where they left off from the previous day. Side-by-side they worked, all the while sharing so much of themselves. It seemed like the more they revealed, the more they realized their passions ran not only deeply on a sensual level, but from within, on a spiritual one. But it wasn't what each said that endeared them to each other. It was how they treated those they were around, as well as how they treated each other. Shemar found Marita so sensitive and attentive that he found himself wondering out loud about something that made her seem to the contrary. "It's hard to believe that you're the same woman who didn't return my calls or write me back, or even acknowledge that she'd received the ticket I sent her to graduation."

"What?" Marita frowned. She didn't know what he was talking about.

On a break, she was leaning against the house while he stood before her. "You know what I'm talking about, baby." He brought his arm over her shoulder, propping his hand against the wall and facing her.

"No, I don't Shemar. When was this?"

"Years ago, after my family and I moved. I called you so many times and left messages with your mom. I sent letters, too. Lots of them. And I sent you a ticket to my graduation."

Marita thought back. Her mother had never told her Shemar called her. Neither had she received any letter or ticket. Because her mother always came home for lunch, she would usually get the mail first, and occasionally would open Marita's. Now aware of Shemar's correspondence, she didn't have to wonder what had happened to it. Her mother had destroyed it. Loving as she was, she thought she'd been protecting her. From her way of thinking, she didn't want her daughter to wind up poor, with a poor man who couldn't take her out of the ghetto that had enslaved them.

Wanting to be honest with Shemar, Marita began explaining what had happened. When she finished, she thought Shemar would be enraged with her. Worse, she wondered if he would begin thinking the worst of her again, since she was her mother's daughter. "Are you angry with me?"

Staring at her, he smiled. "How could I be angry with you? Actually I'm relieved."

"Relieved?"

He played with a long tendril of hair that cascaded onto her cheek. "Yes, relieved. All this time I thought that you were just that inconsiderate."

"Oh, Shemar. Don't you know I would have called you back or wrote you back? My only regret is that I just didn't write you out of the blue like you did me. But this is a new time for us."

"It damn sure is." He was moving in close to her.

She felt his breath on her face, heavy as those escaping from her. "And please don't hate my mother."

"I could never hate your mother. How could I hate the woman who created you?"

Shemar carried his fingers across her lips, playing with them as he looked into her eyes. Then he parted her lips with his tongue. Tasting her sweetness, never feeling enough of it, he gripped

the back of her head, bringing her face and succulent mouth deeper into his. Unquenchable desire rushed through him, tightening his limbs, and
hardening his lower body to an explosive point.
"Let's go home."

Marita could barely contain her stirred passion
enough to separate from him once they were in
the house. But she had been working strenuously
and wanted to be fresh for him. She rushed upstairs for a shower. Agreeing that he needed one,
too, Shemar hurried into his bathroom.

Stepping out of the stall, Marita went over her
body with a towel. Afterward, she searched the
shelf. She'd decorated it with numerous bottles
and was looking for her beloved cherry after-bath
lotion. She was bending over, massaging the thick
pink cream at her feet and ankles, when she felt
something firm, long, warm, and sheathed come
up behind her. The titillating pressure against her
buttocks straightened her posture. Her head fell
back against Shemar's chest. She felt him grip her
waist as he slightly increased his vigor. A light-
headed sensation swept over her.

Planting chill-igniting kisses along the sides of
her face, neck, and shoulders, he removed the lotion from her hands. Pouring it into his palms, he
brought the creaminess around to her breasts and
amorously rubbed it there.

"Oh," Marita moaned as if it hurt her, "you do
that so good."

He wanted to do all that he could, and continued his insatiable quest to please her by rubbing
the lotion more and more, centralizing it now on
her hardened nipples. All the while Marita felt the
increasing pressure from behind.

"I want it . . . Shemar."

He couldn't wait to give it to her. He slathered the cherry froth down her stomach, toying with her belly button, and not soon enough for her, reaching the tip of her hairy triangle. There he caressed the sweet thickness downward, feeling his breath catch in his throat as he reached her little folds. He played inside her moist warmth until neither could withstand any more. He turned her around.

"Give it to me." She pulled him close to her, crushing her lips into his.

Kissing her, he felt his arousal reaching an aching point. The bed wasn't near enough. He gripped the sides of her hips and pushed her up against the wall.

Shemar looked down to guide himself within her; then he held her arms above her head. Insatiably, ferociously, unable to get enough, he moved.

Marita was quiet. Too overwhelmed by the powerful thrusts, she simply held on, never wanting the man who was loving her to stop, never wanting him to deny her the ecstasy she was feeling at that moment, nor the amazing gift of him in her life. Nothing on earth had been as exciting, pleasurable, or as right and perfect as it was at that moment.

Shemar, moving with a passion that he hadn't planned, was overcome with the pleasurable sensations fire-rocketing through his flesh. He had wanted to be tender with her, but she had brought something out of him at that moment that made him so hot, it was as if the rapture of her body had possessed him.

"Oh, I love being inside you. I love it, baby. I love it . . . I . . ."

An intolerable feeling of pleasure gripped where they were joined. Wanting to hold on to it forever, Shemar didn't move. He simply held her with all that he had until he began to shake from the loss of control. "Oh . . . Oh, Jesus!"

His outcry echoed her inner one. Marita felt like a waterfall had burst within her, sending a downpour of its intoxicatingly sweet sensations through every inch of her flesh. It felt so good, tears of joy welled in her eyes.

After a night filled with the most creative lovemaking in nearly every room throughout the house, Marita woke up with Shemar's arms around her. Sunlight was peeking through the chiffon curtains and she even heard birds singing from the palm trees around the house. They sounded as happy as she felt.

Curving her head to look over at him, Marita felt astonished at the ecstasy this man could fill her with. Their sensual chemistry together seemed almost inhuman in its bliss and intensity. They were bonded physically as well as spiritually. During their breaks of lovemaking where they had slept and wakened, they talked endlessly. Anything she had to say was important to him. He listened. He shared. He was as open with her as she was with him. He understood her as she understood him. He was interested and fascinated in everything about her. And he was so attentive.

She also loved other things about him. Like the love that showed when he talked about his family and friends. He was not only caring, but a man of such great integrity. He had such an uncommon insight into life and the world. It was how she felt about things, but could never express. It was just there inside her. He expressed them for her. More than once, she encouraged him to share his thoughts with the world, either in speeches or in publications. At that, Shemar had the strangest smile.

After kissing his sleeping face for several moments, then moving down to his chest, Marita could see that she really had worn him out. He was stone out of it. Thinking about what a tiger he had been with her, it should have been expected. All the lustful scenarios they had shared made her smile and smile.

The afternoon was approaching and since he wasn't up, she thought she'd busy herself until he woke. Wanting to check on Ms. Elizabeth and her grandchildren, she showered, dressed, and headed outside. Since the grandmother lived toward the back of the town house and in walking distance, Marita decided to hike through the woods to her home.

Over an hour later, she was headed back home beaming. Shemar had known what he was talking about when he stated that the organization would come through. Ms. Elizabeth told her they not only had been taken very good care of financially, but they were getting a new home. She gave Marita a long hug, and her eyes welled up with tears.

Thinking about all this good stuff, Marita proceeded back home. She hoped Shemar was awake. She could only imagine how wonderful the day would be with him. Leaves rustling and crunching

made her turn around slowly. Oddly, she didn't
see anyone. *Must be an animal,* Marita concluded.

The rustling seemed more pronounced as she
kept a steady pace toward home. More than that,
the crunching leaves became methodical thumps
like footsteps. Freezing, she spun around. Her
scrutiny scattered from side to side, before peering
into the distance from where she had just come.
There was no one. It had to be an animal. Still,
something told her to speed her pace. She didn't
slow it until she closed the front door behind her.

A blenderlike sound drew her to the kitchen.
Shemar was clad only in tiny red briefs, juicing
oranges. Shamelessly, Marita admired his muscular,
nearly naked form. She could take a bite out of
him.

"See something you like?" he teased.

"Too much that I like." She eased toward him.

"Think you can handle it?"

"I already did, baby."

"Yeah, you keep looking at me like that, I'm going to throw you up on this counter and I'll handle you right here." Shemar watched the plastic
receptacle filling up to the top with butter-yellow
liquid.

"You'll do it anywhere, won't you?"

"And you love it anywhere, don't you?"

She didn't know that about herself until last
night. It made her snicker. She had heard older
women say that it was amazing what the right man
could do for you. She'd lived the truth!

"And where were you, young lady?" He reached
in the cabinet, removing two tall glasses.

Marita eased toward him. "Just went to check
on Ms. Elizabeth. She's in walking distance, back

up there past the woods." She watched him fill
one glass, then the other.

"Aren't you the sweet one." He handed her a
glass. "But I know how *bad* you can be, too."
Reaching behind her, he smacked her on the butt.

"Ouch!" Mischievously, she stared at him, joining him in sipping some juice. "This is real good."

"I know it's good." He rested his glass on the
counter. "That's why you couldn't get enough of
it last night." He swept her into his arms. After a
long heady kiss, he released her. "You are so tasty
this morning."

"You taste real good, too."

"Can't wait to get back in that bed with you.
But first I have to give you some nourishment so
you can deal with me."

She chuckled. "Is that right?"

"I'm going to fix you the best breakfast you ever
ate."

"And I'll go upstairs and read that Sherman
Dawes book while you're getting it ready." She
couldn't resist one more peck of the lips, before
heading toward the door that led upstairs. Suddenly though, she stopped, turning back toward
him. "Shemar?"

"Yes, baby?" He let go of the refrigerator handle
to grant her his full attention.

"Do you ever get the feeling that someone is
following you?"

"Following me?" Frowning, he came toward her.
"Was someone following you?" He didn't much
care for her being alone in those woods, anyway.
"When you went to see Ms. Elizabeth?"

She shrugged her shoulders. "I don't think so.
I didn't see anyone. It was just that I heard leaves

rustling and thought I heard footsteps. But I'm fine. So it was probably nothing."

"Probably right." He lightly gripped her by the arms, caressing them. "This is an island, baby. Animals run around like crazy. Small ones that move so fast you can't even see them. I'm sure that's all it was."

"You're right. Now that you've eased my worry, let me go read my book. I can't wait to go to his lecture."

"You're going to enjoy it. And I'll call you when breakfast is ready."

Marita proceeded up the stairs and entered the bedroom. She fully intended to enjoy the book. However, there was something she needed to do first.

"Hello, Mama?" she said moments later. Clutching a black cordless phone, she moved about aimlessly across the floor.

"Oh, hi, baby, it's so good to hear from you."

"And you sound so good, Mama. How is your therapy going?"

"Fabulous. I'm getting there. I keep pushing myself and I'll be back to my old self. And I thank you so much, baby, for sending me to such a lovely place."

"Only the best for you. But don't push yourself too much. You'll be out when it's time."

"That's true. But enough about me. How are you enjoying your vacation?"

"Loving it. Loving it more than I ever dreamed." She tingled with thoughts of Shemar.

A lighthearted joy suddenly filled her mother's voice. "What is it that you love so much? Have you met a man?"

"Yes, you can say that. He is *soooo wonderful.*"

"Oh, I'm so happy for you, baby," Carol Sommers gushed delightedly. "After this terrible year you had and those problems with your last boyfriend, you deserve a good man who is going to appreciate you and treat you right."

"I have to agree with you, Mama."

"So who is he? What's he like? What does he do?"

Marita went on and on about what he was like. When it came to his profession, she couldn't answer totally truthfully. A somewhat truth would have to do. "He has done lots of psychology work."

"A doctor? My, my, that's just what I want in my family."

"Don't jump the gun now, Mama."

"It sounds serious to me. And what's his name?"

Marita paused. Other than checking on her mother's condition, the point of her call was to let her know she was involved with him despite what she'd done in their younger years. "It's Shemar, Mama."

"Shemar? You don't mean . . . ?"

"Yes, I do. Shemar Dalton, Ms. Nell's grandson."

Her mother was silent for several seconds and then, "That is right. I did hear that he was a psychologist."

"He's more than a psychologist, Mama. People are more than their occupations and their salaries."

"I know that, baby."

"Mama, I know. I know about the letters, the calls, the ticket to his graduation. Why—"

"Baby, my nurse is here. Can we chat later?"

"Sure, Mama." Marita couldn't discuss it any longer, anyway. She heard that trembling in her mother's voice. She couldn't bear to make her cry.

After hanging up, Marita made her way back over to where the phone cradle rested. During the stroll, she passed the window. The vast greenery outside captured her attention. Had someone been following her out there?

Shemar moved about in the kitchen, getting his seasonings together. All the while he was thinking deeply. Yes, he'd been honest in telling her that an animal could have been behind her. It could have. Even so, he, too, wondered otherwise. He didn't want to frighten her. He didn't even want to bring up Cliff's name. Yet if he learned that he was following his woman, scaring her like that, trying to do anything to her, the doctor would need a doctor.

And she was his woman. Every fiber of his being screeched that when they had made love, and when they were just around each other. Its energy emanated in how they were with each other now. The way they spoke to each other. The way they were concerned for each other. Also in the consideration and caring. It came forth when they laughed, when they were playful. Shemar felt that she was his woman from the tips of his toes to the top of his head, because that's where he felt the love for her, all over. She was his woman, and he knew that she felt the same—he was her man.

He could be himself with Marita. The way they talked had blown his mind. He could share his deepest insights and she would understand them.

Now he understood why he'd felt connected. They were connected. They were as connected in spirit and soul as they were in body. It all went together. That's why their lovemaking had been so explosively erotic. He was beyond that point of seeking the satisfaction of mere sexual tension. It was the love that made their intimacy so earthshaking.

Just thinking about it made his body harden with the need for some more. He couldn't wait to get back in bed with her. Though before the sex, before even finishing the breakfast, he had to check on something. Those woods. If Cliff or anyone else was out there, tailing her, they would have him to deal with. Shemar dropped what he was doing, went upstairs, and dressed quickly. Soon after, he headed out the back door.

About a half hour later he returned. Picking up where he left off with the breakfast preparations, he also turned on the radio. An oldies station was the one that suited him. The Temptations were crooning about it just being their imagination. Shemar was getting into the groove. Popping his fingers and singing along, he was sure glad it was his imagination that someone had been stalking Marita in the woods. He checked it out thoroughly. No one was there. And he didn't want to think about anything else unpleasant today. Today, he was thinking all about pleasure. Pleasing Marita and pleasing himself in all kinds of creative ways. What else could he think with that seductress upstairs waiting for him?

Marita thought about her conversation with her mother for a while, then read some of the passages of Sherman Dawes's book. Except all that lovemaking throughout the night had exhausted her body more than she knew. In the middle of a page, she found it hard to keep her eyes open and head up.

All of a sudden there was the hazy scene of grass, trees, and a colorful garden all splashed with vivid sunshine. There were even the birds singing, though their sweet chirping faded as his voice became prominent.

"Marita," Remmy called, stepping through a small passage within a flower bed. "I missed you, Marita."

"I miss you, too." She tried to touch him, to at least get closer. The more she tried, the more it seemed she remained in one place. He was so far away.

"Marita, I told you to hold on to him. Listen to me. Hold on to him stronger than ever. You're really going to need him. Evil is coming. Don't let it take you away from him."

"What evil?"

"The evil you know so well. You know, Marita."

"No, I don't. What are you saying? What evil?"

"You can fight it if you hold on to love. And believe. Believe that love will keep you safe and it will. It already has. Believe in all good and that anything your heart desires can be yours. Believe, Marita. Don't ever stop. You can do anything. You can be anything. Because your soul is good, just like his. You two hold together." He picked up some red roses and held them out to her.

Marita reached, but Remmy disappeared before she could reach them.

"Remmy, come back. Come back! Come back!"

"Marita, wake up, baby."

Marita fought off the heavy feeling of slumber, struggling to open her eyes. Before long, she saw Shemar sitting on the bed with her. A tray of food perched on a night table.

"I was dreaming," her voice slurred.

"Yes, you were." He reached for a napkin on the tray, then wiped the dampness off her forehead.

"I was dreaming about Remmy again." She eased into a sitting position.

Shemar blotted the napkin over her cheeks. "Must have been a whopper because you were yelling for him to come back. You seem worn out, too." More slowly he blotted the softness over her mouth. He started to kiss her, but he didn't want to be inconsiderate as she began talking.

"He was telling me to hold on to someone again." She paused, staring at his warm, steady gaze. "He must have meant you. Oh, this must all sound crazy to you. The dead giving the living messages."

"Not at all, baby." Reaching for her hand, he began stroking the knuckles and delicate outer skin. "I believe those who care about us and have passed on do give us messages and guidance. I firmly believe that."

"And he went on to talking about the power of believing." She went on to share the entire dream. They snuggled in each other's arms as she talked.

"What Remmy was telling you in the dream is very important," Shemar spoke gently into her ear. Then he kissed it. "Believing in something is so powerful. Believing in it and having the faith that God will see you through it. You long for it, you speak it, you see it exactly how you want it to be, and you know in your heart that it's right and you know that God wants it for you, then you can have it. Rely on that always. Belief is powerful. It makes anything possible."

Feeling his breath leaving its tingling warmth

along her ear, she went on to share more about
the dream when she noticed something. A rose
petal was on the floor. "Do you see that?"

Shemar rose, peering in the direction that she
was. Spotting the fragrant petal, he picked it up
and gave it to her. "You said he was trying to give
you roses in the dream."

"He was." This was astonishing. "And you didn't
give me any." In amazement, she sat up, gawking
at Shemar. "Do you think Remmy was actually
here? In this room?"

For a moment, he just stared at her.

"You're thinking your little sex kitten might be
a little nutty, aren't you?" she said, breaking the
silence.

"No." He caressed her cheek, and pulled her
back down where she nestled within his arms.
"The thing is, I was thinking about something that
happened to me several weeks before you arrived."

"What?"

Shemar smiled at the memory. "I believe I had
an encounter with an angel."

"An angel? Like Remmy is my angel visiting me
in dreams?"

"No, this wasn't a dream. I was laying in my bed
in the dark, unable to sleep, just thinking about
my life, my failed marriage in particular, and as I
began to finally doze off I heard a voice coming
from the side of me."

"A voice?"

"I was so startled, but at the same time didn't
want to move to turn on the light. I knew whoever
the voice came from wasn't an intruder. It was
soothing. I just turned in that direction and I
didn't see anyone. I just heard it. It was a voice

that wasn't male or female, and it said, 'Don't worry anymore, Shemar, your love is coming. And she will love you the way that you've always wanted to be loved.' And then the voice just went away.''

The reality of the encounter left Marita speechless. Finally, she leaned over his chest. "That's awesome."

"It's true," he said, looking up at her. He couldn't resist sliding his finger across her lips. "And I'm no more nutty than you are."

"I've heard about angels and things like that on television. Never paid much attention." She pecked his finger as it gently touched her mouth. "But if you're telling me this, Shemar, I believe you. But I think it's only the kind of person that you are, that made you have that special experience. You're open to things like that. You're open to miracles. Lots of people can't tune in that way. Probably so many times angels are speaking to them, but they can't tune in. They've let so much stuff in their head and hearts that they can't hear anything else."

He pulled her tight against him. "We think so much alike." It was as if she had opened his heart and mind and took those words straight from there.

"And you're so secure, Shemar. Whenever I talked about Remmy to other guys I was involved with they resented him. Richard, my ex used to call him the ghost that I was still in love with."

"That's because they were insecure. They weren't sure."

"Sure?"

"Sure that they were your man. Sure like I am. Because I am your man." Shemar rose, his intense eyes locked within hers. "Only *your man*, your God-appointed man could love you as much as I do. I knew I was your man when I made love to you last night. I know I am your man when I look in your eyes. I know I am your man, because I can feel. I can *feel* it. And it feels so right."

Her eyes lingering on his, Marita felt her whole body beating as hard as her heart from the confession. "And I definitely know what that angel told you is true." Easing closer to him, she held the sides of his face in her hands. "I'm who the angel was talking about. I was heaven-sent to love you."

Days later, Marita was very much on Valerian Tate's mind. In a paneled conference room, he sat across from several of his new foreign comrades. They'd just shared the details of their operation, how highly lucrative it was, and asked Valerian what he had to bring to the table.

Reaching inside a briefcase, he removed what he had to offer. It was the portrait he'd painted of Marita, and from the smiles of the gentleman, he knew he was about to become a very prosperous man.

"Here is the exquisite creature I was telling you about. I don't even have to ask what you gentleman think. I can see it on your faces." Pausing, he watched their grins broaden. "So you guys make me an offer I can't refuse. Then we'll get down to the nitty-gritty and get what we all want— all except her. Once I meet up with Marita Sommers she will never have what she wants again. But I kid you not, what she has coming to her is what she so deserves."

Fourteen

Magic felt like it was cascading over Marita at each second during the succeeding weeks. It was the summer of her life—the happiest time she'd ever had. With Shemar she enjoyed the sultry playground of Bermuda like a newborn creature first discovering every ravishing particle of the world. During mornings they would feast on breakfast at luxuriant outdoor cafés or have a picnic at the park, or even among sunbathers at one of the enchanting beaches. More fun wasn't far away after that as they indulged in snorkeling, parasailing, deep-sea fishing, rock climbing, tennis, and her favorite sport—shopping at an assortment of boutiques. Strolling with her, and sometimes behind, weighed down with bags, Shemar treated her to everything her heart desired. He loved seeing her so happy. He'd even partially revealed what he did by saying he was working on a special assignment with Sherman Dawes.

Long rides of exploring the mountainous landscapes, caverns, and tourist attractions were also entertaining. There were even those star-sparkling nights where they danced at the clubs to steel and reggae bands as well as R&B American music. Above all the merriment, though, Marita loved the cruises they went on. For she was mesmerized by the beauty of the water and loved the fact that she was sailing across it.

Swept up in the high of making her happy, Shemar surprised her one late afternoon. After blindfolding Marita, he guided her along some wooden planks. Beset by the scent of saltwater and subtle splashing sounds, she deduced that the shipping dock had something to do with her surprise. When he untied the blindfold, Marita's mouth flung open. A white yacht with the cherry-red inscription *Marita* boldly towered before her. She was flabbergasted.

"It's yours, baby. My gift to you," Shemar told her, watching her staring up at the boat. For him it was like watching a little girl who had just received the present she'd always wanted. "And I am going to show you how to move this baby, one of these days."

Speechless, Marita continued staring up at the yacht, stone-still with awe.

"Can't you say something, woman?"

Smiling impishly, Marita grabbed him by the hand. Not knowing where she was going, she did know what she was looking for. "I'd rather show you something." She guided him through the first door she saw.

"Ooh, yes," Shemar howled moments afterward. "Ooh, yes, you sure are showing me. Keep on. Keep on and don't ever stop. You can show me something anytime that you feel like it. *Anytime!*"

They enjoyed each other so much during that moment and throughout the night that Marita woke up the next day in the afternoon. She blinked her gaze into focus as the neon green let-

ters of the clock on the nightstand read 1:15 P.M.
Baffled at why Shemar wasn't next to her, or that
she couldn't hear him nearby, Marita called out,
"Shemar? Shemar?" She was about to go search
for him when the note on his pillow summoned
her attention.

> *To my sex kitten,*
>   *With the super exciting night that we had, you prob-*
> *ably forgot that today is the lecture. But it is. As part*
> *of the committee, I have to get there before everyone*
> *else. Hence, that's why I'm not making sweet love to*
> *you right now. Tiss . . . Tiss . . . I've filled the closets*
> *with some of those new outfits you bought the other*
> *day. The ones that I loved the most when you modeled*
> *them for me, I have hung in front. Please wear one of*
> *them today. And, baby, don't be late. It starts at 5:30.*
> *It's in the lobby of the Coconut Grove Hotel. Looking*
> *forward to seeing you there. You'll be pleasantly sur-*
> *prised.*
>
>   *Love,*
>   *Your lover man*

Feeling a flood of tenderness, a smile tipped up
the corners of Marita's lips at the windup of the
touching note. She had never known love like this.
It made her feel so good inside, she had to just lay
there and revel in it all. Besides, there was a good
amount of time before she had to get dressed. So she
sank back underneath the covers and closed her eyes.
A fantasy that was now reality played across her mind.
Except that she was so fatigued from their previous
night's love play that she soon drifted off to slumber.
    A gray-cloaked figure who had been lurking, waiting
for the ideal time to strike, believed this was that moment,

as they turned into the bedroom. They were certain that Shemar was gone. Watching and waiting, they had seen him drive away. Therefore, they were sure it was her *with her head and body completely covered with the sheet. Carefully moving, their footsteps thumped lightly into the Persian rug, proceeding to the bed. They ceased movement beside the outline of her head.*

Tossing and turning, Marita could hazily see herself in this very room. But then there was . . . There was someone there. A fuzzy face of a person wearing something large and gray. They leaned down toward the bed where Marita lay. Knowing that they were intending to hurt her, Marita tried to jump out to the other side. They grabbed her by the throat. Instantly, she grasped her attacker's hands.

"No!" Marita shrieked, feeling the air being choked out of her. "No!" She scuffled and scuffled, soon waking. Uncovering her head, Marita sprang up in bewilderment. She looked around at every angle of the room but saw no one there. Scouring everything far more scrupulously, she still didn't see anyone. It was a dream. She was dreaming again. One of those ones so real that she couldn't help bringing her fingers up to her throat. Oddly, it felt like she had worn a necklace that was too tight.

Marita managed to shake off any doubts of the incident not being a dream by the time she arrived at the lecture hall. Hundreds lined the outside of the auditorium where the guest speaker was supposed to be. Clutching a copy of Mr. Dawes's book that she wanted personally autographed, Marita couldn't help listening to the women on line in front of her. Of about the same age as she was, she felt they didn't behave that way. They were talking about their personal love relationships so loudly that anyone could hear them. Following that, they started chattering about what they knew about the reclusive author. Everyone couldn't wait to see him.

"I read that Sherman Dawes is his pseudonym," one of them asserted. "At first he wanted to be private about his identity, but as of late he's had a change of heart."

"I know someone who works at his publishing house and she says that the man is not just fine but *finnnnne.*"

"I hear that," her buddy tacked on.

"And I hear he was on Black Enterprise Magazine's list of wealthiest blacks," the first woman babbled again. "They say he's worth seventy million."

"Seventy million?"

"Millions?"

"Uh-huh, millions."

"Well, my million-dollar smile is going to be working on him today."

With that, all the women laughed.

When finally they were at the ticket booth and paid their entry fee, Marita watched them. Once inside they all stopped, their breath seemingly taken away at the famous author who graced the stage. "He is so fine!" was repeated over and over.

Anxious to get a peek herself, as well as see what Shemar's function was in all this, Marita stepped inside behind them. One look at the podium and she ceased all movement. For she was in breathless awe, too.

"Welcome today," Shemar addressed the crowd. "My pseudonym for many years has been Sherman Dawes. But now I've come to the point where I'd liked to be a little more outwardly involved in spreading my message, spreading it through lecturing, and I will be using my true name, Shemar Dalton."

Shemar went on to speak, numerous times invoking boisterous applause from the packed house. However, Marita could barely concentrate for all that was circling in her head. Neither did she acknowledge Shemar with a smile or any sign of affection when he made eye contact with her. With her head cocked aside, with her arms folded, she simply observed.

Shemar started off speaking on matters presented in his book about making dreams happen. The audience went wild, and he was fueled to go in a different direction. "I would like to now talk about love. Romantic love. And I will title what I'm about to speak about similar to what I have in my book. *Romantic Love is a Delicious Thing. Don't Let Bitter Experiences Deny You of Its Taste.*"

Watching him watching her, Marita listened as he reiterated one of her favorite passages in the book.

"Quoting a line from the eloquent Susan Taylor from one of her 'In The Spirit' articles, *romantic love is a delicious thing*. It's an unforgettable and perfect description. The world looks different through love's eyes. The words of a song have more meaning. Folks seem nicer. Outside looks prettier. The air smells fresher. Swept up in the feeling you can understand why it is that from the beginning of time people have been crying, dying, and living just to taste a little bit of it. But what happens when someone shatters your heart? All your love was lavished on someone undeserving. Now you refuse to let another person hurt you. It's hard to trust anyone. You have vowed to keep your distance from the opposite sex.

"Sometimes the pain rages in our conversations. Women will gripe that there are no good men. Men will gripe that there are no good women. False. Plenty of good women coupled with good men can attest that those are the biggest lies around. Certainly, there are some men that disgrace their gender. On the other hand, there are some women who would scare the devil. However, just as there are negative individuals, there are caring, sensitive, purposeful, hardworking, beautiful men and women. Moreover, they desire the same that you do from a relationship: to be loved like they're the most precious thing on the earth, and they ache to love you that way, too.

"A simple way to prove you shouldn't give up on love is never forgetting this statement: nothing has a perfect score, not even failure. If in the game incessantly, having your heart broken each time is impossible. The score will eventually become imperfect. The odds guarantee you have to win at least once.

"Being alive means welcoming experiences that may awaken your spirit to something magical. Each one of us deserves all life's fruit. Yes, indeed, romantic love is delicious. One of the sweetest joys we will ever have in life. When you're in your last days and sitting in the rocking chair, scanning over the memories of a lifetime, what will you remember most? Surely, it will be how wonderful that special someone made you feel; how safe you felt in his arms; how indescribably passionate what you shared was; how much you loved each other. You'll never know that kind of love unless you give someone a chance to know you—the real you, the you without the baggage of a broken heart, the you who isn't giving a past love

such power, but you, the best of you. Understand that
bitter experience was a lesson for growth, not a failure, then forge ahead. Imagine the sweetness that
could await in the future. So share with someone a
smile, a little conversation, the twinkle of your eyes
across a candlelit table. A new chapter of your life
has to begin somewhere."

The audience became even wilder with the con-
clusion of this oration. Marita didn't clap, didn't
smile, didn't do anything except look at Shemar.
As he held out his hands for the crowd to simmer
down, it was clear he wasn't finished.

"And speaking of new chapters," he went on,
"I must share with you all the new chapter in my
own life. I just have to introduce the beautiful
woman who has made love a delicious thing for
me again. Please stand, Marita." He beckoned her
with his hand. Everyone looked in the direction.
Nevertheless, instead of standing Marita ran out of
the auditorium. Everyone was stunned, but no one
more than Shemar. More than anything he longed
to run after her, but he had more of the lecture
series to continue.

Out in the hall, Marita ran, her eyes so filled
with tears, she didn't notice the person who she
slammed into. It was Pam. Also in the corridor,
she was making her way toward the auditorium.

"I'm sorry," Marita apologized for her clumsiness.

Pam narrowed her eyes, holding them on Marita's.
"What are you sorry about?"

Combined with the bizarre question, Marita
again didn't like the way Pam was looking at her.
Not answering, she continued down the hallway
and out the door.

When the oratory portion of the series ended, Shemar dialed Marita immediately at the town house and the yacht. She wasn't answering at either place. It worried him. Where was she? More importantly, why had she run out like that? But he couldn't ponder on it long. Readers were lining up at the tables with copies of their books to be signed and he was really looking forward to meeting them.

Having a wonderful time meeting everyone, Shemar saw Pam was waiting in line with a book to be signed. "Young lady, I gave you a signed book as soon as I received my promotional copies. So this can't be for you." He was smiling up at her.

Pam lost herself in the seductive swirl of his lips. "It's for a new friend of mine. He's a big fan, just like me."

"I appreciate it. I'm so glad that so many are enjoying the books. And it's nice to see you, Pam."

"It's nice to see you, too." Handing her book to him, Pam's dimples poked into her tanned cheeks. "I really enjoyed your speaking, Shemar."

"Thank you," he said, scrawling his good wishes for her friend.

She patted at her hair. "But I did see that Marita ran out. What was wrong?"

He hid his discomfort with the question, simply handing the book back to her. "I, uh, don't know." He glimpsed the other patrons behind her who were waiting.

Pam got the message. She tucked her book beneath her arm. "I'll be seeing you."

"We'll get together for dinner soon."

Having returned to the yacht to find that Marita wasn't there, Shemar hurried to the town house.

He found her in bed, her back propped against the headboard. Her eyes were glossy.

"Baby, what's wrong? Why'd you run out of there like that?" Shemar came toward her, aiming to wrap his arms around her.

Marita pushed him back. "Get off of me!"

Feeling the winds of her rage, Shemar did as she demanded. "What's going on? Why are you so upset?"

"You really don't know?" She folded her arms.

"No, I don't, Marita. You have to tell me."

She took a long deep breath. "All this time . . . all this time . . ." It made her so mad she couldn't get the words out.

"All this time what? Baby—"

"Don't 'baby' me. You have some nerve. You actually thought that I came to Bermuda because I knew you were a multimillionaire and that I was scheming to get your big bucks. That's why all this time you didn't tell me what you did for a living. You didn't trust me! I remember all those questions you asked me."

"You're right. I didn't trust you at first. And when I started to trust you some, I wanted to see if you would just love me for me. But now I know that you do."

"But all this time. Even since we've become closer you've been keeping your little secret. You still don't quite trust me. You were making sure that I didn't want your fortune."

"Marita, I stopped feeling that way weeks ago. The reason I didn't tell you after that was because I wanted to surprise you at the lecture."

"I was surprised all right." She unfolded her arms, then folded them again. "Here I was just being totally open with you, and honest, and you're just thinking the worst of me."

"I waited because I wanted to surprise you and see the happiness of that surprise on your face. I wanted to introduce you to the audience as my woman, my soul mate, the love that I'd been searching for who I'd finally found."

She refused to show him how good those words made her feel. He wasn't getting off that easy. "That's all talk. You don't love me."

"How could you say that?"

"Because you don't love me."

"Woman, you know I love you."

"If you can't trust someone how can you love them?"

"I do trust you now. And I do love you."

"You don't."

"I do."

She watched him get up. Hurriedly, he removed his jacket and started pulling at his tie. "What are you doing?"

"Getting ready to solve this argument." He threw aside his tie.

"Solve the argument?" She observed him undoing his shirt buttons.

"Yes, solve this argument." His shirt hit the carpet. He went for his pants and shorts next.

Marita felt her insides turning to cream. "How are you going to solve it?"

"Like this." Shemar stood naked and exceptionally ready. After sheathing himself, he approached Marita.

Marita turned aside, feigning disinterest. Ignoring her game, Shemar climbed on the bed, soon easing on top of her. Marita continued to play, but

Shemar still proceeded with his desirous crusade. Thrusting his tongue into her mouth, she couldn't resist as he kissed her deeply.

Fanning the pent-up desire that had been mounting with her anger, Marita felt his fingers playing across her back. Once he located the zipper to her dress, Marita felt it coming off of her. Shemar soon tossed aside the floral sundress and swiftly began working on the bra and panties. Before long, Marita was naked beneath his scorching gaze and being treated to his pleasure-stirring tongue.

Arousal pulsated through her as he kissed her neck, shoulders, and not soon enough, the engorged tips of her breasts. Flicking his tongue around them, he found equal rapture in the taste of the full mounds. With her head swaying from side to side with the elation of unquenchable bliss, she felt his tongue make a sweltering trail down her stomach. For a moment he teased her navel. When he reached her hairy garden, he buried his face there, kissing every sensitive place.

Marita squealed, shooting her hips upward from the excruciating delight. Thrill after thrill sent her into a frenzy, and when she felt his fingers separating her thighs, she braced herself for the ultimate joy. Gripping her buttocks, he raised his pelvis to the level of hers. Then with one guide of his hand, he entered her.

"Oh," Marita whimpered, feeling the shock and ecstasy of him gently pushing inside her.

Then he began to move. Liquid fire seemed to shoot through her. Loving what he was doing to her, she moved, giving back all that he gave. Clutching his back tightly, she couldn't get enough. Wildly, she swung her hips and the wilder she did, he matched her movement with eroticism that made her throb with intoxicating satisfaction. The bliss coursing through every thread of her being assured her answer as he yelled, "Do I love you?"

"Ye . . ." She could hardly speak for the onslaught of his lovemaking.

"Do I love you?"

"Yes," she moaned.

"Do I love you, woman?" Shemar asked again.

"Yes!" Marita cried as they shook together and then collapsed from the pinnacle of emotions that became too good to hold back any longer.

Outside on the window ledge, the onlooker nearly collapsed, too. Passion of a different kind had taken hold.

"I know you love me," Marita divulged as she peered down at the bottom of Shemar's bed. They had made love in every place in the house. His room is where they wound up. Now Shemar played with her feet.

"And I know you love me, too. Even if you did get nutty on me yesterday."

"But that's all behind us. What's in front of us is good loving."

"Yes, indeed." Shemar brushed his lips across her toe.

Marita winced from the sweet feeling, closing her eyes. "What are you doing to me?"

"Making you fall more and more in love with me."

"I can't fall any harder than I am." Then she thought of the boat he'd given her. "I can't wait to get back to the boat. I was too mad to go there yesterday. It's so beautiful, Shemar."

"Like you." Switching his position, he planted a kiss on her lips. "Are you happy?"

"Down-to-the-bone happy."

He smiled. "That's all I want. You to be happy. You sure have made me that way."

"I'm so glad. And speaking of glad, I have to call Aunt Dollie and tell her about my boat. She will flip."

"Right now?" Inching closer, he started fingering around her thighs.

Marita felt that old familiar tingle, but Aunt Dollie was expecting a call from her anyway. "I won't take long."

"All right." He picked up the phone. There was no dial tone. Evidently, it hadn't been charged. "You're going to have to use the phone in your room."

"OK, I'll be right back."

With his hands folded behind his head, Shemar watched Marita walk out of the room with his shirt on. He grinned, remembering her with it off. It all urged him to close his eyes. Mentally, he recreated their lovemaking.

Marita was thinking the same thing as she made her way down the hall and to her room. Except when she reached the door, all that she saw made her forget the erotic images. *"Nooooooooooooooo!"*

Fifteen

Shemar hopped up from the bed and sped toward the screams. He found Marita wailing by the entrance of her bedroom. Grateful that she wasn't hurt, he rushed next to her to see what was so horrifying. Stone-stillness gripped him at what he saw. Marita's clothes were strewn about the room. Most shocking, they were slashed and ripped to shreds.

"Now you say that a Dr. Clifton Harrison probably did this," a teal-eyed officer summed up his report. He'd taken three pages of notes from Shemar. Most of it consisted of who Shemar suspected of doing this and why.

"Of course he did it. He was angry enough at her." He glanced at Marita. Peering out of the window, she'd hardly spoken since the officer arrived.

"All right, sir. We'll speak to Dr. Harrison and investigate this further. We'll let you know what we find out. In the meantime, we advise you to stay away from Mr. Harrison. If he did anything, we'll handle it."

As soon as the officer left, Shemar came up behind Marita, gathering her in his arms. Both faced the window. "It'll be all right, baby. They'll handle Cliff."

Marita remained oddly quietly.

Shemar curved her around. He could see that this had really terrified her. "Baby, don't worry. Cliff will be taken care of."

"But what if it isn't him?" She crossed her arms, rubbing them to soothe her mind. She still cringed at the idea of someone invading her private space. Someone so sinister. She felt like scrubbing everything. She even recalled that dream. Someone was choking her. It was so real. Could it have been? "What if it wasn't Cliff who came in here but someone else?"

"Like who?"

Those eyes flashed. "Don't get mad at me for saying this."

"I won't, baby. Tell me who?"

"Pam."

"Pam?" He chuckled, but stopped when he saw how serious she was. "Pam?"

"Yes, Pam. I saw her at the lecture. She looked at me in such a way. And I bumped into her as I was running and apologized. And she asked me what I was apologizing about. It was eerie."

Shemar didn't let her see how funny he thought this was. He embraced her again. "Pam couldn't hurt anyone, and certainly not you."

"But . . ." That choking dream.

"What, baby? You know you can say anything to me and I'll listen."

Marita took a deep breath. "Before . . . Before I left for the lecture, I had this strange dream that someone was choking me."

"Choking you?"

"Yes, his face was fuzzy so I couldn't make it out. But he was wearing something big and drab. It was so real that when I woke up, I looked around the room, looking for the person. But there was no one there."

"Thank God for that. You know how real your dreams can be. Look at the ones you've had about Remmy."

"I know. But it seemed so real. And afterward it felt like something had been around my neck. Like a necklace that was too tight."

Shemar believed it was a dream. It had to be. "Baby, I don't think anyone was actually trying to choke you. Because if they were what stopped them?"

That was a good question. "You're right. It was a dream. But this Pam thing, I really get bad vibes from her."

Wishing he could soothe her thoughts about Pam, Shemar hugged her. "Baby, her feelings became a little distorted about me. But she's fine now. We're fine. Believe me, she isn't thinking about us."

Pam hurried to her date waiting for her at a table at the Tropical Breeze Restaurant.

Spotting her, stocky Lance Taylor went around to the other side of the table to pull out her chair. "You're looking especially gorgeous tonight."

Pam laughed as she sat. "And you don't look so bad yourself." She slid her seat forward. "Forgive my tardiness."

Lance eased down into the velvet-backed chair across from her. "Forgiven." He picked up a menu. "Now what would you like, ladylove?"

Pam held the menu up to her face, scouring it. The vegetarian dishes caught her attention. "How about that tofu lasagna? You told me that one was good."

"Me? Tofu lasagna, yuck, no way," Lance balked.

"You did. You told me."

"I did not." Lance looked across at her. She had the menu up so high he couldn't see her. He had to see if she looked like she was joking. She didn't sound like she was.

"Shemar, you did."

"Shemar!" Lance pulled the menu down from Pam's face so she could see him. Really see *him*. Had she lost her mind? "My dear, you're mistaken."

"You are horribly mistaken in wanting to see me about anything!" Cliff was outraged as the police officer escorted him off of the golf course to a secluded suite of the exclusive men's club. "Now, what is this all about?"

"Vandalism," Officer Farkley responded.

Cliff leered into the lucid blue eyes. "Vandalism? Vandalism?"

The officer saw the veins bulging in the doctor's neck. "That's right, sir."

" 'That's right, *Doctor*'! I am Dr. Clifton Harrison and I don't appreciate being harassed this way!" Cliff recalled how his colleagues on the golf course had gaped when the officer came up to him, requesting to speak to him privately. "I haven't vandalized anything!"

"I didn't say you did, Doc. I just want to ask you a few questions."

"Questions about what?"

"About a Ms. Marita Sommers."

"Marita?" What kind of mess had she implicated him in? He hoped not those attempted-rape charges.

Policeman Farkley proceeded to question Cliff about his friendship with Marita, the circumstances of the last time they were together, and his whereabouts on the night her clothing was shredded. Cliff was further enraged that Shemar and Marita had claimed that he attempted to rape her. Vehemently, he denied it, stating that it was her word against his. Fortunately, though, he had an alibi for the night her clothing was destroyed. He was attending a family reunion. Over two hundred people saw him there. Officer Farkley didn't hesitate to call some of those people right in front of him. His story checked out as true.

In summing up, the officer offered, "Please stay clear of Ms. Sommers and Mr. Dalton. And remember that she can press attempted-rape charges against you."

Cliff watched the officer walk away. He wanted to make some snappy remark at him for the degrading treatment. Nevertheless, the possibility of rape charges dangled above him. He didn't want to rile that officer just as he didn't want to rile Marita or Shemar into going forth with charges. He was certain that he couldn't endure losing his fortune, career, and being labeled a criminal.

Parole Officer Johnson wondered about the most mysterious criminal he'd ever been assigned to. Was he mistaken in taking Valerian Tate's case? Standing in his vacant room at his brother Kenny's

home, Johnson couldn't believe that he was gone
and hadn't told anyone his whereabouts. The
brother and his wife claimed that when they woke
up, Valerian and everything he owned was gone.
Johnson scratched at his head, as he thought of
that nice old woman and her niece. Could he have
gone after the woman—in Bermuda of all places?

"I'm so glad I came," Marita said, biting into a
rib and looking around at all the fun everyone
was having.

Shemar and she were attending a barbecue
thrown by Trent and Michael. There were so many
people, so much scrumptious food, and the music
had them dancing constantly. After working up an
appetite, the two relaxed underneath a tree with
plates piled high with food.

"I'm glad we came, too." With his greasy lips,
he pecked hers.

Marita watched him biting into a hamburger.
"Now, I thought that you don't eat that kind of
stuff."

"It's a soyburger." He broke off a piece and
placed it in her mouth. "Like it?"

Staring at him, she purposely chewed seductively.
"Ooh, it's good. Oh, oh . . ." She played as if she
were having an orgasm.

Shemar grinned at her antics. "Don't start with
me now." He scanned around. "I'll find somewhere around here to take you and take care of
any little problem you might have."

"I don't think you can."

"What!" He was amused.

"I think you're too worn out from the last time. I don't think you have any more left in you."

"OK, that's it. I'm taking you right here." He pushed his food aside and came at her, forcing her backward on the ground. Since people were around, he tickled her sides and stomach instead of doing what he really wanted.

"Stop! Stop!" she pleaded. "No! I can't take it! Stop!" Eventually, when Shemar saw her unable to bear anymore he eased up.

Marita sat up, groping at her mussed-up hair. "You messed up my 'do."

"And you messed with my . . ." A flirtatious glint flashed from his eyes. "I was just sitting here minding my business and now look what you did to me."

"What did I do?" Marita laughed.

"Come find out." He patted his lap.

She couldn't resist feeling his steel erection against her bottom; neither could she resist bending her head so she could meet his lips. His kiss was so deliciously erotic she momentarily forgot where they were.

"Cut that out!" Trent's jesting jarred them from afar. "No kissing around here. Especially when I'm not getting any." He eyed his girlfriend. Everyone chuckled.

Marita and Shemar continued flirting with their eyes while eating their meals. She was having so much fun. "Today has been so great. It doesn't even seem like that incident happened just days ago."

Shemar stuck his fork into some pasta salad. "That's why I thought it was such a good idea for us to get out to this barbecue and just have some fun, period." He tasted a few noodles. "It'll take our minds off all that crap. But I know it won't happen again."

"How can you be so sure? Especially since the police said it couldn't possibly have been Cliff. We don't know who did it."

"I know. It was Cliff. I don't care how many alibis people covered for him with."

"Oh, you think that's what happened?"

"Of course."

Marita sipped some fruit punch, then set the cup back down on the grass. "Could be." Pam came to her mind again, but since they were having such a great time, she didn't want to damper it with a dissension about Pam.

"The new alarm system in the town house and on the boat should keep out all intruders. Just let them try it. And you don't need a bodyguard. I'll be guarding this body for the rest of the summer." He eyed her up and down. "Woman, how did you get so fine?"

The barbecue area was lit up with colorful lights by the time night rolled around. Nearly everyone was on the floor dancing. Shemar and Michael watched Marita and Trent doing some sleek moves.

Michael was shaking his head with swearing conviction as he gawked at Marita. "I think she's too much for you, Shemar. Let me take her off your hands."

"I'd like to see what your wife says about that." Shemar couldn't get enough of how Marita's hips were shaking. It made him think of things.

Michael hit him on the arm. "Man, she is bad."

Proudly, Shemar smiled. "Yes, she certainly is."

"Does she have a sister?"

"Don't you have a wife?"

Michael laughed. "All right. Be like that." He swished his fingers through his curly locks. "But you're a lucky man, Shemar."

"Yes, I am."

Michael shot Shemar a mischievous look. "Bet it's hot?"

Shemar refused to let Michael upset him. "Michael, I'm not even going there. But I will tell you this. What I feel for this woman goes a lot deeper than falling for her looks. We are connected."

"Yeah, I bet you do connect."

Shemar just looked at him. "No, we are really connected in every way. And one of these days . . ."

"One of these days what?"

"I'm going to ask her . . . I'm going to ask her to be my wife."

Later that night, Marita and Shemar decided on a stroll along the beach. It was well past midnight and they'd found a secluded area. Deciding to relax, they reminisced about the fun they'd had during the day. Marita even talked about the basketball game she'd watched Shemar play with Trent and Michael. She felt like she was in high school, watching her boyfriend dribble up and down the court, filled with pride because that fine creature was her man.

There were so many positive sides to him. She loved the way he enjoyed each day. He'd even awakened her interest in another area of law that she'd studied in college—contract law. In looking over his plans for a series of upcoming lectures, she found the work exhilarating. She found him exhilarating. Taking this life journey with him forever would be spectacular. If he ever asked to marry her, she would say yes in a heartbeat.

Marita was on her back in the sand, staring up at Shemar leaning over her when he whispered, "What do you think is next for us?"

"Next?" When he was looking at her like that, it was hard to think beyond what her body did. Her heart was raging and her insides were beginning to drench with desire. "I hope this is next." She found his pants buckle, undid it, then speedily went for the zipper.

"Jesus," Shemar moaned as she thrilled his soon bare body and titillatingly covered him with her own. "Woman, you drive me crazy."

Feeling his desire escalating, he couldn't contain his anxiousness to shed her of her clothes. Once they were off, he wasted no time in touching what he wanted.

"Oh, Shemar," she cried, feeling his fingers caressing between her wet folds.

Her moans and body fluctuations drew him to do more. Kissing her lips, high from her sweet nectar, he became more brazen, kissing her neck and breasts. With each erect nub he took his time, just as he did touching her sweet dripping place. When he knew she couldn't stand any more foreplay, Shemar coaxed her around, assisting her onto her knees.

Kissing her beautiful buttocks, he then grasped the sides of her hips, and in one gentle movement of himself into her, he felt her moist warmth. Slowly, he loved her, switching his hands from stroking the sides of her hips, to the fondling of her breasts. He was turned on by how much

Marita seemed to love it. Her lustful motions indicated all he needed to know and urged him to do more.

With more force and more erotically, he then excited her, giving all the love within him that he could give a woman he loved so deeply. She was his everything. High from the maddening feeling, he was intent to give her more. Swiveling her back around, he kissed and stroked her as he positioned her atop him.

Gripped with his hot throbbing inside her, Marita knew nothing could feel any sweeter. Being loved by Shemar was the most awesome experience that she'd ever encountered. His love was felt all over and through her, as she pumped, venturing for him to feel as much of the heat of ecstasy that he was pleasuring her with. Much too soon, neither could withstand the rapturous tension. The excruciating bliss rushed to the core of them, before bursting, sending them both into near convulsions of indescribable joy.

Sixteen

Shemar had dozed off when Marita decided to go for a swim. Clad in nothing since there wasn't anyone around, she dunked herself in the water and felt the warmth of it stroking her skin. Because she was an excellent swimmer, she dared herself farther and farther out to sea. The water felt too good. With the full moon beaming down upon her, and her beautiful man lying ashore, it all felt like a dream.

She thought the feather-light stroke across her ankle was a fish. Curious about it, she went underwater. Seeing nothing, she believed it hid behind a huge cargo carton that had probably been lost from a ship. She went back above water. The feathery brush she felt again. This time higher. It touched her calf, then her thigh. Marita bent to go underwater again to see the fish who wanted to play, when she felt herself being pulled. Both legs were clamped around by an iron grip.

"No, get off of me!" she screamed. "Help!"

Someone from behind her was taking her down.

"Help!" She glanced at Shemar at the shore. Someone swiftly covered her eyes. Struggling, she managed to still scream and kick, one kick so forceful it bent the other person over. Her eyes uncovered, from behind she saw a gray-hooded person, clutching their stomach with one hand. With the other they swam away.

So terrified she could hardly breathe, she had turned to go toward shore when Shemar emerged with a hysterical expression before her. "What happened, baby? I heard you screaming."

The police were not taking care of business, Shemar thought as he barged in Cliff's medical office the next morning. Even the near-drowning incident they had treated too lightly for Shemar's comfort. They would investigate it, they had claimed. What was there to investigate? Shemar knew who had tried to drown Marita. After leaving Marita at Trent's girlfriend's house, he went to take matters into his own hands.

The red-haired receptionist tried to be pleasant. "Do you have an appointment, sir?"

"No, I don't have a damn appointment. Just tell that animal to come out of there." He glared at a closed door with Cliff's name inscribed on it.

The receptionist stretched her eyes at the insult. "Sir, you can't see the doctor without an appointment. And I assure you there are no animals here."

Shemar leaned down on her desk, steadying his glare in her face. "Woman, you don't want me to have to break that door down, do you?"

"Sir, you don't have an appointment and you can't see the doctor without one. The doctor is seeing a patient. And we have other patients waiting."

Shemar scanned around at the seven or so people

looking up at him in bewilderment. "Sorry, folks." He then diverted his attention to the woman. "I must speak to that animal. He is in some serious trouble for what he tried to do last night."

The receptionist noticed the patients were mumbling among each other. She knew Dr. Harrison would hate for his patients to be uncomfortable. "Wait one second." A rust-polished finger pressed the intercom button. "Doctor, there is gentleman out here insisting that he see you right away."

"Hattie, how dare you interrupt me with a patient," blared over the machine.

"But sir, he is insisting."

"And he's very angry," Shemar shot, bending down at the machine.

Cliff bolted out of the examining room at the sound of Shemar's voice. "What in the hell are you doing here, disrupting my office?"

"What the hell were you doing last night?"

Cliff glanced at his baffled patients. He couldn't have this. "Get out before I call the police. I don't care what you're here for, just get out and don't bother me."

Shemar stepped around the desk, meeting Cliff's level gaze with his own. "You tried to drown Marita last night."

An uproar of gasps filled the room.

Cliff looked at his patients. "Now he's lying. There is no need to listen to a word of it." He then leered at Shemar. "Let's go in my office."

Shemar slammed the door behind them. "You were watching me and Marita make love on the beach last night and you couldn't stand it. So you tried to drown her when she swam."

"This is ludicrous!" Cliff couldn't believe this accusation. "I'm getting sick and tired of being accused of everything that happens to Marita. I have better things to do with my time than stalking her."

Shemar stepped up close in his face. "You were more than stalking her. You tried to kill her."

"Oh, you're both nuts!" Waving him off, Cliff backed away a step. "Kill her for what? Kill her because of a little ass?"

Shemar swung. "Here's your ass-whipping."

Cliff stumbled from the blow to his jaw. A small line of blood spilled from the corner of his mouth. Clutching at the wound, he straightened his posture and didn't strike Shemar back. All too well he remembered the last time he retaliated. "I don't want her anymore. I have a woman."

"Then leave mine alone." Shemar restrained himself from striking him again. "I really should encourage Marita to bring you up on attempted-rape charges."

"It's my word against hers." Cliff lifted a handkerchief from his white coat pocket. He dabbed at the blood. "Mine against hers."

"Wrong. Yours against ours. I saw what you were doing, remember."

"Who cares what a nobody has to say? I'm a respected orthopedist and who are you?"

"Look at today's *First Morning Press,* third page and you'll see."

Cliff couldn't figure what he was up to. That particular paper was on his desk. He located the page.

Shemar watched Cliff's expression as he saw his picture, beneath an article he'd been happy to read with Marita that morning.

Stern-faced, Cliff looked up, tossing the paper

aside. "So that's how you got her from me? You're some multimillionaire writer."

"It's not about money. It's about love. Something you know nothing about since you're into hate crimes like rape. Now do you still think my credibility won't be that great with the authorities?"

Cliff swallowed the ball of fear that knotted in his throat. "Look, I had nothing to do with those clothes being destroyed. And I had nothing to do with her being nearly drowned last night. I can provide an alibi."

"You'll pay anyone to say anything."

"No, really I didn't do it."

"We'll see about that. Marita will be pressing charges and we will get to the bottom of this drowning incident."

Deafeningly, the door slammed behind him, the sound further stirring Cliff's fury. Not so much did the accusations bother him. He could refute them with his alibis. No, what bothered him was dealing with those threatened rape charges. Moreover, his entire savings could be eaten away in attorney fees.

After spending several hours with the authorities, putting pressure on them to give Cliff what he deserved, Shemar stopped to get some gas. Filling up his Jeep, he was surprised when Pam pulled her car up next to him.

"Seems like I keep running into you," she greeted him, stepping out of her car.

"How are you doing, Pam?"

"Great. Super, if it wasn't for having a problem with my machine at home."

"What machine?" He was dividing his attention between her and the gas pump.

"My, uh, washing machine. You know what, since you're out already and not too far from my home, would you mind just stopping by my house and seeing what's wrong with it?"

Shemar didn't mean to be insensitive, but he really wanted to get back to Marita. She really needed him after such an ordeal. He wanted to do everything in his power to ensure that nothing or no one ever harmed her again. Furthermore, he longed to erase the horrid memories with moment after moment, day after day, of good times. "Why don't you call a repairman?"

"I did," she lied. "They're couldn't come until tomorrow."

"What about the guy you're seeing?"

Pam patted her hair. "He, uh, he's not good with things like that."

"And you think I am."

"I've seen you fix things at the town house."

"Yes . . . I have." Shemar saw how helpless she looked. With his gas tank now full, he opened his vehicle's door and got inside. "All right. You lead the way. But I can't stay long."

The washing machine looked fine from what Shemar could see after inspecting it. In fact, when he performed a test run, it couldn't have run more perfect. "Pam?" he yelled to her in the other room where she'd disappeared to. Wiping his hands on a rag, he was sure glad it wasn't a big problem. Now he could leave quickly.

"Did you find the problem?" he heard Pam yell from another room.

"I didn't find anything wrong. And where are you?"

"Come and see," she beckoned.

Shemar didn't want to feel as impatient with her as he was. After all, they were on good terms again. He wandered into the living room. She wasn't there. The office and the patio were vacant, too.

"Come here," he heard again, and heard it come from upstairs. "I have something else you can fix up here."

Scratching at his sideburn, Shemar sure didn't feel like being bothered with some other repair. He glanced at his watch. It was getting late. He grabbed hold of the staircase rail and looked up to the second floor. "You know, Pam, I really need to get going. Maybe I can come by another day and take a look at what other problem you may have up there. And maybe you should call a real repairman."

"Please, Shemar. You can fix it right away."

Trying to contain his annoyance, Shemar ascended the stairs, searching the various rooms for her.

"Yes, you can fix it," she announced when his stunned face peered into the room where she was. Sprawled in the nude across her thick satiny brown covers, she smiled and rolled her tongue across her lips. "You can fix me."

Shemar couldn't believe how she'd deceived him. Not saying a word back to her, he went in the hall and hurried down the steps.

Pam ran after him, catching him in the living room. "You know you want me." She tried to detect the lust in his eyes. However, she grew frustrated at what she saw and heard—disgust.

"Pam, I told you I'm not interested in you that way!" He tried to walk toward the front door.

She grabbed him by the arm. "Look at me! Look at me, Shemar."

"I see you. You're naked. You should put something on before you catch a cold."

She wanted to kick something. "Look at me! Don't you want me?"

"I want you to stop this!" He eased out of her grip.

"Don't I do something for you? Anything?"

He didn't want to insult her anymore. "Let's leave it like this, Pam. And I thought you were seeing someone. So why are you doing this?"

She abhorred this hold Marita had over him. "How can you reject me like this? Look at how sexy I am. At how beautiful. Look at how much I want you. We would be so good together." She eased against him.

Shemar gently pushed her back. "Pam, I'm not the one for you. You'll find someone. I thought you did, but maybe he isn't the right guy if you're carrying on like this. But you will find someone. You're a nice person."

"Nice! Do you think all I want to be is nice? I want to get it on! I can make you forget that bitch was ever born!"

"Bitch?" Shemar's eyes narrowed. He'd never seen this side of Pam. "Who are you referring to?"

Pam quickly collected herself and spotted a camisole that was draped over the couch. She reached for it and put it on. "I was just talking nonsense. Just talking."

"About who?" Marita's musings about Pam came to mind.

"About anyone?" She fumbled with her hair. "About any woman that you're seeing."

Shemar attempted to get Pam's strange behavior, Cliff, and all other negative thoughts out of his head and Marita's the rest of the day. They were insepara- ble as they tried to busy themselves with more uplift- ing things that had to be handled with his career. Hence, Marita thoroughly enjoyed going over his contracts for more lectures and additional books. As well, she was a great source of inspiration as he shared a passage of the new book he was writing.

Afterward, they went for a two-seater bike ride along one of the many bike trails throughout the island.

"I'm having a ball." Marita sighed as they stopped to take a break at a park. She hurried off the bike and sat in the fresh-cut grass.

Shemar leaned the bike against a tree, before joining her. "I'm having a ball, too, baby."

"You always make me feel better." She reclined against his side, looking out at some teenage boys playing soccer.

Slipping his brawny arm around her shoulder, Shemar faced that direction, also. Nevertheless, he saw what he'd been fighting off in his mind. "I don't know what I would have done the other night if I had lost you."

"But you didn't lose me, thank God."

He pecked her forehead. "I'll be thanking Him forever for that."

"It was so scary, Shemar. So, so scary."

"Your screams scared the heck out of me."

"It was like . . ." She remembered that awful time.

"Like what, baby?"

"Like when Remmy died."

"That's right. You saw him get shot. Was it by a gang or something?"

"No, it wasn't a gang," she thought aloud. She could see the evil now—the evil of Valerian Tate's face. She hated to even say his name. For somehow it had an energy that sprinkled bad feelings all over her. But she felt comfortable enough with Shemar to recount her first hand experience with evil—with Valerian Tate.

When she finished, Shemar was compelled to hold Marita even tighter. "I hope he's somewhere rotting and rotting, thinking about all the pain he caused."

Marita chuckled wryly. "He would never think about that. Evil like that doesn't care about remorse. He just thinks about all the more evil he can cause. He has no soul. You can see that from his eyes."

Shemar felt her trembling. Grasping her arms, he turned her toward him. "Baby, don't let what happened do this to you. Let's press those attempted-rape charges against Cliff and he won't hurt you again. And as far as that Valerian character, you never have to see him again. All you have to do is be with me and be happy."

She smiled. "I am happy. More happy than I knew happy could be. Even my career. I was ready to just totally give up the law, but I do believe I want to do contract law. I'm good at it and I like it. You've reawakened my interest in it."

"You are good at it. And I'm glad that I was part of your new career decision. But I can't take the major credit. It was all on you. You just had to do some soul-searching and see what you liked."

"And I do like it. I feel so full now. So complete in every way. It's almost scary. When life is so good you're just so on guard that nothing comes to take the magic away."

The bike ride had been so much fun for Marita and Shemar, but the love ride was even better. Inside the town house, Shemar and Marita made love until Shemar tuckered out in exhaustion. But still feeling from his love and all that was going so well in her life, Marita just couldn't sleep. She couldn't stop counting her good fortune. Shemar and her new career path made the world seem so different. She felt so full. She felt so much good in her life, it would have been impossible for that frightful incident to really steal all of her joy. She guessed that's what true happiness did for you. It made you see the hopeful things no matter what destructive forces tried to cross your path. Feeling unstoppable and so energetic, she decided to go for another bike ride.

She rode along a different bike trail, one that she'd read about in a tourist brochure. Secluded, it was filled with a pathway of palm trees and the most vividly colored flowers she'd ever seen. A waterfall complemented the surroundings. Marita was sure going to tell Shemar about this one. They were going to explore it together. For it sure looked like heaven. At one point, she just had to stop riding and marvel at it. That is until the heavy blow on the back of her head cut out the light. Everything went black.

Seventeen

Dazed, Marita woke, her eyes struggling to open and catch the bits of escaping light. Dirt was surrounding her, wedging against her and being thrown over her. As she fought off the piercing pain from the back of her head, she woke more fully. As she did, the reality of what was happening to her jarred her into a panic that had her struggling to hold on to her fleeting breath.

"That's right," she heard from a mysterious person shoveling and closing the hole. She couldn't see, but it sounded like a woman. The woman's voice was familiar. She struggled to recognize whose it was. "That's right. Catch your last bits. Breath is a precious thing. And it doesn't come easy to sluts." The shoveling stopped and a face loomed larger than life over the small hole.

Marita gasped at Pam. "What are you doing?" She was struggling to breathe. She even reached up to touch the hole and open it more. Her fingers wouldn't reach. She was too deep down in the ground.

"You ever heard of being buried alive?" Pam sounded amused. "Well, that's what I'm doing. Burying your butt alive."

"No, please. Please, Pam. Don't do this."

" 'Don't do this. Don't do this.' " She was amused.
" 'Don't do this'." Abruptly though, the amusement
was gone. Stone-cold rage reverberated almost
through the earth covering Marita. "I have to do this!
You tried to take my man. So I have to get rid of you!
He's always been mine. He's always been best for me.
Yes, we've been apart sometimes, but somehow we
would come back together. Now that I have him again
I'm never giving him up. Shemar is mine!"

She started to shovel again, covering Marita's
only air passage.

"Please," she pleaded.

"No! Beg all you want. You had too much time
with him, anyway. I couldn't go through with what
I planned before. That was me in the woods. That
was me at your house, shredding all your clothes,
and that was me who choked you and pulled you
in the water. I wanted to kill you, but something
just wouldn't let me go through with it. It kept
saying, 'Don't do this, Pam. Maybe you can get
him on your own.' So I tried. I tried to seduce
him. There I was giving him everything and he
didn't want me. He didn't want me! And it was
because of you! But now you're gone. You're no
more!"

Pam covered the tiny hole, laughing as Marita's
wails for her last breath filled the air. Soon Pam
knew they would stop. They did. Finished with her
work, she picked up the bike and tossed it in the
water beneath the fall. She wanted no trace of
Marita around. The shovel was thrown in with it.
Shemar would just think Marita disappeared.

Pleased with herself, she felt like skipping. Only
when she started to, a huge, hairy arm clamped
around her throat from the back. With it pressing

against her windpipe, she overwhelmingly knew what it was like to desperately need air.

Groggily, Marita woke up in a room that was so pretty it looked like it belonged in a Victorian period movie. Wondering if she was dreaming, as she woke more she realized she wasn't. An elderly woman wearing a turban caught the corner of her eye.

"Where am I?" Marita sat up, praying she was in some fancy hospital. The restraints on her legs and arms told her otherwise.

With a dead, unreadable stare, the woman just looked at her.

"Where am I?" She jerked her wrists and ankles trying to free herself. "Get this off of me! Who are you? Why are you doing this to me?"

The woman continued staring at her, her lips never moving, although her body did. She headed out of the room and into one across the wide hall. Peeking into a room, she eyed her employer. He had been speaking with another guest.

"She's awakened," she announced in a Middle Eastern accent.

"Excellent," Valerian said, nodding for her to leave. When the door closed, he focused back on the attractive woman in front of him. "You really hate her, don't you?"

Restrained in a chair by buckles, Pam was furious. "Why did you bring me here? Let me go. You're obviously not the police."

"No, I'm not. Far from it." He shifted his position on the desk that he sat upon. "And I will let you go if you tell me why you were so angry with beauty in there."

"So you're under her spell, too. Honestly, I don't see what you men see in that woman."

Valerian removed a cigar from a gold case behind him. "Have one?" He extended one to her.

"No way. I just want to get out of here." Pam observed him as he lit it and began to puff. That unique scent circled the room. She loved cigar smoke. It reminded her of her dad. "My father smokes that brand."

"Does he now? So we have two things in common."

"We have only the smokes in common. The other is out. You have a thing for Marita. I hate her."

"A thing?" He puffed. "A thing could be anything."

"Are you trying to tell me you're not hot for her, like everyone else?"

"Hot can have many meanings. But you never mind that. Just tell me what I need to know and I may let you go very soon."

Pam felt she could be honest with this character. After all, he'd taken her to this faraway mansion instead of to a police station after he caught her attempting to commit murder. More than that, he held Marita captive and away from Shemar. "Yes, I hate Marita."

"That's for sure. You've been followed." He blew out smoke. "We saw you doing some very naughty things."

"So. Do you have any more questions?"

"Why? Why do you hate her so? Is it really because of that clod that's been ushering her around?" Valerian held a vivid memory of the two on the beach. "Or is it much deeper? I've done my homework on you, Ms. Wingate. The private investigator I hired to find Marita told me much about you."

"And what have you found out?"

"You've always gone after what you wanted and you hate to lose."

Pam smiled. "I hate to lose something that I want more than my own life."

"And that's Shemar Dalton."

"Bingo."

Valerian laughed. "We are much alike. I hate to lose, too. Years ago, I did lose. Lost money and my pride, when a beautiful young woman rejected me for a dumb kid. I could have given Marita Sommers everything, but she betrayed me. She testified against me. For eighteen years I've thought of nothing except how I want to pay her back."

Pam was enjoying this. Being tied up didn't even matter now. "You should have let me kill her."

"Oh, no, Ms. Wingate." He squashed his cigar in the ashtray, depositing it there. "I have other uses for the lovely Marita. She will pay me back for all my lost time."

Pam noticed the glint in his eye when he spoke Marita's name. "What you feel is bittersweet, though. I can tell. You hate her but you want her at the same time."

"You never mind that. But I am certain that we can help each other." He bent down, freeing her restraints.

Glad to be free, Pam wasn't so anxious to flee. "Let's help each other."

"That is exactly what I was hoping, Ms. Wingate. And here's how we can work together."

At least for now, Valerian thought.

Togetherness is what Shemar ached for when he woke and found Marita gone. That wasn't supposed to happen. He'd had special plans for her when she woke. A diamond was waiting on the dining room table in a cupcake that they were going to snack on while they watched a movie. Then he would have done what he'd been mentally practicing for days. Oh, well, he would have to wait for later. Though he hoped not too much later. Glancing outside the window he could see that it was getting dark.

He wasn't relieved, either, when he saw that her bicycle was gone. She'd been dying to try this alternate bike trail, but he hoped she hadn't ridden it alone. Yes, the authorities were going to put a heavy hand to Cliff since Marita had decided to press charges. But until he was where he couldn't hurt Marita, Shemar didn't want her going anywhere alone. As he pondered more, he had to acknowledge that someone else's behavior bothered him, too. Pam had really gone weird on him. There was something going on with her. Now he could see what his baby had been talking about. Could Marita have been right in thinking that an eye should have been kept in Pam's direction?

Marita saw the door to the room opening and didn't know whether to feel frightened or hopeful. Seeing Pam did neither. She was incensed.

Pam nodded to the woman sitting with Marita. Recognizing a signal, the woman left and Pam granted Marita her full attention.

"Look at you now," Pam teased. "Shemar's big willie can't help you now."

"Pam, why have you done this? Have you lost your mind?"

"Lost my mind! Lost my mind? Because I love him and need him, that makes me a candidate for the loony bin?"

"But Shemar doesn't want you."

"You shut up. You just shut up!" Pam reached over to her.

Marita's cheek stung from the slap.

Pam smirked that she couldn't strike back. "Doesn't feel nice to be held back, does it? To have someone take away something you want. In your case, your freedom. In my case, my man."

"But he wasn't yours. You—"

"Shut your mouth! Next time instead of slapping you, I'll just finish killing you, like I started."

Marita held back the tears. "Please let me go. I won't press charges. Don't hold me here against my will. I'll just let it go."

Pam was tickled. "You think it's me holding you?"

"Who else could it be?" Cliff crossed her mind, but she just knew he wouldn't do something so foolish. He had too much to lose. So did Pam. "Pam, what about your career? About your life? Your future? If you keep me here and hurt me, you're going to jail. Everything will be ruined. Totally ruined over some jealousy for a man. You'll be in prison for all of your precious years."

"And you would love that, wouldn't you? Send-

ing me away. Well, wait until you see what he has
in store for you."

"He who?" What was this all about?

Pam looked over her shoulder at the door and
called, "Come in. Show our captive who has really
captured her."

On cue, the door opened. What Marita saw
sucked her breath away.

Eighteen

It had been so many years it seemed like another lifetime. Time had taken him through some changes Marita could clearly see. He was much heavier. Where there was once smooth skin, there were sags everywhere. The posture wasn't as straight as before. The lips didn't have a cut near the corner like the one on them now. There wasn't a mustache before. There was no double chin. Yet what did remain were those eyes. Eyes that seemingly had much more black than white. They had always resembled a fish's eyes to Marita. Now she saw them otherwise. Those were the devil's eyes. Valerian Tate was the embodiment of evil.

The energy in the room had clearly become more tense with his presence. It even took her back to those days. All she could remember was Remmy. His young life robbed from him by Valerian. He did it so fast. He did so easily, as if blinking an eye. Remmy had been someone's child. Someone's friend. Her man. He just had been, period, and no other human being had the right to remove him from this world.

"You . . ." She couldn't utter a comprehensible word, she was in such shock.

Valerian's slick Italian shoes scraped across the tile as he made his way toward the bed.

Pam smirked. "Wait until you see what he has in store for you." She laughed.

"You . . ." Marita couldn't get beyond that. It was actually him. So many years and years she'd thought about this real-life nightmare. Now here he was.

"Yes, it's me in the flesh, my sweet, sweet Marita."

Smiling, he sat in a chair before her. "How are you?"

"Why did you bring me here? What are you do-ing out?" She jerked at the restraint. "Let me out of these things."

"When you calm down I will."

"Calm down? You have me here like an animal and you ask me to calm down!"

Pam started laughing. "Oh, you'll never know the meaning of calm, when you see what he has in store for you."

Valerian was annoyed by Pam's outbursts. "Go outside until I tell you to come back in."

"Outside?" Pam frowned. She was enjoying Marita being tortured.

"Do as I say."

Oddly enough, he was smiling. However, Pam beheld something in his eyes that told her he meant business. She didn't want to find out what disobeying him would mean. "I'll be right out-side."

Alone with Marita, Valerian couldn't resist the urge to touch her. He brushed her cheek. "Soft as ever."

She turned her face away. "Don't put your hands on me."

With his fingertips, he turned it back toward him. Staring at her, he shook his head. "Oh, time has been so very kind to you. You are even more beautiful than you were before. You'll be so perfect for my plans."

Her heart jumped. "What plans?"

"My plans, Marita. My plans for you."

"What are you planning to do to me?" Pam had alluded to it and now that he'd said it, her anger subsided. Exploding terror replaced it. "What do you want?"

"The same thing you took from me. My life, my youth, my fortune, my years and years gone to waste." His smile grew. "That's all I want from you."

"But you did that to yourself. You were involved in counterfeiting. And you killed Remmy! You killed the man I loved! I couldn't just let you get away with it."

"Why not?" His smile transformed into a snarl. "We could have been together."

"What?"

"You heard me. If Remmy was out of the picture, we would have been together. But no, you had to be with him. You chose him over me."

Marita had never known how sick he was. She thought it was merely evil. But he was insane. He had seen something that clearly wasn't true. "You're wrong. There had never been any contest. I was with Remmy."

"And you should have been with me."

"You were supposed to be his friend."

"I hated that kid. Hated him even more when he had you. You see, I could have any woman I wanted. Anyone back then. All I had to do was look at her, and she would look at me in that way. And I had plenty of Remmy's little girlfriends before. But not you . . . You played hard to get. But still, I could see that you wanted me."

"I wasn't playing anything."

"You played hard. You would look at that little bastard the way I wanted you to look at me. The way I want you to look at me now."

"I can't see you in any other way but disgusting. Look at what you're doing to me. Let me go!"

He hated the way she was looking at him. Her desire for him wasn't there anymore. If only it was . . . maybe . . . maybe he would have changed his mind about what he would do with her. "If you were different toward me I wouldn't do to you what I'm planning to."

This plan of his was suffocating her with fright with each passing second. Maybe she could handle him differently. She had to do something to get away. "What do you want me to do?" She prayed not *that*.

Suddenly Valerian's face became vulnerable, almost boyish. "I want you to look at me that way."

"What way?"

"The way you used to look at Remmy." It would make him feel wanted. So wanted by her. "That's all I want for now."

More and more, Marita could see how sick he was. It made her all the more desperate to do anything to get away from him. Hence, she attempted to look at him tenderly.

Valerian saw through it, seeing her disgust with him. It reminded him so much of how his mother

used to look at him. It made him feel just as un-
wanted.

Abruptly, he stood. "You'll never know life again
as you knew it." He opened the door. "Get inside," he called out in the hallway.

Pam came in smiling. "Can we put your plan
into action now?"

Not knowing what they were going to do to her,
Marita was terrified. "What?" She saw Pam approaching her with a pad and pen. "What are you
going to do?"

"Relax, bitch." Pam sat beside her and undid
the arm restraints.

Promptly, Marita rubbed her sore wrists. "What
are you going to do to me?" She looked at Pam,
who looked back at Valerian.

He nodded. "Do it."

Pam placed the pad and pen before Marita. "We
want you to write a note to Shemar. We have to
make sure he doesn't come looking for you."

"Oh, he's going to be looking for me."

"Shut up." Pam squeezed Marita's hands when
putting the pen among her fingers. "Now write."

"Write what?"

"Your good-bye note," she answered.

"No."

Valerian nodded. "Oh, yes. It is good-bye. You'll
never see him again."

Marita tried to hold back the tears. "Please, if
it's money you want, then just let me know how
much. Shemar will give it to you."

Pam seethed. "You actually think you mean that
much to him?"

"I obviously mean enough to get under your
skin."

Pam drew her hand back to slap her.

"Stop!" Valerian's voice held her back. "We need her to look intact for my purposes."

Marita wiped at the tears she couldn't fight back. "What purposes?"

Pam smirked. "You'll see soon enough."

"Enough of this cat snipping." Valerian tossed his head at Pam. "Just get on with it."

"Is this a ransom note?" Marita wiped at her tears again. "Shemar will give you what you want. And he won't call the cops. Just let me leave here and unharmed."

Valerian was amused. "I don't want his money. I'm going to have plenty. And you're going to get it for me."

Marita was perplexed.

Pam nudged her out of her confusion. "Now start. Dear Shemar . . ."

Marita refused to write. Seeing her unwillingness, Valerian walked closer to her. "Do it or you'll learn my plan sooner rather than later." With that, his gaze burned into hers.

Tearful, Marita felt she had no choice in writing the words that Pam recited for her.

Dear Shemar,

Although it has been wonderful spending time with you this summer, I feel it is time for me to move on. I'm still searching for the meaning of my life and have decided to go on a world cruise to help me discover it. I hope you will understand my need to be alone. Please think of me fondly, as I will think of you. And please move forward with your life. I'm sure there is some wonderful woman out there for you. Unfortunately, it isn't me. Since I am starting all over, I am purchasing a new wardrobe, but I will send for my things. Take care.

                                        Marita

The instant Marita finished the note, she knew Shemar would never believe she wrote such an unfeeling piece of ice. Not after what they shared together. However, if Pam wanted to deliver it, it was fine with her. After reading it, surely Shemar's alarm button would go off. Hopefully, it would be in time to save her from whatever plan Valerian had conceived. All she could do was pray.

Shemar had not slept the entire night. If he wasn't nagging the authorities about hearing anything from the missing person's report he'd put out on Marita, he was having all types of thoughts about what could have happened to her. Did Cliff hurt her . . . or even . . . even Pam? Was she in an accident? Was she lying somewhere unconscious and beaten? For surely something wasn't right. He could feel it. His imagination was sending him into a frenzy when he noticed the envelope slid underneath the front door.

Pam checked her face in her compact mirror, making sure she looked extra beautiful as she stood on Shemar's porch. Finally she knocked on the door. When he opened it, he looked just as she'd predicted: distraught.

"What are you doing here, Pam?" He braced himself for his performance.

"I came to apologize for my behavior. I'm really

sorry, Shemar. I want to get back to where we were
before. If only you can forgive me for what I did."

Looking as if he hadn't heard a word she said,
Shemar nodded. "It's all right."

"It is?" She brightened.

"In fact, come in, Pam."

Pam was thrilled to go inside. She took a seat
in her favorite spot and looked up at him. "You
know, Shemar, you don't look well. Is everything
OK?"

He sat across from her, bowing his head. "Not
really."

"What's wrong?"

"It's Marita. She's gone." He looked up. "And,
Pam, I might as well tell you, our relationship had
gone beyond friendship. And I hope this won't upset you, but I really love her."

Pam let the confession settle in a few seconds.
"And she left you?"

"Found a good-bye note this morning."

"It's all right, Shemar. Any woman who could
leave you like that isn't worth your time. She was
heartless."

"I guess you're right." He stood, hoping she
would get the hint. "I want to be alone right now.
I have to just get over this."

"Sure. I'll check in on you later."

"You don't have to."

"But I want to. What kind of cousin would I be
if I just left you hanging at a time like this?"

"You're something else, Pam." He gave her a
hug and sent her on.

When he locked the door behind her, Shemar's
chest heaved with his fury. There was no way in
the world Marita would write him that pitiful little

note. No way. She was in trouble. That was her handwriting, but those words weren't from her heart. And if Pam, Cliff, or anyone else was holding her somewhere, the earth would have no peace until he found her. Because sure as he was breathing, he knew he would be with her again. Making good on that promise to himself, he listened as Pam's car drove away. He then hurried into his own.

What was the real reason she'd come to his house? That apology excuse didn't fly. So was she snooping? Checking on something? Or just trying to get something she had taken great pains to get? If Pam had anything to do with Marita's disappearance, she was going to be the one to lead him to her. He couldn't wait for the police. He couldn't wait for anyone. Every second of not knowing what was happening to Marita was killing him. He had to find her before both of them died.

Valerian sauntered into the room where he was holding Marita and was surprised that the breakfast tray his maid had left for her was uneaten.

Marita rolled her eyes up at him. "You will not get away with this."

"Don't you know you'll get further being sweeter?" He glimpsed down at the tray. "Why haven't you eaten?"

"Because I don't have a taste for poison today."

"Do you really think I would poison you?"

"You can kill as easily as you breathe."

He chuckled. "This is true. But I have plans for you."

She hated the way he kept saying that. She

fought off the panic that was trying to overtake her. She had to remain calm. She had to believe that she was going to get out of this. Didn't Remmy and Shemar tell her how important belief was. It was like magic. "My boyfriend is a multimillion—"

"I know who the hell he is." And he didn't look happy about it.

"Like I said, if it's money you want, he can give it to you. As much as you want. Just let me go."

"Never." He bent down, getting down on the bed.

With her hands free, but her ankles still bound, Marita moved back as far as she could. She couldn't imagine him touching her.

He hated the way she was rejecting him. "Don't worry," he told her, sitting instead of lying as she thought he was trying to do. "I won't take you. I want you to come to me of your own free will. And like I said, it may delay my plans for you. It may even stop them."

"What plans?"

"Maybe you won't have to find out." He brushed his hand across her cheek.

Marita turned away in disgust. "Don't . . ."

Valerian gritted his teeth. "You see, that's what I hate! I hate your rejection. Your not wanting me! Do you know how that feels to not be wanted? No, you wouldn't. Because everyone wants you." Pausing, he leered at her. "I want you to respond to me the way you did to that Remmy. The way you do to your millionaire. That's what I want from you. If you can do that, maybe it will save your life. But I won't force you. The turn-on is you wanting me. You, the one who put me away because of your hatred, will finally love me so much, you give yourself to me."

"Never."

He stood. "Then you'll know the consequences of that decision." He started walking toward the door.

Not knowing what he was planning, Marita had to do something to prevent whatever it was. "Wait."

Valerian stopped. He spun around. "Is there something that you want?" He stared into her eyes, hoping that it was him.

"Please just let me walk around in here. My legs feel like the circulation has stopped. How can I want you when I feel so imprisoned?"

Valerian thought for a moment. He could let her free. And when she was, they could do something else he'd been dying to do with her. For years in prison he'd dreamed about it. "Let's dance."

"Dance?" After being freed of all restraints, Marita walked about the room. It felt so good to move around. She glanced out of the window.

"It's too far to jump out," he said, studying her.

She looked back inside and at him. She didn't want him to touch her, but she had to try anything so she could get out of there. Well, almost anything. "There isn't any music to dance to."

"Oh, yes there is." He reached into a corner, pressing a button. An overhead speaker began to play a slow jazz tune. Valerian looked introspective. "In prison they had nothing like this." He eased toward Marita.

She forced herself not to back away. "There was no music?"

"Not like this." He was easing closer.

She held her breath as he came so near she could smell cigars on him. She saw him reach for her. "You really want to dance?"

"If you want to dance with me. Only if you want me. If you don't want me it does nothing for me."

Hiding her abhorrence, she raised her arms so he could sweep her into his. Before long, she felt his arms come around her and his body swaying gently, coaxing equally soft movements from hers.

Valerian smiled. "Now this . . . This is worth a man living and dying for. Being in the arms of a beautiful woman who wants to dance with him." He leaned back, looking down in her face. "I can see that you like it." He held her tighter. "Can't you feel that I like it, too?"

Marita couldn't take any more. He was so sickening to her, she felt the nausea rising up in her stomach. She dashed to the bathroom, leaning her head over the bowl.

In the other room, Valerian listened to her and his rage grew to a fever pitch. So he disgusted her. She found him so unappealing she was physically ill. That riled him. He'd given her a chance to save herself by showing him affection and she couldn't do it. Well, there was something he could do and would. He had to leave and make preparations.

When Marita came out of the bathroom, she was relieved that Valerian was gone. Neither could she help jerking the doorknob, hoping it would open. As she suspected, it didn't. At least she was free to walk around and look out of the window. Though with this freedom, she only desired more. How was she going to get out of there? Did Shemar believe that ridiculous note? If he knew her like she knew him, he wouldn't have. He couldn't. There was no love in that note, no heart.

She had to believe. She had to believe that she would get free. And with this determination at heart, she looked out the window. It was too far for her to jump. However, the pen and paper that Pam had left were still in the room. She could write a note and throw it out. Perhaps someone would find it. She had to believe. She had to believe she would be free. She had to believe that Shemar's love would save her.

Nineteen

"This can't be happening!" Dollie paced about her living room's antique carpet, shaking her fists because of what Parole Officer Johnson had just told her.

She was too upset to cry, or scream, or sit, or do anything. She just had to move. Even so, nothing would rid her beloved great-niece of the danger she had just been warned of. So she looked to where she always looked in times of crisis. "Oh, my dear Lord," she implored. Her head raised, she closed her eyes. "Please, keep my Marita safe from the devil."

"Mrs. Brunswick," the parole officer offered. He was strolling up behind her. "I assure you we will do everything we can to make sure that Valerian Tate comes nowhere near Marita."

Her chest heaving, Dollie swerved around. "You all should have kept closer tabs on him. You should have told me the second that he turned up missing from his brother's house and missed his meeting with you. The second it happened."

"We did as much as we could."

"He's up to no good again. I can smell it." Lord knew she had compassion for those who had made mistakes. She knew that some people came from backgrounds that one could partly blame for their winding up on the wrong side of the law. But this man . . . He didn't even seem human to her.

Watching the elderly woman, Johnson wished there was something he could have done to ease her anxiety. He laid a consoling hand on her shoulder. "The authorities have been alerted. Now, as I told you before, there may not be any real need to worry. He may just be hanging around here in the city somewhere."

"And he may be in Bermuda where my niece is."

"We've alerted authorities there to be on the lookout for him. They have wanted posters of him at all airports and federal buildings. But there is a possibility that he may have had access to a private plane. At least that's what his sister-in-law said. He bragged to her about meeting some foreign friends and that he was going for a ride on their private plane. But he told her it was just a day trip, not far from where he was staying."

"I don't care about all that nonsense." Dollie scowled up at Johnson. "I just want my Marita safe."

As soon as he left, Dollie was on the phone. Certainly, she couldn't tell Carol about this. Stress at this time of her recovery could reverse all the healing she'd done. No, she needed to call Marita and Shemar. Shemar would keep Marita safe.

"Hello?" Hoping it was Marita or the police with good news, Shemar swiped up the phone on the first ring.

"Oh, Shemar, baby, how are you doing?"

Shemar hadn't wanted to hear Dollie's voice. He couldn't tell her about Marita and he didn't want her to detect something wrong in his voice. "I'm fine, Ms. Dollie. How are you doing?"

"I was doing all right, but . . ."

"But what?" He wondered if she'd heard from Marita. Still, he had to let her talk to find that out. "What's wrong?"

She went on to explain the nightmarish news from the parole officer. When she asked to speak to Marita, he lied that she had gone shopping. Dollie summed up the call by stating that the authorities in Bermuda had been alerted about Valerian Tate and had been looking for him.

When Shemar hung up the phone, he had to just sit a moment and gather his thoughts. Now he had to worry about three people being after Marita. Though for some reason, Cliff was dwindling off his suspect list. It was just a feeling he had. That same feeling was telling him that someone else should have been higher on that list.

Yesterday he'd traded his car for Trent's. That way Pam wouldn't recognize that he was following her. It was easy to do since he knew her routine for that particular day of the week. She did nothing out of the ordinary. Though she did have dinner at an outdoor café with an older man he'd never seen before. As he thought of that older man, he recalled Dollie's description of Valerian Tate. He was a heavy man with a mustache. The man Pam dined with fit that description, too. Could there have been a connection? Could Pam . . . and he? How? He would get a picture of Valerian Tate. If it was him, he would follow Pam again today. Only this time he would be accompanied by the authorities.

* * *

Marita was standing about the room, praying as she'd done since she woke in this place, when two burly men grabbed her by the arms. Practically dragging her, they answered none of her questions about where they were taking her. Her curiosity was answered when she was pushed in a room. Her face lit in shock as she looked around it. There was Pam, smirking. Valerian also stood there, stern-faced. And around an oblong conference table, there sat several men, some speaking in a foreign language.

"These are my friends," Valerian announced. "They will be your friends, too, Marita."

"What's going on?"

"You," Pam raved. "You'll be getting it on. And I will be with Shemar."

Valerian nodded. "Yes, they will be your friends. You see they operate the best . . ." He smiled. "The best and most sophisticated pleasure services around the world. It's underground but highly refined. They take beautiful women such as yourself and market them among various countries where the law is very lax. I'll be living in one of those countries with you. You'll be working for me. Women like you can make a man very rich."

"No!" Marita just knew this couldn't be happening. "No! No!"

Pam snickered. "You're going to be a slave, missy. A modern-day love slave."

"Yes, you will," Valerian added. "You will repay me for the loss of my years. From sunup to sundown, you will work on your back, and the money will be split between these gentlemen and myself. This will be your life. Your freedom, your family,

your everything will be taken away, just like it was
for me."

"No . . . no . . ." Marita knew this had to be
some nightmare, some game. She'd watched a pro-
gram about this early in the year, about how
women were being captured and sold into prosti-
tution in foreign countries. Their families would
try to find them, but they never could. The first
lady was even working to fight this. They called it
the trafficking of women. "No . . ." Her knees
went as numb as her heart as one of the men
stood from the table. Grinning, he mumbled something in a foreign language, then approached her.

"Yes, you will be going with them," Valerian
said, "and me, too. We'll be taking a private plane
in a few moments."

"No, you won't!"

Officer Farkley, accompanied by several other officers burst into the room. They drew guns. Seizing
Valerian, Pam, and all the men, they read them
their rights and handcuffed them. Marita's stilled
heart began again when she saw Shemar.

Hugging her, he began explaining how Pam unknowingly led him to her. They both watched Pam
as she was dragged away in handcuffs. Her eyes
glued to Shemar, Pam began jerking away from
the officer holding her, coaxing him toward Shemar until she finally stood in front of him.

"I only did it because I love you."

"I loved you, too, Pam." The words sounded
buried and whispery.

"Do you still love me?"

He just looked at her. He'd never really known
who she was.

"Well, I'll always love you." She narrowed her

eyes at Marita. "She'll never love you the way I did."

"Let's go!" the loud officer holding her demanded. Roughly, he led her through the doorway and out of Marita and Shemar's sight.

"It's all over, baby," Shemar hugged Marita tight within his arms. "All over."

The rest of the criminals were being led out. Valerian stopped, giving them both a lingering glare, before he was shoved out the door.

Marita shivered, watching his back, and she couldn't stop crying. "They were going to . . ." She couldn't even say it, it was so upsetting.

Shemar blotted her tears with kisses. "Don't say it, baby. I just need you to do one thing for me." He pulled her tumbling hair back from her face. "Just one thing. I've been trying to get you to do it for days now."

Sniffling, Marita looked up. "Anything for you. You saved my life. In every way."

"Then you can't deny me."

"I'll do whatever it is. I'll do anything for you."

"Will you marry me?"

Epilogue

It appeared like slivers of silver were scattering over the mellifluous turquoise sea. Beneath the late-afternoon sunshine, Shemar shifted his captivation from the ocean. He eagerly traded it for the heart-stopping beauty of the white-draped creature who suddenly stood beside him. Donning a simple, shoulder-baring silk gown, Marita was a vision like no other. Enthralled with her loveliness, he couldn't believe how blessed he was. This exquisite woman was actually in love with him. She was as much in love with him as he was with her. So much so, her bare toes bore into the pinkish sands alongside his. On a secluded area of the beach, with her aunt, his grandmother, before a minister, she was waiting to promise to honor him forever as his wife.

Marita being with him wasn't about his money. His being with her wasn't about being with someone so that he wouldn't be alone. Their being with each other wasn't about the passionate sexual chemistry that they created together. Shemar recognized it was beyond that. It was all that they were to each other, and the dream of so much more to come. Overall, it was a feeling—that mystical feeling that draws one human being to another and never lets them go.

Feeling as soft as the way Shemar was looking at her, Marita knew this moment was incomparable to any other. It wasn't so exceptional because she was seconds away from exchanging marital vows. For she'd always believed she would marry someone some day. Marita just didn't believe that she would feel the way that she did when she married.

Sure, she would have loved the person, been content with him, and gone through the motions of the ceremony. For she would have had a life-long companion. Still, there was such a vast difference in what she would have accepted and what she now lived. She just didn't love Shemar; she was *in love* with him. She just wasn't content; she was down-to-the-bone, intoxicatingly happy. She just wasn't going through the motions of the wedding ceremony; she was feeling the immense power of their love at every second and always beheld it reflected in his eyes.

Never did she dream of experiencing magic again. Only this magic was real. Yes, Remmy's affection and the emotions he inflamed in her were unforgettable. Yet *this,* what she shared with Shemar, could be counted on. His love was as strong and steady as the fierce pounding now claiming her heart.

Marita smiled at Aunt Dollie, her radiance gracing her side like a pink flower, and Ms. Nell glowingly standing beside Shemar. Her heart filled that they were there despite she and Shemar insisting it wasn't necessary. For there would be a large ceremony with family and friends attending in DC within weeks.

Cloaked in russet-and-gold hued African garb, the middle-aged minister commenced the nuptials. "The bride and groom would like to start off with expressing sentiments to each other."

Marveling at the precious sight, Dollie was blurred to all else he was saying because she was too preoccupied with her pride for Marita. Equally, she was proud of the woman she spotted approaching from the distance. Marita had told Dollie about Carol's wrongdoing. Dollie knew that this would make Marita so happy.

Gripping a cane, Carol Sommers found her way quietly behind her daughter and her son-in-law-to-be. Her large, luminous eyes watching, she was distant enough so that she wouldn't distract Marita.

At that moment, all Marita could see were the eyes that were as much a haven for her as they were an unspoken beckoning of eroticism. "Shemar, you filled me up inside where I used to be so empty. I had loved before, but no one could touch that place inside of me that made me feel as alive as I do now. You made that happen. No one else could before. With you, I feel protected and warm, as much as I do excited and desirable. Your support makes me feel as if I can do anything, and with you I know that I will. I thought I had found true love once before with someone who had a good heart, but did bad things. So I tried to look for the opposite, a practical man. But those kind of men never made me happy. You do. You are everything to me. Your heart is good, and the way that you live your life backs that up. I thank God for you, Shemar. I thank Him for bringing you into my life. And I love you so much."

Shemar withheld the kiss that her trembling lips summoned him for. Instead he held her hand, looking deep into the brown eyes as clear as the sea beyond her. "Marita, so long you've been part of me. Ever since I met you as a very young man I was affected by your presence in my life. I was spellbound by your beauty at first, though it was all of you that maintained that spell, your tender heart, your courageous spirit. When we became part of each other's lives again, something inside me was telling me you were everything I ever needed. But I fought it because of my own insecurities, built from pain from my past. But after spending the most wonderful time I'd ever had with anyone, with you, I knew that what something inside was telling me was the gospel truth. You felt like my woman long before I confessed it. You were in my heart. I know you were sent to me, God-sent, and I will honor that every day of my life, loving your body, mind, and soul. I will love you forever, Marita Sommers. I will be thankful to God forever for your love."

The minister added traditional marital scripture, along with his personal blessing for the bride and groom. Finally, he announced, "I give to you, Mr. and Mrs. Shemar Dalton. You may kiss your bride."

Shemar tipped his head down and with ravenous eagerness brought his lips to hers. Relishing the sweet taste of each other, the minister's clearing of his throat reminded them of where they were.

A breeze cooled Marita's aroused state as she eased back from her husband, her eyes lingering on his, only lured away by: "Marita, baby?"

Her mouth agape at the familiar voice, Marita's head turned aside. Gladness rippled over her at seeing her mother and she rushed toward her.

"Mama, I can't believe you're here." Emotionally, Marita wrapped her thin frame in a hug.

"Yes, I'm here, baby." Carol patted Marita's back. "I couldn't miss your special day. I wanted to surprise you." Carol gently let go of Marita as she saw Shemar approaching. Ashamed, she peered up into his handsome face, wondering how to begin her apology when his large arms came around her. Carol felt the subsiding of her built-up tension.

"I'm glad you came."

The sincerity in his voice further soothed her worry that he might hate her. "I'm *so* glad God enabled me to be here, too. I've had so much time to just think about my life. I want to make up for the things I did to hurt you." She wiped at that line of water that ran down her cheek.

Watching the two, Marita huddled together with Dollie, Nell, and the minister.

Shemar slackened the embrace while still holding onto Carol's arms. "Mom, you don't have to make up for anything. We're not holding on to anger here today. We're all starting over, and we're holding on to love for a lifetime."

Hours later, sometime past midnight, a half-moon shined down on the yacht *Marita* as it sailed the serene waters. Inside of the homelike vessel, Marita's head nestled against Shemar's chest as they lay entangled among satiny blue sheets.

"Do you know how lucky we are?" Shemar whispered into the after-love silence.

"I sure do." Marita looked over into his eyes. They were slowly dragging across her face, making her feel beautiful. "Because I know how I used to feel. There's probably some woman out there right now thinking the way that I used to. Thinking that she'll never find real love." She watched him bringing his face closer to hers, his mouth parted and seeking hers. "But she will. She . . ."

Dear Reader:

Love is one of the most beautiful gifts given to us in this life. I hope you felt its power in Marita and Shemar's story. I tried to entertain you with passionate characters that you could relate to or be inspired by. Marita settled for relationships that didn't make her truly happy; something was always missing. Shemar held on to the hurt from a past relationship so that it prevented him from experiencing an even greater love.

I hope this story shows that we all deserve to feel real happiness in a relationship. We should also never give someone who hurt us so much power that it stops us from feeling the love of that special someone that God has out there waiting for us. We all deserve the best that life has to offer, whether it's in a romantic relationship, loving family and friends, or a long-desired dream that we want for ourselves.

Thank you for reading and being such a blessing to me. Thanks to those of you who write to me, too. I love hearing from all of you and hope I can continue writing stories that you enjoy. May you be blessed in every way.

Please feel free to let me know what you thought of *Dangerous Passions* or any of my other books.

Write to: PO Box 020648, Brooklyn, New York 11202-0648
E-mail: LoureBus@aol.com
Web site: http://www.LoureBussey.com

Until next time,
Louré Bussey

ABOUT THE AUTHOR

Louré Bussey is the best-selling author of seven novels: *Nightfall, Most of All, Twist of Fate, Love So True, A Taste of Love, Images of Ecstasy,* and *Dangerous Passions. Amazon.com* has recognized her books on their list of top selling 100 multicultural romances, and her work *Images of Ecstasy* was recently nominated for an Emma award. Her writing career began with publishing 56 short stories. A multimedia artist, Louré is also a singer/songwriter completing a CD based on her novels.